LAST FERRY SOUTH

Hal Dorin

DEDICATION

Dedicated to:
My wife, Doris Dorin
Our children, Joanna Dorin Brandt, Adam Dorin, and Paul Dorin
For their editing assistance and continued support;

And to Dan Jones, a retired Towson University professor who formed a Writing Club we now call the Dan Jones Writing Group—in his memory.
The critical appraisal by the DJWG of my monthly chapters over a five-year period, made it happen.

PROLOGUE

A lone and adrift at sea*—the Zodiac bounced off a rock jolting Homer awake, and with it the memory of decisions that shattered his life.*

The winds picked up rocking the small boat and spraying a salty mist into his eyes. To keep from being tossed about he grabbed a rope attached to the perimeter of the inflatable craft. During his brief nap the fog cleared revealing a clear star-studded sky, but without a moon to help light his way.

He remembered his parents telling him he always asked to be lifted up to touch the moon.

He knew the stars—they were old friends, welcome friends. They helped guide his way during years at sea. Now the ship's GPS negated the need for following a course with the aid of the sun and the stars. However, he'd kept his old sextant and original slide rule to show others the way it once was. Now they too—were gone.

What he needed was more gas for the outboard engine. There are no stations on his sea route ahead. "I'll end up using the oars," he mused. "I can row".

The soft-sided boat bounced off another rock, probably the last of the shoals before the open ocean ahead. Aboard ship he never considered the sea between small coastal islands, as the ocean. Then, the times he was surprised by immense waves and treacherous winds close to shore.

Even without moonlight he saw some whitecaps on the crest of small swells. "I'd rather have the fog back and not the winds," he mumbled. He wanted calm, not visibility. Visibility was required to see the ocean directly ahead. Winds caused swells and rough seas. Winds kept him from reaching the safety of an island. Winds scoffed at the reliance on GPS' and compasses that helped to keep him on-course.

His small boat and outboard engine were meant for harbors, not the open ocean. He wore a survival suit mainly for warmth, but neglected to put on his life jacket. He wasn't particularly concerned. He'd spent most of his life on the ocean. He was in a familiar environment. Even during the most severe storms he was never uneasy by the happenings at sea as long as he was in charge, and his ship could take the beating.

The ocean was his gracious host, but he also knew it to be a fickle and sometimes—an untrustworthy friend. I must be careful. I need to survive. There are loved ones who would be concerned about my absence, and be devastated if I were to perish. And the loved ones I let down—those I may have recklessly destroyed.

The memories resurfaced. No, the memories never left the surface. That's what frightened him—the memories he was destined to live with.

His mind became like a jungle, with thoughts caught in the vines of contrition and confusion, and overcome with mourning.

CHAPTER ONE

October 15ᵗʰ—Anchorage, Alaska

*I*n the late 1940's, soon after World War II ended, the U.S. Navy sold or gave away thousands of surplus ships. One of these, a three hundred-foot LST, Landing Ship, Tank, once used to deliver American war vehicles and troops to Pacific shores, was bought by Conveyance Cargo, Inc., a company based in Seattle, Washington. They converted the ship to a commercial ferry and named her, *Alaskan Eagle*.

Now, well over fifty years later and under the command of Captain Homer Dixon, the *Eagle* sat at its northern terminus loading cargo and passengers for the return trip south.

Waiting for the Harbormaster to clear the *Eagle* for departure, Homer paced up and down the long concrete dock. He paused to peer up at the ship and at the quickly darkening autumn sky. A stiff wind tousled his bushy brown hair. He ran a hand over his head and down the weathered skin of his face—a face that showed concern, for this was his ship, and for over twenty years, his home.

He knew that over time, wear and tear combined with the sea destroyed all ships.

He took-in a deep breath and climbed the gangway to the ship's deck.

"Hey, Captain, you're right on schedule—the middle of every month. We call you the Ides of Anchorage," the Harbormaster yelled as he negotiated the gangway and came aboard, his face flush from the cool ocean air as he smiled, happy to see Homer. "So, this bucket is still floating. When are they gonna scrap her?"

"She runs just fine," Homer said. "Just needs a little shipyard work."

"Come-on, she's being held together by rust."

"Now, now, you'll hurt her feelings."

They'd repeated the same greeting for many years.

"Some crewmen were looking for the ship yesterday," the Harbormaster said. "I told them when and where to find you."

"They found us—couple of strange birds. From Singapore, but they're not Asian. Company's local agent signed them in Vancouver. A little old for deck work but what the hell, I just need them to get me back to Seattle. I'm still waiting for two officer trainees to stand bridge watches with me and Ernie. I'd rather take twelve-hour shifts than have to baby a pair of youngsters for the next ten days. The way the company has cut the size of my crew, the Coast Guard will ream us out one of these days."

"Homer, the number of times you've taken the *Eagle* south you could stand twenty-four hour shifts by yourself. You're probably up on the bridge all day anyway. Hey, looks like these are your young men coming aboard now."

Homer turned to the two men approaching him. They acted a little hesitant. He could tell they were not comfortable aboard ship. He extended his hand. "I'm glad you made it okay. Find our First Mate, Ernie McInnis. He'll get you squared away."

"Yes Sir, Captain," they answered, before disappearing into the ship.

After completing routine ship departure tasks, the Harbormaster pointed at the boxes being loaded on the ship. "That's the first time I've seen survival suits going back to Seattle. They must be defective."

"First for me, too," Homer said. "I'll ask Davy about it tomorrow."

"Say hi to Davy for me," the Harbormaster waved, as he departed. "See you next month."

Homer called a routine all-hands meeting on the open deck near the gangway. He looked at his crew and some of the passengers gathered. As always, he made a conscious effort to stand erect. His body no longer did that, and though the *Eagle* was only a cargo ship, he wanted to maintain older traditions and look 'in command'.

"Gentlemen, we have two new seamen and two new officers aboard. Get to know them. Presently we have a crew of twenty-two, which should stay the same for our journey south, plus ten passengers. The number of passengers may increase at each port. We'll make our usual stop at my favorite port tomorrow and leave for Juneau the following morning. We'll spend two days in Juneau before heading for Ketchikan, then on to Seattle. Weather looks good for the next week. Ship's activities should be routine. First Mate McInnis will provide more details. Have a fine trip."

"You too, Captain," some of the crew responded.

He waited as Ernie continued the meeting. When Ernie dismissed the crew, Homer wandered over to the deck rail. The last of seventy-six cardboard boxes were being loaded from trucks on the dock. This was the shipment his old friend Davy had consigned.

He looked at two men in suits who were directing the loading. They seemed overly concerned about how the boxes were handled, as if each container was filled with fine china.

"They're only survival suits," Homer quietly muttered. "Or are they?"

The two men glanced up at Homer.

Did they hear me?

They spoke to each other while looking at him—studying him.

The sight of them and their expressions, unusual in the way they fixed on Homer, disturbed him. He turned away to continue his inspection of the ship. Like sailing skippers of old, he looked aloft each time he came out on deck, examining every familiar surface. Lately, it was hard for him to admit certain feelings and doubts about the ship, and also about himself—*we're way beyond our best, you and me.*

As if responding to his thoughts, the frayed mooring lines groaned at each gentle surge of the tide in Cook Inlet. Even with their spring long gone, the lines continued to hold and protect the aging vessel.

CHAPTER TWO

October 16th—Kenai, Alaska

"Davy, you look like hell," Homer said.** "What's the matter with you? I didn't say anything during dinner—it could have upset Maddy even more. She was already sad about losing your dog. I'm worried about you. You're fidgeting and shaking—look at your hands. Are you sick or is it about the dog?"

Davy sat on the divan with his head down and his face showing anguish. He gestured for Homer to wait a minute.

"It's not about the dog, Homer—though we loved that mutt. Maddy can see something *is* wrong. She keeps asking me, but I wanted to talk with you first. I knew you would come here after you tied up the *Eagle*. I'm in a lot of trouble, Homer, and it's all my fault."

"What kind of trouble?"

"I've been threatened, and I don't know how to handle it. They said they'd kill us, Homer," Davy said, forcing the words out. "I still can't believe it."

"What the hell are you talking about?" Homer shouted, jumping out of his chair.

"Keep it down, Homer, I don't want Maddy to hear—at least, not yet. I don't know if these guys are serious, or bullshitting me, or just trying to scare me."

Davy slowly pushed himself off the divan. His usual fighter stance sagged. He closed his sweater and started pacing on the small deck. Even with the wind guards and an overhead heater, the slight chill of a fall breeze got through. "Homer, I'm in over my head. I didn't mean to. I was too trusting. They blindsided me, then backed me into a corner." His face showed pain—he was suffering.

Homer let his old friend take his time.

They were on the back deck of Davy's house in Kenai, about halfway between Anchorage and the Port of Homer. The fading sunset silhouetting snow-topped mountain peaks across the water. The deck faced west, overlooking Cook Inlet. The evening was still and clear. In the middle of winter it could get cold and windy, but never the low temperatures of a few hundred miles north.

From the vantage of this land-based shelter, the beauty of rough and stormy seas could be enjoyed safely, and with indifference—a strange feeling for old seamen.

Captain Davy Masters bought the house years ago after he retired. Said he wanted to watch the ships to and from Anchorage and talk with old friends by marine radio.

"There are two things we need to talk about," Davy said, calming. "I'll take the easy one first. The company might be setting you up for a fall, either to offer you a new job, but not as captain, or force you into retirement. Those two young executives they gave you are worthless. Watch them so they won't be the cause of your downfall. But you still have Ernie as First Mate so you should be okay."

"You're sure full of happy news, Davy."

"That's not the worst of it." Davy grew pensive again. He gulped his beer.

Homer noticed Davy's hands shaking. "There you go, again! What the hell is going on? What kind of trouble are you talking about? Just sit down and tell me what happened."

"No, I can't sit down. I'm too wound up. I need another beer. How about you? Hell, you never turn down something to drink."

Davy stepped into the house and yelled, "Madeline, we got more cold beer?" He turned to Homer. "I haven't told Maddy anything, but just like you, she can see. I'd better not get into any poker games," he chuckled, trying to make light of the situation.

"Okay, you know that now and then I act as a broker for cargo shipments. Gives me something to do and a little extra cash. Well…"

"Here's your beer, boys." Maddy came out looking at Homer. "He tell you anything? He's hiding something that's eaten' him up."

"Maddy," Davy said taking a beer, and with a deep sigh sat back down, "I was about to tell Homer. It concerns a shipment loaded on the *Alaskan Eagle* going to Seattle. You wanna hear about it?"

Maddy glanced over at him. "A shipment? I don't want to hear about a shipment. With all your fidgeting and shaking, I thought maybe you'd lost money gambling, or were upset about losing our dear Kodiak. You can't imagine the thoughts I've had. I don't want to hear about a shipment. You tell Homer about it while I clean up."

They sat quietly after Maddy left. "Kodiak." Davy, said, shaking his head. "Some name for a stray. Remember when we picked her up on a boat trip over to the island? She'd been fine lately. Day before yesterday, I let her out back. We found her a few hours later. Vet said it was something she ate."

"I'm sorry, Davy. I should've said something to Maddy." Homer gave Davy time to gather his thoughts. He'd seen him angry, seen his overbearing authority and sometimes his violence, all brought on by a rigid sense of right and wrong. But he'd never seen him fearful. This wasn't the Davy he remembered as a ship's captain. Homer was saddened to realize Davy was getting old. It happened so gradually, not noticeable the few times a year they met to drink and recall past adventures.

"Okay, Homer, here's what happened. A stranger contacted me to arrange a relatively small shipment to Seattle. You loaded it yesterday. He got my name by asking around in Anchorage. He wanted someone familiar with the *Alaskan Eagle*. Looking back, I can see he targeted both of us. He wanted an independent broker, not a large firm where many people would know of the shipment and might ask questions.

"He said the Seattle supplier of ocean survival suits is recalling them to make improvements in accordance with updated Coast Guard requirements. Usually, when the summer season ends, the distributors and retail marine supply stores keep their excess stock until the following summer's tourists and fishermen come back. I gave it no thought at all. If someone wanted to ship seventy-six survival suits back to Seattle, so what? That's when I made my mistake."

"What do you mean?"

"I should have let it drop. I had no reason to see any kind of problem. I called the guy shipping the boxes just to be friendly—I hadn't met him yet. I joked with him about how Alaska may be the largest state, but with a small population everyone knows every-thing about everyone else, particularly in the marine supply busi-ness. He said he planned to drive to the *Alaskan Eagle* to check on his boxes when the ship gets to the Port of Homer. He asked if he could stop by to say hello. They came today. That's when it took a bad turn." Davy stared at Homer. "Do you get the picture so far?"

"I think so, but I'm getting nervous as hell waiting for the punch line."

"It sure feels good talking to you about it, Homer. I've had a big lump in my chest. I've been scared shitless. It's gradually easing as

I tell you about it, but I'm bringing you into something nasty, and I feel terrible."

"Tell me the rest of it—everything. We'll see how we can work it out."

"We can't work this out. We're in too deep, and we can't ask for help. We'll have to see it through ourselves."

"Damn it, stop beating around the bush! Just tell me!"

"Okay, okay, Homer. I met the two guys. They said there are more of them, but it could be just those two." Davy took a gulp of his beer and paused. "They said they'd kill us, Homer, me and Madeline," Davy said again, whispering hoarsely.

"Holy shit Davy, why? What the fuck did you get into? Now, damn it, tell me the rest that happened! Don't leave anything out."

Davy paused. "Well, it was just a routine shipment until I got curious. You saw the boxes, nothing unusual. I'd already taken possession of the shipment. I didn't question them about it until after the boxes were loaded on the *Eagle*. If I'd thought about it a few weeks ago, I could have refused the shipment, but there was no real reason to do that. About midday today, two guys appeared at the door. They said they were the party shipping the boxes.

"What did they look like?" Homer asked, standing out on the deck. "There were two men in suits watching the loading in Anchorage."

"They were nicely dressed," Davy, said. They mentioned again that they were driving to the ship to see how their boxes made the trip. When you get back to the *Eagle* tonight see if they ever showed up. Now I think they came here just to see me. After my questions the day before, they probably decided to do some damage control."

Homer waited for the rest.

"They said the survival suit packing is deceptive. Yes, they're shipping survival suits, but the suits are packed to cushion a small, sensitive, and possibly fragile package in the center. They wouldn't tell me what's in the smaller package. Then, to my amazement, they laid down fifty thousand dollars in hundred dollar bills. They said it's an incentive for the two of us—for you and for me, and also to bind us to their contract. They said I should share the information and money with you."

"This is weird, Davy."

"I know, weird and scary as hell. At first they were calm and pleasant, but then they started to play hardball. They said the boxes are rigged so toxic fumes would come out of them if they were opened for inspection. 'Of course', they said, 'we wouldn't want any of the crew or the customs people in Seattle to be exposed. Their lives depend on you and Captain Dixon'. They knew that a shipment directly between two U.S. ports is not subject to inspection, but in these times, who knows. And that's why they looked for a small reputable broker, me, and a reliable captain, you."

Homer felt his body stiffen as Davy went on.

"They told me in a matter-of-fact way, if anything goes wrong, or if we go to the authorities, they will…" Davy paused again, breathing deeply, "…they said they'd kill Maddy in front of me, and kill me. And they said, 'we will kill your friend Captain Dixon also'. They told me they know where Lorraine and my granddaughter live, and that we'd be watched. If we managed to elude them, we'd be tracked down. They said they were part of a large organization."

"Jesus," Homer breathed.

"What can we do, Homer?" Davy cried. "This is a fucking nightmare. I don't know what to do."

"My God. I can see why you're twitching the way you are." Homer walked over to the corner of the deck. He saw movement at the end of the street—a car door opening and a man pouring liquid out of a cup. For a moment, with the car light on, he thought he could see two men sitting in the car. "Davy, did the Vet say what Kodiak might have eaten?"

Davy looked up, his mouth open. "No, he didn't say. Oh, no. Do you think they had something to do with it?" Davy sat with his head in his hands. He slowly lifted himself out of the chair, and raised his head to look at Homer. "I want you to take the money. I don't want Maddy to see it. Half of it is yours, anyway. If anything should happen to us, get the rest of it to Lorraine. You know where she lives."

Homer shook his head. "First of all, I don't want any of the money, but I'll take it to Seattle. We have to sit on the money and ride this out. When it's all over, you and Maddy use it to get a condo in Maui, or something. The best thing right now is for the two of you to pack some bags and come down to the ship with me. When we get to Seattle, and everything is okay, just go visit Lorraine for awhile."

Davy looked at him.

In an effort to calm Davy, Homer switched to his—*we've got a problem, how do we solve it approach.* "We don't know what's in those boxes, and we may never know, but they must be worth a hell of a lot for them to give away fifty grand in insurance money. The boxes aren't marked fragile. If they're booby trapped with a toxic gas, there must be a tightly sealed inner wrap. The cardboard container, no matter how sturdy, couldn't seal it. There must be a smaller package in the center with the contraband. I'd like to know what it is. We'll probably never know. If we do find out, we're dead. There's nothing to do but go along with them—and there has to be more than the two of them, just to pack the boxes."

Davy kept shaking his head, *No,* as if he could ward the problem away.

"What did they look like, Davy?" Homer glanced up the street again. The car was gone. "Let's go inside. It's damn cold out here." He locked the deck door behind them and checked the front door of the house.

"What are you doing, Homer?"

"I saw two guys in a car up the street, but the car is gone now."

"What did they look like?"

"I couldn't tell. How about the two guys who came to see you, what were *they* like?"

"Their English was good, but they spoke with a slight accent. I don't think they're American born." Davy turned to walk into the bedroom. "I'm gonna check on Maddy."

While he was gone Homer went back on the deck to look, then checked the living room and kitchen windows. He did not see the car. When Davy returned, Homer asked about Maddy.

"She's all right. Just finished her shower."

"Listen," Homer said. "I really think you should drop everything and come with me. You can stay in my Seattle apartment. When the goods are delivered, you can go down to California to visit Lorraine. We can't confront these people, or try to double cross them. We wouldn't know where to start. We *could* tell Customs about it in Seattle. Then Customs would have the goods but not the people, and we'd be looking over our shoulders for the rest of our lives. There's too much unknown at this time for us to do anything except go along."

They'd both dealt with unscrupulous people in their careers but never faced apparent evil.

After a quiet moment, Davy said, "I asked Maddy and she doesn't want to go right now. I couldn't explain the situation to her. If we're being watched, or if one of them sees us board the *Eagle*, we could be in trouble. When the ship leaves, things should calm down."

Homer thought about it, nodded, and got up. "Keep your gun handy. I mean it. Keep it out, loaded, and available." He gave Davy a brief hug. "Goodbye, old friend."

They shook hands. Davy held onto Homer's hand. "I feel a hell of a lot better now." He handed Homer the bag with the money.

"You should feel better, you old fart. You've transferred the burden to me."

"What are you going to do?"

"I'll see. I have to secure those boxes and put a barrier around them so no one gets close. It feels like we're being threatened by fanatics, but instead of fighting we've joined them to save our own skins. Are we saving ourselves, or just delaying the end? As for my job, I'll see how this trip goes and see what the Company wants to do with me."

Maddy came out in her bathrobe. "Good-bye, Homer dear." She paused, then said, "You know, Homer, whenever we say good-bye I always wonder if we'll ever see you again."

Homer and Davy exchanged glances.

Homer cleared his throat, "Thanks for dinner, Maddy. I'm sorry about Kodiak."

"Thank you, Homer."

"Take care of this old man here."

"I'll try, Homer, I'll try."

CHAPTER THREE

*D*avy walked out of the house with Homer. They both looked up and down the street. As Homer climbed into the truck Davy grabbed his shoulder and held onto his arm. "You be extra careful, now. These guys could be anywhere. In fact, check your passengers, and even some of your crew."

"Good point." Homer patted Davy's hand and started the truck. "And you get back in the house, be cautious all the time, and keep Maddy with you. You'll have to tell her something to make her aware, but try not to scare the hell out of her."

Davy nodded. "I know." He watched as Homer drove away.

Homer kept his high beams on. He glanced down each of the side streets. Nothing appeared out of the ordinary. Not yet on the main highway, his seemed to be the only car on the road.

His body slumped. He no longer needed to keep up the façade of being in control. "I've got to focus," he whispered to himself. His whole career he'd dealt with ships, cargo, and people. The problems that arose, and there were always problems, were handled utilizing past experience. Problems that couldn't be solved were just that, but decisions were made to get past them. Problems with imminent consequences were always solved, in one way or another, to some degree of satisfaction.

The present dilemma was so new, with so much unknown, he had a difficult time aligning his thoughts. It was as if they were fighting blurred ghosts. Circumstances at sea required rapid decisions, but those decisions were almost automatic. They were rarely without precedent, in that, they were always the same, or a variation of situations with which he had experience. Also, he was part of an organization, part of the ship. Problems were never aimed at him personally.

He felt anxious for Davy and Maddy. Why hadn't they come with him? It would be easier to control if they were all together. He needed a drink. There was nothing in the truck. Thinking about Davy and Maddy made him less concerned about his own danger. Once back on the ship, with Ernie for support, he'd be in familiar, secure surroundings. He was confident he could manage. *You live your life day by day and get hit with an unexpected situation, totally beyond your imagination.*

Coming out of the residential and commercial area he turned east on the Kenai Spur Highway leading to Sterling Highway, for the seventy-mile drive to the Homer Spit. He pulled a cell phone from his jacket. "Ernie, I just left Davy and Maddy. We've got a problem."

"Are they all right?" Ernie asked.

"They're fine. I won't go into the details right now, but it's about those boxes we loaded in Anchorage. Did anyone come aboard tonight looking for me or asking to check on them?"

"No, no one. What's going on, Captain? Fill me in."

"I will, as soon as I get there. It should take me an hour or so. Will you be around?"

"I will now. Skipper, just got a message—we won't have to worry about coddling those two trainees. They'll be leaving in Juneau. Why, I don't know."

"What do you mean, leaving in Juneau? We need them all the way to Seattle."

"Not gonna happen. The company didn't say why. They would've left from here, but it's a hassle trying to get back to Anchorage for a flight."

"Shit, Ernie, we need watch-standers. We can't be on the bridge around the clock. Goddamn new management. They don't give a rat's ass about us. Why are they doing this? Davy heard something was going to happen, but didn't know what. They've probably written us off already. They might give us our walking papers when we tie up in Seattle."

"They told us to pick up some people in Juneau or use the senior crew to fill in," Ernie said. "Almost any decision could be a Coast Guard violation."

"This is a royal pain in the ass."

"Skipper, how about signing Nick Banner? We hauled his equipment up from Seattle last winter. He's due to board in Juneau for the trip back, and he's got a Mate's ticket. Maybe he'll help us out. Be better than picking up a stranger."

"Nick could work out fine. Call him tomorrow. Meanwhile, keep an eye on the gangway so the seaman on duty doesn't let just anyone on board. I'll sign off now. Boy, I need a drink."

"Go easy, Homer, we'll throw down a few when you get here."

The drive and talk with Ernie calmed him, just as telling Homer had relieved Davy's anxiety.

Sterling Highway ended at the Spit, a strip of land jutting out four miles into Kachemak Bay. It provided a natural seaport for the city. The *Eagle* was tied up at the Alaska State Ferry Dock out on the Spit. During his career Homer had plied only the waters of the Alaska Marine Highway from Seattle to Anchorage. He came to the states of Washington and Alaska after his Maritime Academy graduation, and rarely left. He had an apartment in Seattle but thought of Alaska as his home.

Traffic was light late at night, but visibility was never good on this unlit winding highway making it difficult to see cars ahead or those overtaking from behind. The weather, as usual, was overcast and misty, leaving a wet film on the surface of the road and on his windshield.

He drove one of the *Eagle*'s old pick-up trucks at a moderate speed. Everything connected with the *Eagle* was old. The trucks were kept in the hold of the ship utilizing the cargo loading-unloading ramp. Although it looked a mess, the truck was well maintained by the crew. Used only for limited transportation and the loading of ship's stores, it had low mileage.

He reached for a tape in the glove compartment. The music would help keep him awake, not that there was a chance he would doze off. Glancing over, he saw a new note on the dashboard. Notes were common in the truck. Everything from grocery lists and telephone numbers to basic vehicle operating procedures. Some were in Spanish. He was surprised he hadn't noticed it before. He grabbed it off the dashboard and held it close in the dark to read the printed words: 'We are watching you Captain Dixon'.

Homer looked at his rear view mirror. There were headlights a few hundred yards back. He hadn't been paying attention. *How long had they been there? At his speed, cars should be passing him regularly. A few had.* The headlights lingered behind him. *Is it a cautious driver, or someone following me?* Homer increased his speed. The headlights kept pace. They were not trying to pass, but seemed a little closer.

He speed-dialed Ernie. "I'm almost to Anchor Point. There's a car following me, but before you ask me a lot of questions, I've got some."

"You okay, Captain? Should I call the police?"

"No, don't do that. They're not going to do anything. They just want to tail me. Those two new seamen we got in Anchorage, have they been aboard?"

"Yes, and no, Skipper. They were here for most of the day then asked for the evening off. I saw them get into a car, probably a rental. I guess they didn't want to take a bus or walk the four miles into town. Pretty costly for seamen at their pay rate."

"Did you notice the type of car, or color?"

"Not really. Let me think; it was two-door, dark color, not too big. Will you tell me what's going on?"

"Not yet, Ernie, only about 15 minutes to go." Homer ended the call.

Now he felt certain they were following him. *Were they the guys parked on Davy's street?* He kept his pace fairly constant, hoping they were unaware that he knew he was being followed. *They probably don't care if I know. They want to intimidate me, and they are. Had they wanted to do me harm, they could have done that anytime in the past hour. But why? Their goal is to get the boxes to Seattle with my help. Davy's no longer in the picture. It's up to me. Their intimidation was another way of saying, yes, Captain Dixon, you are being watched.*

He was now within the Port of Homer town limits. His pursuer stayed very close. *Maybe they're just playing games?* He felt agitated again but resisted the urge to slam on his brakes or just pull over. Pioneer Avenue, the main east-west road through the town, came into view. He saw two large trucks slowly approaching up the grade. On impulse, Homer swung left onto Pioneer just in front of the lead truck. The truck driver blew his horn. The car behind Homer jerked his wheel starting to follow, then continued on Sterling Highway. In that instant he saw two men in a small, dark, two-door car.

"Why did I do that?" he wondered out loud. They're getting to me, he realized. *I've got to stay rational.* He slowed as he approached the Police and Fire Stations. Again an impulse took over. He wanted to go to the Police, show them the money, and get the burden off his back. If not for Davy and Maddy's safety, he would've done just that.

Instead, he pulled into a closed gas station and parked while keeping an eye on his rear view mirror. He picked up his phone again. "Ernie, I cut off at Pioneer and they didn't make the turn. There's no sign of them. Before you start asking questions, I'm going to sit here and tell you what happened tonight. While I'm doing that, be sure you're in a spot to see if those two come aboard, and if they get out of the same car."

Homer went over the events of the evening, including the drive back. He had no doubts about taking Ernie into his confidence. He considered himself fortunate to have had Davy as a mentor and friend, and Ernie, someone he could trust without hesitation. Ernie was one of the reasons Homer hadn't looked for other jobs when management and company policies changed.

"Skipper," Ernie interrupted, "They're walking down the dock. No car in sight."

"I'll be there in ten minutes. We'll talk more in my cabin." He turned right on Lake Street, leading him down a hill back to Sterling Highway. The full four miles of the Spit was now visible. The volcanic upheavals and glaciers left this thin piece of land, just a few feet above sea level, for use by the town.

He drove out on the Spit, scanning all familiar locations, searching for the chase car. He parked the truck on the dock near the *Eagle's* loading ramp, still holding the note. *I'll show it to Ernie.* He got out of the truck glancing around for anyone or anything strange. He wondered if he was being watched. As he climbed the gangway, the pounding of his heart belied his casual manner.

Ernie waited for him in the Captain's Stateroom.

"Ernie, I don't know where to start," Homer said, thinking he sounded like Davy earlier in the evening, and how it'd only been a few hours since these events began. "I forgot where I left off. I'll go over it again."

After a lengthy and emotional conversation, interrupted by Ernie's questions, they sat in silence.

Homer showed him the bag of hundred dollar bills before locking the money in his safe. "I'm too beat to mess with the cargo now. We'll have some hands re-stow it in the morning. I'm dry as a bone. Let's go down to the saloon for a beer." Again, he felt relieved to have shared the burden with Ernie, as if the more who knew of the situation would somehow lighten its weight. He knew Ernie could analyze the problem from a less emotional point of view.

"We've got some crew and passengers still ashore," Ernie said, as they walked down the gangway. "I told them to be back aboard by five. We'll have to vacate this dock early. The Alaska State Ferry is due at six. I checked the crew roster for anyone who could be classified as suspicious. Just came up with the two you've identified. As for the passengers, I didn't see anyone unusual. We'll have to look closer and check those coming aboard in Juneau and Ketchikan."

They drove a short distance along the Spit Road.

"Skipper, do you remember that fancy yacht, about an eighty footer, that was parked up-stream from us in Anchorage? Take a look to the right. Isn't that the same boat?"

"It sure looks like it."

A few minutes later they entered the old Spit-Boaters Saloon, a throwback to days gone-by. Most of the ports they serviced, including the Ballard seaport area of Seattle, had similar funky bars. Homer and Ernie knew them all. A loud three-piece band at Spit-Boaters helped mask their conversation.

"We'll need a work-crew of six seamen to secure those boxes," Homer said. "I want to direct the job myself and to observe those two new guys. Don't tell them what the work entails so I can see their reaction.

"Bastards want to intimidate me—this should make them sweat a little."

CHAPTER FOUR

October 17th–Departing Port of Homer, Alaska, 5am

"I *see you guys decided to come back," Homer yelled,* kidding a few tardy seamen as they walked up the gangway. Standing on the outer bridge of the *Eagle*, he surveyed his ship and all the pre-departure activities with what appeared to be a relaxed smile.

Still dark, the Spit was asleep but aglow with lights. The October sun would not show until later in the morning. The *Eagle's* winter departures and arrivals were usually early in the morning or after dark. From mid-September through mid-May the shortened days and lower temperatures drove the cruise ships back to the Caribbean.

A shame, Homer always said, because the area of Alaska from Ketchikan to the Ports of Homer and Seward, were spectacular during the winter, and quite tolerable, with less snow and warmer temperatures than much of the lower forty-eight. Someday they'll realize that.

His favorite town, somewhat influenced by its name, had always been Homer. Year after year he endured the same kidding—was he named after the town, or was the town named after him? Occasionally, a more scholarly bar mate would cite the Homer of ancient Greece, or a younger seaman would bring up Homer Simpson.

"What are you grinning about, Skipper?" Ernie asked.

"It's been less than twelve hours since the shit hit the fan. I slept less than three, and I might be fooling myself, but for some reason I feel like we're in control, not them. You'll need to take the ship out while I inspect those boxes and see how best to secure them."

"Aye, Captain. As soon as we have our departure meeting and pull away from the dock, you'll have six seamen down in the hold, including our two newcomers."

The brief all-hands meetings were held out on deck in tolerable weather. "Gentlemen," Homer greeted them, enjoying the moment and his role as Captain. "And Ladies," he nodded to the two women in the crew. "It saddens me to leave beautiful Homer, but we can look forward to coming back next month." He knew they could judge his disposition at these meetings. He was rarely anything but cordial, treating the crew almost as passengers.

It was up to Ernie to impose a reasonable balance and strict discipline similar to the Executive Officer on a Navy ship. Both Homer and Ernie had personalities that fit their roles.

"The weather looks good for the next week and will probably stay that way until we get to the sheltered islands south of Juneau. Our roster is at the standard level of twenty-two. Passenger count is still at ten. First Mate McInnis has a few words for you. Have a fine trip."

"You, too, Captain."

Homer went down to the cargo hold storage area on the ship's lowest deck. The boxes were packed three high against the outer starboard bulkhead. Held by a flexible mesh fence they were secure as stored, unless something in the hold got loose and smashed against them. He noticed they were loaded almost in sequence, with the numbers one through seventy-six prominently displayed.

They were hauled into the hold this way from trucks. He was easily able to identify and count all of them.

"Captain," one of the senior crewmen said as he entered the area, "I've got the other men on their way. How do you want these stacked?"

"Place them on that port side ledge above the lower deck. This cardboard will turn to mush if we ship any water. There's only room to stack them two high but we have plenty of open space on the ledge to spread out. Also, use a double mesh to secure them, each mesh tied-off independently."

Homer looked at the crew coming in. Those he knew either nodded at him or accepted his presence. The other two, whom he'd seen briefly when they reported aboard but not since, glanced at him and followed the others.

The forty-pound boxes were cumbersome to grip without rope ties or hand slots in the cardboard. The ledge was twelve feet off the deck of the hold. A basket suitable for lifting two boxes at a time was fitted to a moveable hoist. The four experienced seamen were positioned on the ledge to grab and secure the boxes while the two new men lifted them off the lower stacks to load them onto the hoist.

About halfway through the project Homer felt the *Eagle* make a sharp right around the end of the Spit incurring a head wind and an ocean swell. It made the ship roll about ten degrees to port. Not significant as such, but it caused a box to slip out of the hands of the lower crew. The box fell about six feet to the deck and bounced with no apparent damage to the cardboard or the structure of the container. Homer tensed.

The two men showed no concern and immediately grabbed the box to continue working.

"That's what I saw," Homer told Ernie later. "There's no way both of them could fake it that well. Either they were not told of the inner bag with toxic gas, or there is no gas, or these two guys are not even part of the organization threatening Davy. My gut feeling is that the toxic scare is a lot of bullshit, but these two are here to watch us and to make sure none of the boxes go missing."

"I'll keep their work assignments away from the hold," Ernie said. "That way we'll notice if they're spotted down there. During the two days we're in Juneau we can see if they meet with anyone, or if we notice anyone who fits Davy's description of his two visitors.

"I've tried to get in touch with Nick Banner in Juneau. He should be happy to help us out with the incentive of free passage to Seattle. I'll ask him to drop in at the Coast Guard Station today to certify his papers."

"That shouldn't be a problem," Homer said. "At some point, if he agrees, we'll have to tell him what's going on. If all hell should break loose, he'll be needed to back us up."

"Could be tricky. He might balk at being kept in the dark. We don't know his frame of mind in situations like this. We'll have to feel him out. I'll open our gun locker today to see the condition of our guns and ammo. You should check the one you keep in your cabin. And, with your okay, I'll search the personal belongings of our two strangers while we've got them occupied elsewhere."

"Do it," Homer said. "I know you've looked over the passengers and their papers, but I'm going to do it again and greet each of them properly, as The Captain."

They steamed through Kachemak Bay heading for Cook Inlet. Most of the trip to Juneau was transiting the Gulf of Alaska, the open ocean leg of their route to Seattle, with seas most susceptible to weather extremes.

Occasionally, Homer ran into fifty-knot winds and forty-foot swells while making this crossing. On some trips he would need to seek shelter for one or more days in nearby ports. The only time during the voyage he felt comfortable staying off the bridge, and trusting the officer on duty, was when the seas were calm.

Upon leaving Juneau, the journey south past the lower Alaska Islands, through sheltered straits, was rarely weather threatened but presented tricky feats of navigation and ship control. Sometimes fog or rough seas would hamper their trip in the more open ocean areas, as in the Canadian waters south of Ketchikan.

Homer waited until seven to call Davy. There was no answer after about a dozen rings. He tried a second time. Again, no answer. *Either they're out, unlikely this early, or he's on the line and didn't want to switch over.* Homer didn't want to consider other possibilities. "Jesus," he muttered. His feeling of being in control waned. *I can't call his daughter. It's too early and I'd scare the hell out of her. Should I call the police? If so, I should call them now in case it's an emergency.*

Ernie knocked and came in. "What happened to your happy face, Skipper? You look like death warmed over."

"I tried to call Davy, twice. There was no answer. It just knocked the shit out of me." Homer took several deep breaths. "What should I do?"

Ernie was about to respond when Homer's phone rang. "I thought that might be you," Davy said. "No one else would call me twice at this hour."

"It *was* me, damn-it, you scared the hell out of me," Homer snapped. "I wanted to give you an update. Are you okay?"

"Yeah, we're fine. That was our friends from Anchorage on the line. It seems they know you re-stowed those boxes, which pleased them. I didn't know you freaked out on the ride back to the ship last night. The whole thing amused them, no end. Obviously, you've got some spies on board, as we suspected."

"You seem pretty casual about the whole thing," Homer said. "I've briefed Ernie and have this call on speaker phone."

"Hi, Ernie," Davy greeted. "The reason I feel casual is that they're happy, which makes the whole thing less threatening."

"Bullshit," Homer said. "Don't let your guard down for a second. I don't trust them. We're pretty sure we've identified the two new seamen as the only people on board to watch. I'll talk with them as soon as we hang up."

"Well, be careful."

"You be careful," Homer warned. "You're more vulnerable than we are. I'll call you often as long as we have a signal, so answer the damn phone."

"I will. One more thing. Sneak off to a bank in Juneau and get one of those bills checked to see if they're real. I saw something in the news about phony money being circulated in the Seattle area."

"Good idea, but I can't just walk into a bank. They might ask questions, and if the bill is bad, they'll confiscate it and report it. I'll figure something out. You stay well, now." Homer ended the call and turned to his first mate. "Ernie, find those two and send them here for a chat. We might as well get this whole thing out in the open. I'll meet with them alone. As yet, they don't know you're in on it. Let's keep it that way so our options remain open."

"Aye, Skipper. I'll come in after they leave. If they give you any trouble, buzz for me."

Homer's quarters consisted of a small suite befitting his position as Captain, with the bed and his personal items in an adjoining room. His desk occupied an imposing part of the office.

Fifteen minutes later, the two were standing in front of him. Homer stayed seated. Their papers were on his desk. "You're both from Singapore and one of you is named John Smith and the other John Brown. Who has the sense of humor?"

"Those are our names," one replied. "We have the official papers to prove it. What do you mean by 'sense of humor'?"

"And you are who?" Homer asked.

"My name is John Smith," the tall one responded in an agitated manner.

Homer repressed a smile.

He seemed like a typical hardened, thug-type character, right out of old movies. John Brown was his shorter sidekick, but more normal in looks and demeanor.

"Well, we got that cleared up," Homer said. "Oh, by the way." Homer paused. "Do you know what I mean by the words 'by the way'?"

They both looked at him.

"We have a company policy that no telephone calls can be made from the ship at sea except from the communications center on the bridge. It's standard industry practice. You'll need to give us your cell phones and radios until we get to the next port."

They stared at Homer for a moment. "Cut the crap, Captain," John Smith sneered, "You may be steering the ship until we get to Seattle, but you are not in charge. We are in charge. If you care for your friend Davy and his wife, you better understand that. We should tell you that someone will come aboard in Juneau and again in Ketchikan to check our shipment. We will be with you until the ship gets to Seattle. You will receive instructions on how to proceed during the offloading. Do you understand, Captain Dixon?" Smith grabbed Brown's arm and turned. They left the cabin without another word.

Homer sat stunned and breathless. His feelings were so unusual he just stayed there, red-faced. At no time, or in any other situation aboard his ship, would he have ever tolerated what had just happened. He felt like his hands were tied and his mouth taped. He relaxed. The more he thought about it, he was glad he kept his temper.

Ernie knocked and came in.

Homer continued sitting there with an eerie smile on his face.

Ernie stared at him, somewhat puzzled. "What happened?" After hearing the details, Ernie nodded. "Nothing has changed. In fact, it makes it easier for us. We don't have to pussyfoot around them. Since they don't know that I know, I can treat them like seamen and work them like seamen. And that's the way you should treat them in front of any of the crew. They're not going to do anything. There's nothing they can do. They don't want to fuck things up."

"You're right. I just got burned. It's like the ride back from Davy's house. I can't let myself get intimidated. I've got to get past it. Yeah, we're being watched. They know we know we're being watched. We know they know, etc. Ernie, I'm glad I've got you around to whack me on the side of the head when I need it."

"It's my pleasure, Homer." Ernie smiled. "What I've got to do now is contact Nick Banner. Beyond that, everything should be routine ship's business, at least for the next two days until we get to Juneau."

"Look at us. Two old codgers," Homer mused aloud, "We've been in a lot of battles but never in a fight like this. We'll figure this out. Either see it through to the end or bust it apart. Let's see what happens."

CHAPTER FIVE

October 17th—Juneau, Alaska

*N*ick's phone rang just as he got to his truck. He answered without looking at the number, thinking it might be Minnie or one of the guys in his crew.

"Nick, hey. I'm glad I got hold of you. This is Ernie McInnis, First Mate on the *Alaskan Eagle*. How have you been?"

"Just fine, Ernie. How are you guys?"

"Good. We just left the Port of Homer and expect to get to Juneau in two days, the morning of the nineteenth. You still planning to ride with us from Juneau to Seattle?"

"I sure am. I've got most of my gear stored at the dock waiting for the *Eagle*. Is there a problem?"

"No problem at all, but I wonder if you could help us out. We're short a Mate who can handle officer duties and stand bridge watches. Would you be willing to do that for free passage and a fee reduction for shipping your gear? In fact, we'll pay you the standard Mate's rate if Coast Guard will clear your papers."

"Ernie, you guys must be desperate to need me. Sure, I'll help you out. Actually, the Coast Guard has paid for my passage and the shipment of equipment as part of my contract, so cost is not a factor. I'm on my way over to the station right now."

"Good. Would you ask them about your papers, Nick? It'll keep us from picking up a stranger."

"Will do. I'll let you know what they say. Ernie, is that forward cabin on the starboard side open? I may have company on the way back."

"It's yours, Nick, even if Coast Guard doesn't sign off on it, and I won't even ask any questions. I'll fill you in on the situation aboard the *Eagle* when we arrive. No big deal, really. I'm glad I was able to get hold of you. How did your job go?"

"It went well. We finish up tomorrow and will wait for you the morning of the nineteenth. See you then, Ernie."

Nick signed off the call, climbed into his truck, and headed for the Coast Guard Station. *It could be a fun trip. It'll update my Mate's qualifications, and the accommodations on the Eagle will be better. Ten days on a leisure trip with Minnie, without the guys giving me hell about robbing the cradle. Coast Guard should approve it. My past experience and two-year working relationship with the station will help. Anyway, Ernie wouldn't have suggested it if he didn't think it would work.*

"Hi, Mr. Banner," the Coastguardsman at the front desk greeted him. "Your meeting with Commander Ellings has been changed to the Captain's conference room."

I guess we're going to have a formal wrap-up of the project. Two years of proposals, contracts, and underwater construction, culminating this past summer with the installation. The job was difficult, but personally rewarding. He planned to complete the final report in Seattle with Minnie's help. They would make use of the trip south on the *Eagle* to get it organized.

The Captain's secretary asked him to go right in.

Captain Forrest stood talking with an unknown civilian.

The only other participant in the meeting was Commander Ellings, Nick's usual contact during the project.

Captain Forrest approached Nick and shook his hand. "Nick, we've expanded the agenda of this routine project completion meeting to include a few new items. I'm sorry to spring this on you, but you'll see why as we proceed. First, Commander Ellings will review the Security & Surveillance System you're completing. After that we'll get to the Ketchikan Coast Guard Base S & S System. You've shown an interest in doing that job. With your indulgence, I'd like to keep you in the dark for a few minutes about the presence of our guest here. Commander, you may carry on."

Commander Ellings proceeded to review the project from the proposal stage through the last task, slated for tomorrow, of photographing the installed underwater system for inclusion in the final report.

The level of detail must be for the benefit of the stranger, Nick surmised, as he stared at the only other person in the room.

When he finished, Commander Ellings nodded at the Captain.

Captain Forrest rose and uncovered a wall chart of the Ketchikan Coast Guard Base. "Nick. We issue construction contracts for Ketchikan as well as Juneau. You've expressed interest in providing the S & S System for Ketchikan. As with Juneau, the system will continuously monitor surface and underwater incursions from the shoreline of the Base out into the channel. What we would like to do is by-pass the proposal and bidding stage and negotiate an extension to your present contract that would include Ketchikan, citing cost, scheduling advantages, and government security issues, with Coast Guard providing the necessary ships and personnel."

Nick nodded at Captain Forrest and smiled. "Captain, I'd be delighted to accept a contract extension."

"Fine. I'm pleased. Since I'm certain we can work out the details, you might want to off-load your trucks and some of your equipment at the Ketchikan facility when you stop there. You and Commander Ellings can coordinate that."

Captain Forrest paused a few seconds, looking at Nick. "We received a call from Captain Dixon on the transport vessel *Alaskan Eagle*. You may be aware of their interest in signing you on as Mate for the trip back to Seattle. We'll approve the request. It ties in with the last item we want to discuss."

The Commander spoke next, "Now, the reason for our unusual meeting this morning; Nick Banner, I'd like you to meet Frank Harris, with the U.S. Coast Guard Headquarters in Washington, D.C. I'll let Mr. Harris take over from here."

"Mr. Banner," Frank Harris started, "We have a situation that may involve foreign nationals in this country utilizing bogus passports and papers. They may be shipping contraband loaded on the *Alaskan Eagle* in Anchorage, destined for Seattle. If it is contraband—as yet we do not know what it is. We're late in putting this together. As far as we know, all the suspected contraband is aboard the *Alaskan Eagle*, so the cargo can be controlled at this point. Most of the foreign nationals seem to be together on a chartered yacht called *Mother's Love*, trailing the *Alaskan Eagle*. However, we have yet to identify the rest of them or their locations. Is there a problem, Mr. Banner?"

"Please, it's Nick. Do Captain Dixon and his First Mate McInnis know of this? Will I be getting into a can of worms, here? And, I get the feeling that you're leading up to something."

"We are, Nick. We don't know if Captain Dixon is aware of this. We can't notify him by ship-to-shore radio. The message could be intercepted. We hope you'll be able to assess the situation when you get aboard. Before I complete the broad picture, I'd like to get to the bottom line. Nick, we know your background, your experience, and your capabilities, including your eight-year stint as a Navy SEAL. We'd like your help. As a legitimate passenger and cargo shipper on the *Alaskan Eagle,* and now even better as a crewmember, you can pass us information until we're ready to move in. Your presence should not arouse any suspicion. But before you make up your mind, you should know that this is a ruthless bunch. They are suspected in several murders. In addition, the man who chartered the yacht to a Mr. John Adams was involved in a hit-and-run motorcycle accident. He did not die," Harris paused.

"We have the man under police protection at a hospital in Anchorage. It appears that anyone who makes personal contact with them, and could identify them, is in jeopardy of being killed. You should be aware of this, Mr. Banner. Until we know what is being shipped, and the location of all the people involved, we feel it best to hold off. We're here for the next two days. When the ship leaves Juneau, we'll fly to Ketchikan. We need you to accept or decline by tomorrow so we'll have time to brief you on the details. We'll meet here at the Coast Guard Station. The same in Ketchikan; we'll meet on the Base. None of this information is classified, as yet, but it's considered extremely sensitive."

Nick frowned. "Let me break for a few minutes to check on my crew, ponder this and come back with some questions. I'll give you my final answer tomorrow. My feeling right now is yes, I will do it."

When Nick walked out of the meeting, Frank Harris caught up with him. "Can we have a minute alone? I'm sure you don't know this, but I need to disclose a past association I have with you and your family. I went to high school with your wife, Helen, and I was on patrol with the San Diego Harbor Police twenty years ago this past July 4th. I hope this doesn't affect your decision."

Nick felt his composure slipping as the memories resurfaced. He mumbled something to Harris and made his way blindly to his truck. He was unsure how long he sat alone before returning to the meeting.

CHAPTER SIX

October 18th—Juneau

*N*ick opened his eyes—Minnie was lying with her head propped up by her arm, staring at him.

"Good morning," he said.

Minnie didn't respond. She continued to stare with a frown on her face.

"Okay," Nick said, sighing. "What is it?"

Minnie's face softened. She slid down next to him for a full body hug, and kissed his neck. "We've got to talk," she whispered. "No, I've got to talk."

They lay still, enjoying the feel of each other. Nick embraced her. He ran his hands up and down her torso, resting them on her backside.

She had a slim, well-conditioned body with youthful energy that permitted her to keep up with the men in his crew. Minnie had joined them in May when the spring weather allowed their diving operations to continue. His crew was a rugged bunch closer to her age than his.

At first, he thought of her a little young; associating her more with his college age daughter, Hannah, but over time came to realize she wasn't a kid.

"I know what you're thinking," Minnie said. "It's that condescending way you pat me. You weren't that way last night."

"Minnie."

"Nope," she said, placing her fingers over his mouth. "I'm doing the talking. You can talk later. Nick, it's not our age difference. Twelve years is no big deal. It's that something has died inside you. On the job, you're all business, in charge, and good at it. But sometimes, when you're with me, you pull inside yourself. It's almost as if you remember that you're not allowed to enjoy yourself, that you're supposed to grieve." Minnie's eyes welled. She lifted Nick's hand to her lips.

"Minnie."

"No, not yet, you sweet man. When Hannah was here we spent a lot of time together. We became good friends. She told me her mother died when she was born, but she never went into any of the details. I'm not sure she knows the details. But that's not what I want to talk about. The end of the project comes at a good time. I don't fully know you, Nick. I don't know what you're hiding inside, but I've fallen in love with you. Yet, I grieve for your grief, if that's what the problem is. It's not that you are down sometimes; it's the distance you travel when you're down. It frightens me," Minnie sobbed.

Nick wondered how to explain or even discuss that Fourth of July with her, or with anyone. The pain had eased, but never left him, even for a day. Yesterday's conversation with Harris nearly destroyed his self-control. He cut their second meeting short, feigning a problem at the job site.

Nick drew Minnie to him, holding her until she became calm. They lay there in silence. Gradually, their emotions turned physical in a subdued, tender way, unlike their explosive encounters after long workdays of concealing their mounting attraction.

Afterward, with Minnie asleep, Nick showered and dressed for the remaining tasks at the job site. He left her a note to join him.

His crew was busy packing project gear as Nick drove out near the end of the Coast Guard pier. They kept up a continuous light-hearted banter that went with the feeling of completing a well-done job, and the anticipation of flying home the next day. Nick planned one more dive for a final inspection of the underwater system.

"Hi, Boss," one of his guys called out as Nick approached the work area.

Nick hired a team of six divers, including Minnie, for the Coast Guard contract, each with different or overlapping specialties. Except for Minnie, the group all worked with Nick on and off through the extent of the two year contract. She was a diver, but the only crewmember not experienced in underwater construction. Nick needed her on site for her engineering and computer skills and to help with the project completion report.

"I'll be suiting up for my dive," Nick informed the five men. "You guys decide who will go with me and who's manning the support boat. When Minnie gets here, she'll replace my dive buddy. I want her to see the finished product and take photographs. She'll need as much as she can get for the report."

It was no secret to the men that Minnie was shacking-up with the boss. Most of them had tried to win her soon after she arrived. She evaluated all of them, she told Nick later, but wanted him. When the project was running well, with harmony between her and the guys, he acquiesced, but made her wait until Hannah went home after her summer break. During the time when Minnie hung out with the guys she was careful not to give Nick the impression she was fooling around with any of them.

Although the depths were not significantly challenging, a maximum of about eighty feet, he put on double tanks to extend his time underwater. He planned a circuit of all sixteen bottom-mounted sensors, most of them in the deeper water. He carried a powerful underwater light to supplement the midday sun in the clear, frigid water. It looked to be a good visibility day, but at this depth they could barely see the large white number on each sensor structure.

The area, under constant surveillance, was listed as restricted and off limits to all ships, boats, divers and swimmers not approved by the Coast Guard. The exact location of each sensor was classified. Nick and his crew needed to undergo background investigations for their temporary clearances. A power and signal cable from each sensor was buried a few inches below the ocean floor and run through individual conduits to the main building at the Station. Random height floats attached to anchors on the ocean floor were scattered throughout the area to deter surface ships and underwater diver vehicles. Each float was on an anchored winch and could be raised or lowered from the control room ashore.

Divers were required to wear flexible steel gloves to work near the barbed razor wire connecting each structure. These wires troubled Nick. They were almost invisible even in the best midday light. Minnie had been in the water many times during the months of construction, but carrying the underwater camera was cumbersome. He'd have to watch carefully to keep her away from the wires. Nick insisted that all dives by his crew, since the installation of the wire system, be on a buddy-diver basis; two divers for each dive, no exceptions.

Minnie arrived and suited up. Spotting the bubbles and support boat, she joined them near the bottom, replacing Nick's dive-buddy. "How are you, sleepy head," Nick teased through their acoustic diver-to-diver communications system.

"You rat," Minnie snapped back. "Why didn't you wake me? It's bad enough that the guys give me hell, but the smirks were a bit much this morning."

"Ha!" Nick grinned. "Gotcha."

"You sure did, you motherfucker, but I'll get you back."

"I'm sure you will," Nick agreed, "and I'll probably never see it coming. Okay, let's review the plan. I'll swim holding on to the taut wire between the structures. You follow a few feet above me. We'll stop at each sensor and other points of interest for photos and to record comments. I'll point out a safe area for you to stand on the bottom near each structure. I'll hold onto the wire to show its location. You stay close, within view. The traverse between each of them should take no more than a few minutes. You're going to get quite a workout. Turn your recorder on now so you can describe each photograph as you see it. I'll add information to the written report later. You ready?"

"I'm all ready, MF."

"No kidding around, now."

"Okay."

Before Minnie arrived, Nick had inspected the top of the sensor structures above the barbed steel wires. By staying in-line with these wires, he avoided any of the random buoyed vertical cables with floats. This dive with Minnie would be more detailed, more time consuming, and more hazardous. Minnie wore thin insulated gloves to operate the camera and flashlight.

Weary toward the end of the inspection, Nick asked Minnie how she was doing. She said fine. He could tell from her voice and her swimming that she was tired. As good as their heated suits were, the chill was getting to their hands and feet, and spreading to their torsos. "One more task to go. Are you up for this?"

"I'm really beat, but let's get it done."

They swam along the barbed razor wire to the first structure that needed additional attention. Nick laboriously cleared debris that had accumulated while Minnie watched. She offered to help but he motioned her away, afraid she would get too close to the barbs. They were two hours past peak sunlight. Nick shined his light on the structure, and the number, as Minnie took photographs for the report.

They followed the same procedure at the next one. Instead of paper and trash, this structure was obscured with a large piece of sheet metal framed with thick steel borders—probably dropped from some ship or barge. Nick struggled to free the metal wedged into the structure, and held in by the current.

Defying Nick, Minnie came down and grabbed one end of the sheet metal. As they moved away from the structure, the current hit full on the flat face of the sheet. It swung them around in the water.

"Let go!" Nick yelled.

Minnie released the sheet metal, flipped over and lost the camera. She grabbed for the camera strap, but missed. She yelled out as one hand came in contact with the barbed wire.

Nick let the current take the sheet metal and quickly came to Minnie's aid, pulling her off. Red spots were showing on her light colored glove.

"We're going to the surface," Nick said.

"What about the camera?"

"I'll come back for the camera. Let's go. Now!"

The large soft-sided Zodiac support boat floated nearby. Nick boosted her up so her arms flopped over the side of the boat, and removed both of their facemasks. "Remove her tank and pull off her gloves," he yelled at the two guys in the boat. "Wrap the cuts on her hand, lift her into the boat, and take her to the pier. My computer light is flashing, but I have to go back down to finish. I'll swim to the pier and hang onto one of the lines while I decompress."

The men pulled off Minnie's gloves. Her left hand appeared to be covered with blood. She held it high in the air, as one of the guys prepared to wrap it with first-aid gauze. She looked like a surgeon, holding up her hands, waiting for sterile gloves, or a doctor holding a newborn child streaked with blood.

The sight briefly panicked Nick. He drove the thought from his mind as he descended to the bottom.

CHAPTER SEVEN

*L*uckily, the sheet metal settled in the mud nearby. He found the camera on the bottom and shot the final photographs. Nick glanced up at his completed project, and at the random height floats. He wondered if the crew in the monitoring station was tracking his location. The floats reminded him of photographs of the tethered balloons over London during World War II, installed to protect the city from German bombers. He checked his compass for the correct heading to the pier.

Grabbing the rope hanging from the pier, he slipped his arm through the loop set at the fifteen-foot depth. His time in the water, longer than Minnie's, required decompression. A wrist computer told him at what depth and how much time he needed.

The sight of Minnie's hand had upset him. He hoped they'd taken her to the hospital in Juneau, or at least to the clinic on the Coast Guard Station. His head spun. It felt as if it was twirling around while his body stayed rigid.

He kept swallowing to stave off nausea. He was too experienced a diver to have this happening. The computer read-out showed an eighteen-minute decompression stop with ten minutes to go. He tried to concentrate on the cause of his discomfort. The dive had taken longer than planned, but was not significantly deep. For that reason, they used pure air in their tanks, not a gas mixture. He swallowed and breathed deeply, trying to keep his mind off the image of Minnie's hand. But he couldn't. *Only five minutes to go.* He let his mind wander to other things. He did not want to experience decompression sickness.

His dive school instructors would frighten them with statements like, 'The Bends happens when nitrogen bubbles in the blood get trapped in parts of the body and come out painfully for a few days when you're on the surface, and if there is no pressure tank available to decompress, you're in trouble'.

Up till now, the image of hands streaked with blood had been confined to his own haunting dreams. Minnie often witnessed his nighttime restlessness, but he'd never discuss it. He'll have to tell her about it and about the grief that led to it. He'd grown close to her, more so than anyone since his wife, but he hadn't been fair. Minnie's friendship with Hannah during the summer opened his eyes, and his heart. His shallow relationships with women in the past had followed a pattern of sex and silence, until they gave up. Hannah never met any of them.

They celebrated Hannah's twentieth birthday on July 4th during her visit. The date was like a mixture of delight and anguish for Nick. More than once on her birthdays, even as a child, Hannah would ask him why he looked so pained through his happy face. When she was ten, he told her about her mother dying at childbirth, but waited until she was twelve to tell her the details, both of them crying the whole time. He couldn't wait any longer for fear she would use her computer skills to research the very public events.

His wife, Helen, was eight months pregnant that July 4th holiday. They were on the water in San Diego Bay in a small cabin cruiser enjoying perfect weather. She said, 'It's going to be a long time until we can go do it again—let's take the boat out.' She was in good shape, still running, and hadn't gained much weight.

The images flashed through Nick's mind, almost a catharsis; *Nick at the wheel, Helen standing on the small back deck, the wake of a speedboat causing their boat to rock, Helen's yell, then screams, as she slipped and fell on the deck.*

Nick idling the engine and going back to help her, the boat still rocking, Helen telling him to remove her shorts, that her water had broken. She was bleeding. "The baby's coming," she said. Nick's mind going numb, remembering the doctor had mentioned her good physical condition and joked that the baby could just pop out.

The next thing he remembered; he was holding the crying blood-streaked baby with the cord still attached, Helen crying in pain, Nick yelling for help to a boatload of people nearby, "I need help, I need a doctor!"

A boat coming alongside, someone taking the wheel, a woman comforting Helen, a man cutting the cord, Helen bleeding, Nick sitting on the deck holding the baby, blood on his hands and arms, approaching a pier on Coronado, Helen going quiet, someone taking the baby from him.

Helen carried off the boat, an ambulance, the ride to the Naval Hospital, talking to the doctors, Nick calling Helen's parents, staying at the hospital with the baby, the agony of Helen's funeral.

Afterward; the joy of his daughter, Hannah. Nick asked relatives and friends not to tell her any details; that someday he would.

His decompression time over, Nick climbed onto the pier. He shed his dive gear looking at Minnie.

She stood up with an anxious expression, but seemed relieved as he walked over.

He put his arm around her. "Are you okay?"

She nodded. "I wanted to wait for you to go to the hospital with me."

Nick kissed her forehead and wet eyes. "Let's go get you fixed up, darlin'."

CHAPTER EIGHT

October 19th—5am

Homer glanced at the radar screen on the bridge of the Eagle as they navigated the passages approaching Juneau. It was overcast and pitch black, with calm sea conditions and light rain. He opened the door to the outer bridge to look at the lights of the boat trailing them. The yacht was a constant reminder they were being watched. *Those sons of bitches.*

"What are those guys doing, Captain?" his helmsman asked. "They've been dogging us for two days now. Any closer, we might as well throw them a line and tow them to Juneau."

"Probably someone with little experience at sea, or lousy navigators," Homer said. Through the years, hundreds of small boats along the Alaska Marine Highway route had stayed close to them. Many of them would wave and come alongside asking questions about location or weather. The small boat operators were more comfortable near the *Eagle* than next to the giant cruise ships.

He planned to call Davy as soon as his cell phone picked up a signal from Juneau. He could use the radio, but didn't want to talk with Davy on a public line, open to anyone listening on the same frequency. No doubt John Smith and John Brown contacted the yacht using simple, secure, short-range walkie-talkies.

Homer's cell phone rang, wrenching him from his thoughts. "Davy," Homer yelled into his cell phone, as he moved to the outside part of the bridge. He slid on the wet deck, hit his hand on the bulkhead rail, then grabbed it to keep from falling.

"No, my dear Captain Dixon. It is not your friend Davy. Captain Davy and his wife Madeline are fine. A moment ago I listened to an update about them. They have a busy schedule today. You may not be able to reach them."

Homer faltered, hearing only the most negative implications of the message. "Give me a minute here." He removed the phone from his ear and stood there opening and closing the hand that hit the rail. The pain in his hand was minimal, but he needed time to think. He steadied himself against the rail as the ship rocked, with the ever-present Alaska wind blowing mist into his face. He wiped his wet eyes on a sleeve. Homer was not a stoic person. His emotions and feelings showed on his face, and by his voice and body language.

Ernie often reminded him that the crew was aware of this. Compared to other ships and other Captains his crew had served under, Homer was the most respected. He was their Skipper, their surrogate father. While some Captains evoked contempt, Homer generated affection. The instinct among some of his crew was to protect him.

The helmsman, an old timer, reacted to the Captain's slide across the deck, and obvious discomfort, by buzzing the First Mate.

When Ernie came up to the bridge, he nodded at the helmsman. He peeked out at Homer and at the proximity of the yacht.

Homer gestured for him to stay inside.

"Captain Dixon, are you there?" said the voice. "Are you all right? You seem to have just hurt your hand. You must take care of yourself. We need you."

"What were you doing talking with Davy at five in the morning?"

"We didn't talk with your friend Davy this morning. We talked with our contact near his house."

"Look," Homer said, keeping his voice steady. "I'm going to try Davy as soon as we end this call. I've got to make sure he's okay, because if I can't get hold of him, my next call will be to the Coast Guard in Juneau."

"Now, now, Captain Dixon, stay calm. As far as I know, Captain Davy and his wife Madeline are still asleep."

"You've got their place bugged?"

"Unfortunately, yes. It is difficult watching them from a parked car. You must realize there is a significant investment at stake here. The reason for my call is to instruct you concerning your two-day stay in Juneau. Our representative on your ship, John Smith, has a big mouth and a short temper. He should not have made you aware of their true identity, but having done so is not a great problem. In fact, it might be better this way. We can now converse in a more open manner. Mr. Smith reports that since the conversation in your cabin with him and Mr. Brown, everything aboard your ship seems to be quiet and very cordial. Your crew has not been warm to them, but since they are foreigners and they themselves are not, shall we say, warm people, that could be a factor. We need them aboard for muscle, not their personalities. I'm pleased that the issue of their cellular phones and short-range radios has been resolved."

Homer looked at the yacht as he listened.

"Also, please do not concern yourself about the dropped box while you were transferring them to a safer and more secure location on the ship. My men said you appeared startled when this happened, presumably regarding the toxic gas. Captain Dixon, we would not jeopardize this little venture, I should say the magnitude of this venture, with shoddy packaging. Be assured that the toxic gas will be released only if the boxes are opened in an improper manner. Are you still there?"

"I'm still here, and listening to every word." Strangely, Homer did not feel intimidated. He glanced at Ernie again through the window, motioning for him to stay there.

"Good, I'm happy to converse with you and exchange this necessary information. I understand that you will be shorthanded on the bridge, losing two young men, with no plans as yet to replace them."

"Yes, we will lose two trainees in Juneau, but will replace them with an experienced seaman who will sign on as Mate."

"And who is this man?"

"His name is Nick Banner."

"Ah, yes, Mr. Banner. Trained as a Navy SEAL; a widower with a college age daughter, heads an underwater construction company, recently worked on a contract for the Coast Guard Station at Juneau, and has extensive experience with underwater sensors and surveillance equipment."

Holy shit. They've been planning this a long time. "I'm very impressed."

"Thank you. Now, I would like you to use our two men to replace the two you are losing, instead of Mr. Banner."

"Can't do that," Homer replied quickly. "Coast Guard requires a certified level of training and experience. We've contacted Nick and the Coast Guard has approved his qualifications for upgrade to Mate. If something changes and Nick couldn't go with us, we'd stay in Juneau until we could get someone qualified to stand a bridge watch. Also, Coast Guard usually conducts a surprise inspection of our ship's crew records and our required safety equipment, in Juneau or Ketchikan."

"I see. Well, I insist you use John Brown in some capacity on your bridge. Actually, he has very extensive at-sea experience. Now, to get back to Juneau; I made the original arrangements with your friend Captain Davy Masters, and was one of the two men who came to visit him in his home. After you have loaded your additional cargo in Juneau, I will have someone come aboard the *Alaskan*

Eagle for the purpose of inspecting our cargo. Afterward, you and I will meet aboard my yacht to discuss the remainder of your voyage. I certainly hope you will not be so foolish as to contact any of the authorities. It would be disastrous for you and for Captain Davy."

Homer kept his patience as the voice went on.

"The project has proceeded very smoothly up to now. Let us get it completed and we can each go our own ways, a little richer, a little happier. You realize, of course, that you and Captain Davy are willing participants in this venture. We instructed Captain Davy not to tell his wife any details. As far as our surveillance has reported, he has obeyed this request. I certainly hope you are doing the same. It would be truly unfortunate for any individuals who have this knowledge. I must also inform you that the Anchorage distributor of the survival suits became uncooperative a few days ago. Sadly, he had a fatal automobile accident yesterday. I see your First Mate McInnis looking at you from inside the bridge house. Please assure me that neither he nor anyone else has been informed by you of the details of this shipment."

"I've told no one. I wouldn't put anyone in jeopardy, Mr…"

"You need not know my name, Captain, unless of course you wish to call me John Adams. As you can see, I am a student of American history. I am very much pleased that we have had this conversation of understanding, Captain. I look forward to meeting with you in Juneau. Ah, there is one last thing I must discuss with you. You might think we intend to do harm to you or your country and that you would sacrifice yourself, as a good soldier, to save your country. Nothing could be farther from the truth, Captain. This is merely a business venture."

CHAPTER NINE

October 19th—Juneau, 6am

"*Tell me more about your comments regarding several murders,*" Nick said to Frank Harris.

Commander Ellings nodded in agreement. They were in an early morning meeting at the Coast Guard Station, postponed the previous day after Minnie's accident.

"Will do," Harris replied. "Our sources believe there is a connection between the somewhat suspicious fatal automobile accident of the Anchorage distributor of survival suits being shipped on the *Alaskan Eagle*, and other incidents that happened in Vancouver." Frank Harris hesitated, and said, "This is discussed in strictest confidence. It could louse up our whole investigation of these people if it were leaked in any way." Glancing at Captain Forrest he asked, "Would you look into what the recently changed surveillance requirements call for, if anything, regarding sweeping your facility, vehicles, and base residences for bugs?"

Captain Forrest gave a nod.

Harris turned to Nick. "In addition to what we've discussed this morning, there are many other aspects that must be addressed. Your experience with surveillance equipment comes to mind. You'll need to repeatedly sweep your living quarters, and use only the cell phones and radios we provide. Our information indicates that these people are fairly sophisticated with their electronics. They're obviously well-financed, for example, the charter of the yacht."

"Do we have any idea what they're hiding in those boxes?" Nick asked.

"No. We're hoping you'll find that out for us. Now, back to your question regarding the murders. The Canadian Police informed us of unusual incidents, and a death in Vancouver. A common denominator in their investigation was the *Alaskan Eagle.* As such, they contacted us. Two young seamen were found somewhat beaten up in an alley near a bar where they'd been drinking. They'd been signed to join the *Alaskan Eagle* in Anchorage, but clearly couldn't make it. The *Eagle's* company office in Seattle confirmed that their agent in Vancouver hired two seamen for the *Eagle,* but had no information beyond that. The Canadians contacted the agent's office. They discovered he had died two days before of an apparent heart attack. With a history of heart disease, no autopsy was thought necessary. The family had the body cremated. But before the heart attack, he hired the two walk-in seamen, John Smith and John Brown, the men I've told you about."

"You're joking about their names." Nick said.

"These are the names on their papers and passports. It's funny, but they're not. The information we have shows them to be a vicious bunch. You understand," Harris, continued, "These two men are now part of the crew of the *Alaskan Eagle,* and a Mr. John Adams chartered the yacht that's trailing them, and is probably aboard it. We have surveillance now in place to record open deck activity and personnel aboard the *Alaskan Eagle* and the yacht *Mother's Love,* while in Juneau, and in Ketchikan, if we don't move in before that."

"Again, you don't know if Captain Dixon is aware of this."

"No, we don't."

"Do you plan on telling him?"

"Not yet. We feel that doing so could jeopardize the case and put his life in danger. It would look suspicious if we came aboard for a meeting or asked him to come here. Obviously, he's being watched. Even calling by phone or radio could blow it."

"The accident that my diver had yesterday," Nick said, "seems to be a mixed blessing. She was due to ride back with me on the *Eagle* to work on our completion report, but will fly to Seattle for plastic surgery on her hand, thus keeping her out of harm's way." He avoided any mention of their personal relationship. "The reason I asked for this early-morning meeting is that today is a busy one for me. Besides organizing the loading of my gear on the *Eagle,* now changed to planning the offloading of some heavy gear in Ketchikan, I've got paperwork with my crew and I need to see them off at the airport."

"It'll make our meetings in Ketchikan more normal," Harris said. "Nick, you've been away from this type of activity for a long time, and must have some trepidation as to what you're getting into, but let me emphasize that we will not leave you hanging. We'll be in constant contact and be prepared to act on a moment's notice. So, do we have your full commitment on this?"

"Yes," Nick replied. *What the fuck am I doing? Why am I so anxious to do this? I've backed off from confrontations and commitments for so long, yet here I am jumping at this. What has changed? Why have I changed?* "However, I want you to let me make Captain Dixon and First Mate McInnis aware of the situation and, if they already know something, coordinate all our efforts."

"Okay, I guess that makes sense. We can go into the details tomorrow." Harris shook Nick's hand as they walked out. "Nick, you're now an employee of the United States Government, the Coast Guard. That comes with a lot of strings attached."

"I remember," Nick commented dryly, "from my Navy days."

Nick's phone rang. "Hi sweetheart, wait one minute, a meeting is just ending." He covered the phone. "My daughter in San Diego."

Frank Harris nodded slowly and waved as he walked by.

"Hi, Honey."

"Hi, Daddy. I was wondering what your plans are. Am I going to see you soon?"

"You sure are, Honey. The job's almost over. We're packing our gear on a transport ferry, the *Alaskan Eagle*, to get back to Seattle. In about a week or so, and after I get my report organized, we'll spend a long Thanksgiving Holiday together. How's school?"

"School's good—same old stuff. Your crew leaving also?"

"They're flying out today."

"What about Minnie?" Hannah asked. "Is she riding the ferry with you?"

"Hannah," Nick chided. "Minnie is a good friend and a good worker, but …"

"I know, Daddy, but she's nice and I want you to be happy."

"I am happy, Sweetheart, you make me happy."

"Oh, Daddy, I know, but I think Minnie is kind of special."

"I do, too. Actually, Minnie was due to ride the ship down but she cut her hand yesterday. We thought it best that she fly to Seattle to have it taken care of."

"That's great, Daddy. Not about Minnie's hand. But, I think it's wonderful the way you feel about her. Will she be okay?"

"She'll be fine, but the ship is no place to be if any of the cuts should get infected. I'll meet her in Seattle."

"Do you think she would like to come to San Diego for Thanksgiving with us?"

"I never thought about it. She might have plans with her family. I'll ask her."

"Good, Daddy. I've got to go. I'm just walking into class. I'll talk with you soon. Let me know the plans."

"I will, Honey, bye. I'll let you know."

CHAPTER TEN

October 19th—Juneau, 7am

"**S**kipper," *Ernie called out, "John Smith asked if he could talk with you."* They were on the bridge of the *Eagle* as it approached the dock in Juneau.

"What does he want to talk about?" Homer asked, aware of the other crewmen on the bridge.

"Says it's personal."

Homer moved to the outer bridge as if he were ignoring the request but motioned for Ernie to follow. "Fine, send him to my stateroom as soon as we tie up. I can't give him much time. It's a busy day."

"Okay," Ernie said. "I don't see Nick Banner, but I see his trucks. He told me he'd be here when we docked."

"He could have his hands full with Coast Guard work. I'll be below."

John Smith was waiting for him outside his stateroom. "I see you didn't expect to be refused, Mr. Smith."

"You have no choice but to see me, Captain Dixon," he said.

"What's on your mind, Mr. Smith?"

"Mr. Adams wants you to come to the yacht tomorrow at noon. He will send someone in a car to drive you."

"I can see the yacht from here. Why don't I walk?"

"These are the instructions I have. It would be wise for you to do as you have been told."

After Smith walked out, Homer stayed in his stateroom, thinking, *I feel as if I'm slipping and sliding, unable to stand straight, unable to keep my footing. Why can't I stay in control? Even with the unknowns, why can't I maintain some degree of control and stay on top of this?*

Ernie knocked, interrupting his thoughts. "I've got some paperwork that needs your attention, Skipper."

"I'll meet you on the bridge in a few minutes. I need to mull over a few things."

"Sure, Captain." Ernie stared at Homer for a moment, then walked out.

Homer noted Ernie's hesitance. *That's part of my problem. I've got to keep discussing things with Ernie. He keeps everything on the surface, never lets problems creep inside to louse up his head and drift down to his stomach. I need to take this one piece at a time. For now, I'll concentrate on John Adams. How should I act, what should I say? It's going to be difficult. I've got to keep a lid on the normally effusive Homer Dixon. But, since he investigated the Eagle, and me, he'll know. He'll know me.*

Up on the bridge, Homer waved away the paperwork and pulled Ernie outside. "Ernie, since this all started I've vacillated between we're fucked and we can beat this thing. Right now, I feel like I did when I drove away from Davy's house a few nights ago—totally confused and overwhelmed." Homer recited this in a calm, resigned manner. Yet, as he talked, with some comments from Ernie, he realized his mood was temporary, a process to resolve a problem. His entire career, he'd relied on planning, contingency planning, and immediately confronting a setback with, "Let's see how we can fix it".

Aboard ship, his crew provided a comfort shield. He scoffed at large marine companies that rotated their crew every three to six months. You can't learn every switch, knob and valve, and the history and idiosyncrasies of every vital piece of equipment in that amount of time.

"Skipper, Skipper," Ernie said. "What's going through your head?"

"Sorry Ernie, I get lost in reality. I'll get back to the fantasy that's working itself into our lives, or is it the other way around?" Homer paused. "Ernie, your involvement in this mess and knowledge of what's going on puts you in deep shit. The guy who calls himself John Adams has asked me about you. It seems that between him and the others in his band of thieves, they've used up all the Johns in our early history. Anyway, his people have seen us talking and they think I've told you everything. We have to be very careful, or what's better, you should back off and let me handle everything on my own. They probably feel they know everything that's happening on the *Eagle*. That could be why this John Adams is so calm and confident. I think you should…"

"Homer, stop right there. There's no way I'm going to turn my back and not support you. If anything, it makes our position stronger. In fact, we should get about a dozen more people involved. That would even the odds a little."

"Thanks, Ernie. I knew you'd feel that way but I had to give you a way out. I do need your help and will even more so in the next week. Adams told me that the Anchorage distributer of these immersion suits had an unfortunate auto accident. In other words, he wants me to know they killed him. Whether it's true or not, they're trying to keep us in line and scared. I could call the distributer in Seattle to check it out. Adams probably expects me to. I'm sure there's no way to tie them to the murder. They seem too good to make any mistakes. I just hope they don't hurt Davy and Maddy."

"Okay," Ernie said while heading back inside the bridge. "One other thing, Skipper. When was the last time you saw Sally?"

"Couple of months ago. It's been too long. I really miss her. I'm planning to see her when we get to Ketchikan. Why?"

"She does a good job of keeping you grounded, that's why."

"I've got a good signal now." Homer spoke loudly when the call went through.

"I knew it was you, Homer. This damn phone startles the hell out of me, especially when those guys call me at night or early morning. It upsets Maddy, no end."

"Is Maddy with you or have you gone out of the bedroom?"

"I'm in the kitchen, now. They called about an hour ago."

"I know. I just spoke with a man who would only identify himself as John Adams. His two people on the *Eagle* have papers that list them as John Smith and John Brown. We're dealing with a bunch of American history nuts. Look, we're approaching Juneau and I've got some things to tell you and some questions to ask. He told me flat-out that he's got your house bugged, and probably your car also, and that a guy in a car somewhere nearby is monitoring them. I don't know if it's true or not, but we have to assume it is. Can you get another cell phone for use when you call me, but use your regular phone for everything else?"

"Yeah, there's a phone store about fifteen minutes away. It's not the same company, though."

"That's even better. Get an extra phone, different company and different number, and get one that takes pictures, maybe a throw-away. Do it today. Have you told Maddy?"

"No, nothing more than that it's a complicated shipment. I'm afraid she would freak out if she knew anything more."

"Good. I think you should keep it that way. Davy, this John Adams, probably the lead guy who came to see you, what did he look like? I'm going to meet him on his yacht."

"He had no unusual or ethnic features, Caucasian, clean shaven, short black hair, and, I almost forgot, he has bright blue eyes. I don't know how I forgot that. I was intrigued by those eyes until he threatened to kill us."

"You seem a little foggy, Davy. Are you still half asleep?"

"I've been feeling lousy for a few days now—both of us have. We're going to the clinic today."

CHAPTER ELEVEN

October 19th—Juneau, 8am

Nick sat on the edge of Minnie's bed watching her sleep. He whispered, "I've been a goddamn fool. Did you get that? Are you awake?"

"Mm," Minnie murmured.

"How much pain killer did you take? Are you okay?"

"I'm okay."

"I want to tell you something. I have to tell you before you leave, but you need to understand what I'm saying."

"Mm-hmm."

"All right. It's not easy for me. I'm sitting here looking at you, at your beauty, your perfection, and at the outline of your body. Shit, I don't want to get distracted."

Minnie turned on her back. With her eyes still closed, she pulled up her nightshirt.

"Not yet," he said. Nick bent over to kiss her nipples and the tip of her nose, as he drew the sheet up to her neck and kissed the disappointment from her lips. He sat up and held her gently. "Minnie, you've changed my life. I've become a different person. You've opened me up. I, I love you," he stammered. "I haven't said that to anyone except my daughter in over twenty years."

She opened her eyes wide to stare at him, and started to speak.

"No," Nick stopped her. "I've got to tell you more. I want to tell you about my wife."

Minnie sat up, pressed his hand to her lips, and waited.

The incessant memories that played over in his mind through the years had never been put into words. He started slowly, with many side comments, finally reaching the emotional details. He paused as necessary to calm himself, surprised that he could get through it.

Minnie removed his hand from her wet face, and placed it on her chest. She wrapped her arms hard around his neck. They sat still for a few minutes.

Nick ran his hands along her arms. He loved the feel of her skin, the silkiness of her body. He never tired of stroking her. With the many women he'd had in the past, he would eventually wonder: *Who else has done this? Who else has kissed and stroked this part of her body? Who else has fucked her like this? Who else has brought her to ecstasy with their tongue?* But he never had those thoughts with Minnie. *I've made her mine, and she has made me hers, totally.* "We haven't much time."

"Careful of my hand. It hurts like hell. The painkiller is wearing off."

"I'll get you more pills."

"No, not yet. I'm enjoying this."

"Okay, but we need to get moving. You've got four hours to catch your flight. I need to get you dressed and packed."

"And, you'll have to help me wash—I need a shower."

"That'll be the fun part."

"Behave yourself," she smiled, as he picked her up, removed her nightshirt and undressed himself. "What are you doing, and what's with that shit-eatin' grin?"

"I've got to get in the shower with you."

They stood by the bed. Their bodies blended perfectly. He put his arms around her. They kissed leisurely, then wanted more. Standing there, he lifted her so her legs embraced his hips, just high enough. She wrapped her legs around him, hooking them in back. They both cried-out at the same time. Still panting and entangled, he walked them to the shower to put her down. She stood with her hands wrapped around his neck.

"Now, hold your hand up high so it doesn't get wet." He washed her hair, face and neck, kissing her wet mouth. "Keep your eyes closed. I'm in charge here. Now I do the arms and back, and the front of the back."

"That feels good," she said. "So, your experience goes beyond sea diving, and muff diving."

"No comment. Stop talking. You'll get soap in your mouth."

"That's not what I want in my mouth. When do you get to the bottom parts?"

"Right now," he said, as he washed and explored her crevices.

"My legs are getting weak," she whispered.

"Is that why you're holding on to me?"

"It was the only thing I could find that's rigid, rigid," she teased. "Now, shut up and finish what you started."

"One of your bandages is getting wet."

"I don't care, I love these doubles. Your hands work magic. Now, be quiet, I'm concentrating. The second one takes longer."

———

Minnie snuggled close to him in the truck.

"We've got to stop at the ship," Nick told her, "I need to coordinate my equipment loading with the First Mate. I'll show you my cabin. It would have been ours. Then we'll go to the airport. The guys will stay with you until you get to the hotel in Seattle, and will take you to the doctor in the morning."

"I wish you could come with me," Minnie said.

"I know, love, so do I, but I'll see you in about a week. If you're up to it, we can go to San Diego, see Hannah, work on the report, and stay for Thanksgiving."

"When does the ship get to Ketchikan?" Minnie asked with a smile.

"In a few days. Wait a minute. Don't even think about it. Your hand won't be healed. Call me tonight and tomorrow while we have a signal. I don't know how far south the signal will reach. I'll let you know my other cell number tomorrow. It's a satellite gadget that's more cumbersome, but will always have a signal."

"Where'd you get that, and why now?"

"It's from the Coast Guard as part of my upgrade to Mate status."

Minnie looked at him quizzically. "You're the worst fucking liar I've ever met. What's going on?"

"I can't tell you."

"Well, you'd better tell me something before I leave."

"Okay, I will," Nick said, as they walked up the gangway.

Intent on showing-off the *Eagle*, Nick looked at the ship in a different way. The rare October sunlight revealed the *Eagle's* many structural and surface imperfections. It wasn't a pretty picture.

"Nick," Ernie McInnis greeted them, "And you must be Minnie."

"Nice to see you, Ernie. How did you know Minnie's name?"

"Some of your guys were just here. Said you'd be along. We'll load your gear in the morning. It'll be put on last, since most of it will be first off in Ketchikan."

"Good, that'll work for me."

"They told me about your hand, Minnie. You gonna be okay?"

"I'll be fine," Minnie said. "The cuts aren't that bad. They just need a plastic surgeon's touch to keep from having nasty scars. Ernie, when does the ship get to Ketchikan?"

"Minnie," Nick chided.

Ernie smiled. "We should be there the morning of the twenty-second and be off again the next morning. Nick," Ernie said softly, "You free for a bite in town tonight? I've got some things to go over with you, and it's always too busy on the ship. Say about six?"

"Absolutely. I know all the best eateries in Juneau, from the ear-splitting blues places, to the very sedate." *Ernie's invitation seemed out of character.*

"How about a place with moderate noise, so we can talk privately?" Ernie said.

"Okay*," He may know already.* "Sounds good. Is my cabin open, Ernie? I'd like to show Minnie what she's missing by lousing up her hand, and then we need to get to the airport."

"The cabin should be open, with the keys inside. Nice to meet you, Minnie."

The cabin was located on the starboard side forward, opposite the port side gangway area, and one deck above. As they entered the cabin, Nick put his finger over his lips, indicating quiet.

Minnie's eyes widened. She put her palms up as if to ask, what the fuck is going on?

"It's a good cabin," Nick said, as he pulled her over to lie on the bed. He planted his mouth on hers, and whispered in her ear, "No questions about my Coast Guard phone, or anything, just small talk. I'll tell you on the way to the airport. Okay, we'd better get going," he said, rising.

"That's a hell of a way to say goodbye." Minnie pouted.

"I know, but time is getting short. I'll make it up to you."

"You'd better. How about a repeat of this morning? We should make that a regular shower activity."

"My pleasure." Nick hugged her tight. "I'm sorry about your hand. It was my fault."

"Of course it was your fault. You wanted to get me defenseless in the shower."

They walked out and across the deck. Four people in uniform, all officers, were waiting near the gangway. Nick could see their rank but could not tell the specialty of service. An Army Officer with a silver bar asked him, "Are you part of the crew? We're the Corps of Engineers group that will be traveling with our equipment back to Seattle."

"Ah, yes I am," Nick, replied. "I'm the Second Mate. That sailor over there will find Captain Dixon or First Mate McInnis for you."

"Thank you. I'm First Lieutenant Garcia. Our gear is on the dock, waiting to be loaded. We have two Second Lieutenants, and our boss over there is Major Flowers."

Nick squinted at the female Major.

She looked around with an indifferent expression, her back to the sun. Rays of light appeared to sparkle around her head.

Nick stood there, mouth agape. He pulled in a deep breath, holding it, as if waiting for someone to say—you can breathe now. She had no particular features, but the familiarity was uncanny.

"Nick, Nick," Minnie called from behind him, "We'd better go."

The Major glanced at Minnie and at Nick as they descended the gangway and walked to their truck on the dock.

"Why were you staring at her?" she asked as they climbed into the truck.

"She looked familiar. She reminded me of someone."

"She looks a lot like Hannah," Minnie said. "Oh, god, she reminds you of your wife!"

"It threw me. For a moment, I actually thought it was her."

They drove in silence for a few minutes, Nick with his thoughts, and Minnie looking out the window.

"You're quiet," Nick said. "You were going to ask me about my new phone."

"Fuck the phone. I'm leaving for Seattle and you're looking at all the women."

"All the women!" Nick said, smiling. "When have you ever seen me look at other women when you're around?"

"You just did. I saw you. What do you mean, when I'm around? So, you look at them when I'm not around?" Minnie glared at Nick's wide grin and threw herself at him, punching his body with her elbow, and pressing his gonads.

"Ow!" he yelled.

"That's so you'll behave yourself. Now, tell me about the new phone."

"From what I know, there are two foreign nationals on board the *Eagle* as part of the crew. They're suspected of bugging the ship for some reason or another, and the Coast Guard asked me to use my surveillance skills and equipment to locate and de-bug them. I said I would. You can't tell anyone this. Not the guys, or anyone else."

Minnie stared at him, confused. She continued staring at him, as if she wasn't sure what was going through his mind, or hers. "Well, you be extra careful," she said, quietly.

⊨⊨ ⊨⊨

"Ernie," Nick spoke into his phone, "I'm clearing out of my apartment, should be back about four. We still on for six? Good, see you then."

He put on his running shorts and took off. He headed out along an isolated heavily wooded road, skirting the water. If he could fit it in, he tried to run every day. Half way into the run, he heard a familiar screech. He stopped as close as he could, about twenty feet from the aging eagle. Nick had first spotted the bird months before. He had gotten into the habit of thinking through his problems, if any, and his current activities, and imagining the eagle's response.

I've been looking for you, Nick said. *I almost went right by. It's been a few weeks now.*

I know.

There have been a lot of changes in my life.

I know.

I've signed on with the Coast Guard.

I know.

I've opened up to Minnie.

It's about time, isn't it?

Well, I was preoccupied with the job.

But that's over now.

Then Hannah and the guys were around.

But they're gone now.

I think the epiphany came after Minnie hurt her hand.

I know. I think it did.

I'm going to miss our talks.

And, I'm going to miss you. This last encounter of ours comes at an opportune point in time; your work, Minnie, the overdue openness about the memories of your wife, and this new spy adventure you're on. Then there's the fact that I won't be around much longer.

No, you can't leave. I need you!

You're emerging from a twenty-year vacuum. You need no one but yourself. You're leaving, possibly never to return to Juneau. I'm too old to fly to Ketchikan. Forget me and get out of here, clean. But don't forget Minnie. She's your salvation. You need her. You love her. She loves you. She's feisty and she has balls. But you know all that.

Nick, still breathing deeply from his run, stayed motionless for a few moments, absorbing the words. He slowly lifted up his head to gaze at the old bird. "Yes, I know all that."

CHAPTER TWELVE

October 19th—6pm

"*Is this place okay?" Nick asked,* as he and Ernie walked into the bar.

"Looks good."

Nick requested a booth in the back, with a view of the door and the whole restaurant. He felt amused how easily he slipped into a protective stance. "It's been a long time, Ernie. A year ago, last April. I should have come down to the ship when you guys came through."

"Well, hell, Nick. It's always a busy day when we come here. This time of year, it eases off a bit. Nick, I want to fill you in about the situation on-board. I told you we're losing two young officers. Company wants them back in Seattle. I'm glad you could help us out. Particularly, help me out. Homer's been stressed out lately with that, and there's the situation on the *Eagle.* He's okay, but he's drinking too much. This might be our last trip with the *Eagle,* not that we want it that way but the ship's getting too old, too much maintenance…"

"Ernie," Nick interrupted, "Can I use your cell phone? I don't have mine, and I promised Minnie I'd call when she arrived in Seattle."

"Nick, maybe we should both stop pussy-footing around. I talked with a friend over at Coast Guard. Said you signed on with…"

"How did he tell you?"

"She called."

Nick put his open hand up for Ernie to wait a minute. "Bear with me a second here." Nick took the phone apart, inspected the case and the battery, and scanned it with a palm size object. Reassembling it, Nick found his own phone in his pocket and called Ernie's number. He gestured for Ernie to answer the phone. "Well, looks like it's clean, and I get no other signals that would indicate a bug is attached anywhere on you. Now we can talk."

"I guess my friend was right," Ernie said. "You have signed on with Coast Guard. What's the story, Nick?"

"First, you need to tell me about your friend. Who is she and why would she be spreading classified information? It could be damaging, even fatal, if known by the wrong people."

"She's an old friend. She works directly for Commander Ellings. I've known her for about ten years. She was concerned about me. I cautioned her. She said absolutely no one other than her, the Commander, the Captain and a Mr. Harris out of Washington are aware of your involvement. And of course, she knows what it's all about."

"I assume you and Captain Dixon both know everything that's happening on the *Eagle*."

"Yes, and as far as we know, no one other than two new seamen, with passports from Singapore, are aware of the situation. But, it's possible there are others that are, well, working against us."

"Ernie, for your own safety and that of Captain Dixon's, I've got permission from Coast Guard to tell you all they know. But again, they're tracking these people and don't want any leak, or action, that could louse it up. Now, as you said, we can stop pussy-footing around."

"I'll tell you what's happened on board," Ernie said, "The intimidation and threats. We feel as if we're in the dark, not knowing all the people involved, and what the boundaries are. We sort of react to each situation."

"You've been threatened?" Nick asked.

"Well, Homer and Davy have. The bad guys don't know that I know. At least, we don't think they know that I know. I'd better start at the beginning, four or five days ago. When we get back to the ship, Homer can fill in any blanks."

"Who is Davy?"

"That's why I have to go way back. Davy and Homer are old friends. It all started with Davy and his wife Madeline and the loading of the shipment in Anchorage," Ernie hesitated. "I don't know if I should reveal their part of it. Davy and Madeline are in great danger." He paused again, looking down at the menu.

"Hey, Ernie, I'm one of the good guys. We're on your side. You need us. This thing is too big for the two of you."

"I guess you're right. We do need help."

"I have a meeting at Coast Guard tomorrow morning. It may be the last meeting until we get to Ketchikan. I'll make them aware of everything you guys know."

Ernie related the events of the past week.

Nick interrupted a number of times asking him to clarify details and let Ernie know most of the Coast Guard information he knew.

"Holy shit, this thing is bigger than we thought, and more menacing." Ernie shook his head. "We don't know what's in those boxes, but we're going to find out before we get to Ketchikan. We should get back to the ship now and let Homer know. Let's finish our drinks and get a bite on board, okay?" Also, we've been trying to figure how to check out those hundred dollar bills, to see if they're good. Could someone at Coast Guard have their Credit Union look at a couple of them?"

"Shouldn't be a problem. Ernie, there are two guys at the table near the door. They keep glancing at us. Do you know them?"

"Shit, one of them is our crewman, John Brown. I don't know the other one, the teenager, but I think he's one of the men who helped load the boxes in Anchorage. He may be off the yacht. There's no way this could be a coincidence. They must be following us. It's creepy having them watch our every move. How did we get into this fucking mess? I've made hundreds of trips on this run with Homer without a care in the world other than ship's business and which bar to go to at night."

"I think we should leave," Nick said. "Stop to say hello as we go out and tell John Brown who I am. From what you just told me, they already know about me, about my daughter, and where she lives. That pisses me off." Nick took in a deep breath. They downed their drinks. Nick put money on the table. "I'll take care of it, Ernie. Let's leave before they do, but with no rush. I'm going to take their picture with my phone. I need about three seconds. It has a silent shutter and no flash. They'll never know it happened."

As they approached the table, Nick appeared to be listening to a conversation on his phone.

Ernie, though small in physical stature, more than made up for it by his quickness of movement and his facial and verbal expressions. When he planted his gaze on someone, few could respond in kind. "Mr. Brown," Ernie greeted them. "I see you know the good restaurants in Juneau, even those far from the ship. Meet our new Second Mate, Nick Banner."

John Brown nodded, expressionless, making no effort to introduce his companion.

"Weren't you one of the men loading boxes in Anchorage?" Ernie asked, looking at the young man.

His reply was a silent stare.

"No, you are mistaken," John Brown, said. "My friend is on a yacht cruising for pleasure. His English is not good."

Ernie nodded. "Well, see you on board."

"I saw your John Brown reach for his phone as we walked out," Nick said in low tones. "You might have tipped your hand that you know more than they think you know. Let's be mum until I can sweep the truck for bugs."

At the truck, Nick ran his handheld device over the inside and outside of the vehicle. "See this? It's a tracker, attached to the inside of the bumper. Gives the location of the truck. That's how they knew where to find us. I'll leave it in place for now. No voice transmitter though. The truck noise would drown it out, anyway."

"Let's get back to the ship to tell Homer," Ernie said.

"Good. I want to sweep his cabin, phone and things. We'll have to figure out what to do if we find anything. It'll tip our hand if we mess with them. I'll get some guidance at my morning meeting with Coast Guard."

"Nick, good to have you on board," Homer greeted him as they entered his quarters. He was lounging in an easy chair with a glass of hard stuff. "I'm glad you agreed to help us out on the trip back. Goddamn company's been jerking us around. Job all finished at Coast Guard, huh? How about a drink?"

"Ernie and I just had a couple." Nick smiled. "How have you been, Captain? Sorry to have missed you earlier today."

Ernie gestured for him not to say anything as Nick started checking out the room.

"Job went well." Nick continued his conversation during the survey. "I hope to have more projects with Coast Guard. Good people and satisfying work." He found three bugs in the room, indicating the location with one, two or three fingers as they were detected.

"Sons of bitches," Homer muttered.

Nick put his finger to his mouth, while Ernie slashed his hand across his neck.

"Better than working for my damn company," Homer said, recovering.

"Captain, how about joining me and Ernie for a bite to eat. We didn't like the menu at the place we were just at."

"They have something to drink where we're going?" Homer asked.

"We wouldn't go anywhere else, Skipper," Ernie, said.

CHAPTER THIRTEEN

October 20th—9am

*H*omer **wandered his ship in the morning darkness**—somewhat hung over and with a foreboding tightness in his chest. *I'm having a heart attack. Maddy saw it. She knew I'd never see Davy again.* He nodded at crewmembers and tersely smiled at passengers. As the morning lit up, he saw that it looked cloudy but not overcast. His years at sea had taught him how to predict weather by studying the sky. *The days are getting shorter. My days are getting fewer.* A ray of sun appeared to bounce off the glacier. *I've never walked on a glacier. Thirty years in and out of Alaska and I've never walked on a glacier.* "Ernie, I'm taking off for a while. You gonna be around?"

"Sure," Ernie replied, with a perplexed look. "It's a little early, Skipper. Don't throw down too many. And we shouldn't go near the Coast Guard station," he said as an afterthought, as Homer walked away. There was no response, not even recognition that he had heard. "Newitt," Ernie called to a senior crewman nearby, "The Captain is leaving the ship. Ask him if you can take him somewhere, or if you can help him, or if he wants company."

"He just shook his head, got in the truck, and took off," Newitt said, when he returned a few minutes later.

Homer drove down the dock. The meeting last night with Nick and Ernie played over in his mind. "What you're telling me is that we're fucked," Homer had said to them. "We'll be out at sea with a boatload of cutthroats nearby with Coast Guard holding back while they put the pieces of this puzzle together."

"I'll be meeting with them again in the morning," Nick said. "Then we'll have the whole picture, or as much as any of us have. I don't know what their conclusion will be, but I suspect they'll want us to continue on to Ketchikan while they figure out their best plan. The threats to you, Captain Davy and his wife Madeline, are new aspects of this smuggling, or whatever it is, for them to factor in."

"We're fucked, and Davy and Maddy are fucked," Homer said again. "We're all doomed. We'll let these guys run free until they kill someone again. I hear about things like that every day on the news. It's not going to work."

Driving down the dock, he took little notice of a man hurrying off the yacht and into a car. He turned at an arrow pointing to the glacier road, a route he'd passed hundreds of times. The nearby Mendenhall Glacier was practically within the city limits of Juneau. "See, that wasn't so hard," he muttered. He parked at the glacier visitor center. *I'm too early. It doesn't open until ten, winter hours.* He sat in the truck, breathing deeply for five minutes or so. *I'm falling apart. When did that start? Was it after the meeting with Davy, or before? Is that why the company wants to dump me?* The pounding in his chest was easing. *See that? I'm okay.* He got out of the truck, studied a posted chart of the area, and started walking an upward path to the glacier. One other car was parked in a far area of the lot.

The climb kept him warm, but dressed only in a sweater for traipsing around the ship, he chilled each time he stopped to catch his breath. *Boy, am I out of shape.* The day was clearing. Some blue sky was visible through the trees in the heavily wooded area. After twenty minutes or so, he turned left and followed a side path until it reached the edge of the ice. Homer studied the expanse of the glacier. The slight breeze cut into him. He ventured out over the ice on a short walkway made of rough timbers, holding onto a railing constructed on the downward side of the walkway. Standing near the end of the walkway, he stepped backward placing his feet on the ice.

He continued backwards for about a hundred steps up the glacier and stopped. He found a comfortable footing, looked at his feet and out at the glacier, and closed his eyes. He breathed in deeply through his nose, noting the unusual scent emitted from the glacier ice, different from ocean air.

He planned to stay here as long as he could tolerate the cold. He relaxed, feeling the tension drain from him. *See that. This is what I wanted. I can handle this. No more doom and gloom. I have no choice. What the hell was wrong with me? I can handle this. I've got to get back into my problem-solving mode. Think about things that are right with me. On my ship, I'm in control.*

He opened his eyes to blue sky and bright sunshine. The air warmed. Only his feet felt no relief. Looking down the glacier, he saw a man somewhat hesitantly edging onto the walkway, clutching the railing.

The man kept looking all around, across and down the glacier. When he glanced up toward Homer, he was squinting directly into the sun. He pulled out a phone and spoke frantically in a language other than English.

He followed me. He's one of them! Homer's anger rose, and gradually subsided. *The bastard's face is contorted. He's terrified.* Homer watched him. The man looked back into the woods.

A black bear ambled out onto the walkway staring at him. The bear walked slowly forward, moving his head from side to side, as if searching for food.

The man took a pistol out of his pocket aiming it at the bear.

"Holy shit, he's got a gun," Homer muttered, "and here I am a sitting duck."

The man kept moving away. He tripped, grabbed for the railing and lost his grip on the pistol in his hand. Lunging for it, he tumbled off the end of the walkway. The pistol cascaded down the glacier. Lying on the ice, he held the edge of the timbers and gawked at the bear.

The bear stopped and looked at him quizzically, as if to say, *what the hell are you doing?*

The man slid along the ice to the front side while holding the base of the walkway. He watched the bear amble toward him. He tried to move away when the bear sniffed at his hand.

Somewhat mesmerized by the scene, Homer took a moment to react. As he stepped forward, his numbed feet collapsed, landing him on his back. He slid slowly out of control down the ice. His feet slammed into the walkway. The startled bear backed away, fleeing into the woods.

The distraught man stared at Homer.

He's just a boy! Holding a railing post, Homer reached over to grab his hand. Their eyes met. Their frigid fingers touched without feeling, unable to grasp.

The boy panicked. When he lurched for Homer, he lost his grip on the walkway. He let out a long groan as he started to slide, his fingers frantically digging into the ice.

Homer climbed onto the deck and watched him and the cell phone silently disappear down the glacier. "I'll be damned. Maybe he wasn't one of them." He dialed 911 with the details. Pondering the situation, he called John Adams. "Mr. Adams?"

"Ah, Captain Dixon, I am looking forward to our meeting today."

"Mr. Adams, I'm up on the glacier. Did you, by any chance, send someone to follow me?"

"No, not at all, Captain."

"Well, is it likely that someone else sent him, or that he did it on his own?"

"It is always possible, Captain. Why do you ask?"

"I tried to help someone who fell on the ice but he slipped away before I could get hold of him. He slid down the glacier. I called 911. He may have been able to stop himself somewhere."

"I see," Adams responded, coolly. "Thank you for your concern."

Homer hobbled on his feet until they lost their numbness. He hiked down the trail with a slight frown on his face. *Well, I tried to save him. If they find him soon enough he should be okay. If not, or if he's been beat up badly, that's one less son-of-a-bitch out there.* As he walked across the parking lot, a helicopter passed overhead.

Ernie was still on deck when Homer climbed the gangway. He looked at Homer trying to judge his expression. "Skipper, where the hell did you go? I was about ready to send out a search party."

"Ernie." He put his hand on Ernie's shoulder, a rare show of affection. "I stood on the glacier!"

"No, shit, Captain, you've been talking about doing that for years."

"Yep, but let's go to my stateroom. Nick's cleaned it up, so I can tell you what else happened."

CHAPTER FOURTEEN

October 20ᵗʰ—Noon

*H*omer changed from his casual attire to a clean white uniform for his meeting with John Adams. He expected to be picked up by a driver for the ride to the yacht. At the same time, one of the yacht people would inspect their cargo on the *Eagle* with Ernie and John Smith. At five minutes past noon, Homer walked out to the gangway where they were assembled.

One of the strangers standing nearby glanced at his watch and stared at Homer.

Fuck you. This is my ship! Homer paused and looked at the gathering of men.

Nick seemed to be hanging around, talking to one of the crew while stealthily photographing any new faces.

Homer nodded at Ernie, and headed down the gangway.

His escort led him to a car for the short drive. His stomach tightened as they approached the boat. *Who is this man, this leader, this murderer, and this organizer of such a complicated scheme of crime? But he needs me at this point. I'm part of his elaborate plan. Has he backed himself into a corner? I doubt it. He probably has escape plans if things go wrong. And at that point, he'll no longer need Davy or me. That's when we'll have to watch ourselves. Damn, I could use a drink. I hope he doesn't keep me waiting.*

He was led into a spacious lounge. He waited, taking in the fancy surroundings.

"My apologies, Captain Dixon, I was on an overseas telephone call," Adams said, as he entered.

Bullshit, Homer almost said aloud. He noticed Adams' blue eyes and the way he favored one leg.

"Please, sit down, Captain. What can I offer you to drink?" He openly stared at Homer, sizing him up. "I'm pleased to finally meet you. I know quite a lot about you, your accomplishments, and some of your weaknesses. We have researched the *Alaskan Eagle* and your record."

The opening salvo from Adams unnerved Homer. It was probably calculated to do so.

"We have placed passengers and seamen on your ship this past year to observe you and your crew. Please do not question me about these people, myself, or about our cargo. Cheers, Captain," Adams toasted, with a self-satisfied expression.

Homer, tight lipped, raised his glass and nodded.

"Also, Captain Dixon, I want to thank you for helping my crew member on the glacier. Yes, it was my sailor. All my people have been instructed to observe you, assist you and protect you, in any way possible. As I have said before, Captain, we need you. We need you to get our cargo safely to Seattle. You will be pleased to know that my man survived. Your call to the authorities saved him. He was taken to the hospital. I returned with him a short time ago." Adams turned his head and mumbled something.

A bandaged youth entered, bowing slightly toward Homer.

Homer rose, smiling, taking the young man's hand. "I'm happy to see you. I'm sorry I wasn't able to reach you."

Adams observed Homer's manner with a slight smile, most likely adding to his evaluation of this uncomplicated man. "His English is not good, Captain, but he has told me he is thankful for your efforts to save him." He gestured for the man to leave. "Now, Captain, please sit and accept something to eat. Let me fill your glass. I understand you enjoy drinking. So do I. How is the progress of the voyage so far? I am satisfied. Are you?"

"Mr. Adams, getting your cargo to Seattle is the easy part. My concern is for the safety of Davy and Madeline, and what those hot heads you have watching them may do. Davy can get pretty belligerent at times."

"My people are under control, Captain. I understand that you, also, can fly off the handle, as you say, when you get angry. That is my concern. That is why we are here watching you, and watching our cargo."

"Well, we understand each other now, Mr. Adams."

"Yes, we do, Captain Dixon. Now, we can enjoy our drinks and good food. Tell me, have you shared our secret with your friend, Mr. McInnis? You and Mr. McInnis spend much time together talking."

"You knew, when you decided to use the *Alaskan Eagle,* of my long association with Ernie McInnis. The time I spend with him is not only official business, but our friendship."

"I understand that, Captain, but you have not responded to my question. Have you kept our secret?"

Homer looked directly at him. "I would not put Ernie's life in danger by telling him."

"Very well, Captain. Now, about Mr. Banner's close association with the United States Coast Guard. We know of the work he's done for them, but find it strange that he continues to have early morning meetings at the Coast Guard Station." Adams observed Homer closely as he spoke, "And he's quickly approved to be part of your crew. Again, I find it strange. As so, we have been monitoring his activities."

"We've discussed Nick Banner before. When you say monitoring, do you mean you have established electronic surveillance on my ship, as you have at Davy's house?"

"You forget, Captain, the magnitude of this business venture."

"I'll take that as a yes, that you have bugged my ship. If I find any I will destroy them."

"Calm down, Captain. Shall we eat?"

"You're right, Mr. Adams," Homer said smiling. "Now that we are friends, are you going to tell me what's in those boxes, other than survival suits?"

"Ha!" Adams roared. "I like you, Captain. Just like most Americans, you are very open. During my education here I was astounded at how naïve and innocent you people are."

"That's because of our freedoms. We are able to live relaxed, open, and free lives."

"You are correct about that, Captain. I have traveled the world observing people and societies. The freedoms here are unique. Yet, this trait, and your successes, can also be your weakness. People and countries around the world take your money and use it against you. I have observed foreign people in your country steal from you, subvert your laws, and hide behind those laws. The reason I conduct my business here is that the profit is high, and the penalties are not as extreme."

"Mr. Adams, in another time and place, I think we could be friends."

"Possibly so, Captain. However, I am using my knowledge of Americans, with their openness, to exploit you for my gain. Just so you understand how serious I am about this venture."

"Mr. Adams, you've got me by the balls, if you know what I mean."

"Oh yes, I know that. We have similar expressions in my language."

"What language is that? I can't quite pin it down."

"I expect someone will. For now, let us keep it my secret. It's safer for all of us that way."

"In any other situation, I'd be fighting you all the way. But you've cleverly prevented me from any resistance by your threats and surveillance of Davy. However, if any harm comes to Davy or Madeline, or their family, all bets are off. I'll be fighting you in any way I know. I'm not as timid as my personality might indicate."

"I am well aware of that, Captain. For that reason, we must continue as we started. We must maintain our surveillance. Please let your friend Davy know that, to keep him from doing anything foolish."

"That's exactly what I've been telling him," Homer said.

"Also, Captain, tell him that once this venture is over, we will vanish into the wind. We will be gone. Our paths will never cross again. Unless, of course, you are foolish and notify the authorities."

"Again, exactly as I told Davy. I told him to take the money, see it through, and hope for the best. But you probably know that with your bugging of his house."

"Ah, Captain, we are going around in circles. Have more to eat. Let me fill your glass. How do you like this fine vessel I have chartered? At our next meeting in Ketchikan, I will show you the excellent accommodations."

"I'd like that."

They stood and walked to a large window. "You seem to be in a little pain," Homer noted, trying to diminish Adams somewhat. "Did that happen when you were observing the cargo loading in Anchorage?"

"Ah, I did not think you noticed us, Captain. Yes, I had an error in judgment at one point; however, I rarely misstep. I see that my representative has left your ship."

"This is a good time for me to return. I have a lot to do this afternoon. I will have our usual all-hands meeting of which you should get a full report."

"Yes, I will. I hope that my two people on board are not too troublesome. They are a vital part of my plan."

"What if we hadn't needed two additional seamen in Anchorage? What would you have done?"

"We would have found a way. We are very good at finding a way. The turnover rate of seamen is high. They quit, get sick, have accidents. You know that, Captain. What time do you plan to depart to maintain your schedule? We too, must make preparations."

"We'll have our all-hands meeting at seven in the morning and leave as soon as we can after that."

"Fine. Again, we will use your ship as our navigator."

"You should not stay too close, though. Some passages between here and Ketchikan are tricky, with narrow clearance. Also, we can expect some fog and limited visibility."

"We have fine navigation equipment, Captain, but our people lack experience. If we lose sight of you, we can set our radar to maintain contact. Our Mr. Smith and Mr. Brown report that some in your crew have expressed concern that we are too close. I hope you will ease this concern. To end our meeting on a more serious note, Captain, I must again warn you of the consequences of deviating from our procedures in any way that may jeopardize this venture."

"I hear you loud and clear, Mr. Adams."

CHAPTER FIFTEEN

October 20th—3pm

*N*ick stood on deck near the gangway, looking over the Eagle. I *hope I'm not over my head here.* 'I don't know exactly what I'm getting into' were the words he had used at the early morning meeting with the Coast Guard, his last meeting before the *Eagle* departs for Ketchikan.

"We'll keep you informed," Harris told him. "We'll call you daily, hourly if necessary, day or night. We'll expect you to do the same. Now, let's recap new events. We're processing the photos you've given us of all definite and possible terrorists. We're using that term to describe them for now, even without proof of their intentions. Better to approach this from an extreme, more serious point of view, and back down from that if we're wrong, than to underestimate the severity of this and get surprised or attacked. We hope it's merely smuggling of contraband."

"But, keep this in mind, and stress the point to Captain Dixon and the First Mate—this is a well-funded operation, and more importantly, we're convinced that they have murdered two or more people. We've checked the hundred dollar bills. They're real, not bogus. Amazing how they would part with that kind of money. This operation has got to be costing them close to a million dollars; the yacht, travel, extensive research, phony papers, survival suits, the fifty thousand dollars, and God knows what else, even considering that their credit cards are bogus and payment for their boat may never be honored." He paused as if thinking along a mental list.

"You must find a way to break into one of the boxes. With that information, plus the extra time to for us to determine the location and extent of their people on shore, we may be able to move in on them in Ketchikan and impound the cargo. If not, then definitely the minute you get to Seattle. We may want you to stop in Bellingham, the first U.S. port after you leave Canadian waters. It's a small port, easily controllable and we'll have more concentrated resources and personnel to do it. A large port like Seattle would give them more opportunity to jump ship, abandon the yacht."

"Mr. Harris, they're tailing us and tracking all of our activities on and off the Eagle. Since my involvement became known, they might be trying to monitor Coast Guard interests as well. Have you thought about a possible mole among your people?"

"We have. Recently, Coast Guard has adopted more stringent security codes and other security measures, for example, the underwater project you've just completed. Regarding Captain Davy and Mrs. Masters, the two men who are watching and listening to them are now under our surveillance. You might let Captain Dixon know that, lacking other resources in their small community, we've enlisted the police lieutenant in Kenai to look after them. We won't contact them ourselves, for obvious reasons, and Captain Dixon should not let them know this. Also, because of the implied threats to their daughter in California, we've got her house and phones covered. Again, no one should let them know this. So, to address your concern about getting in over your head…"

Nick mentally dismissed that statement. He thought to himself, *it all comes down to keeping my head above water—on all fronts.*

Harris continued, "We now think that, with Captain Dixon and the First Mate on your side, you should be more comfortable with the situation. We didn't know that four Army engineers were going to be on board. We don't expect anything to happen, but if all hell should break loose, you might be able to make use of them. For that reason, we have a travel case for you to take back. It's loaded with guns and ammunition to beef up the ship's supply of weapons."

Nick thought about the meeting. Rather than ease his concerns, the more he knew increased his burden. *Should he have asked Harris to include the monitoring of Hannah? But until the adversaries know of his involvement, she should be okay.*

While he was crouched down to re-tie his shoes, a shadow passed over him and a voice said, "Mr. Banner."

He stood up.

"Hi, I'm Angie Flowers. We haven't been introduced."

"Of course," Nick said. "I'm Nick Banner. How are you Major Flowers?"

She wore running gear. "Are you going out for a run?" she asked. "And if so, can I come with you? I don't know the roads or trails around here."

"I am, and you may, but you'll probably run rings around me," he said, looking at her face. *My god, she's beautiful.* He glanced at her left hand. *No ring.*

Noting the glance, she grinned. "No, I'm not married, and never have been, and that's a closed subject."

"Wow, look how much we know about each other after just five minutes," he joked.

"Well, I still don't know anything about you," she said.

They started on Nick's usual route, passing the empty perch often occupied by the aging eagle. Nick slowed, looking around. His expression must have changed to one of guilt, as he thought of Minnie.

"My, my, Mr. Banner, you look like a bad boy caught with his hand in the cookie jar."

"Am I that transparent? Reminds me of the time I was in the men's department of the Seattle Nordstrom's. I saw a man hand-cuffed by two people, probably cops. I saw his expression change from fear, to guilt, to shame. Never forgot that. As for me, we can talk about my expressions over a beer sometime. So, what are you guys doing here, and how did you get to where you are in the Army?"

"As we told the First Mate, we were inspecting bridges over some of the small streams at the Misty Fjords National Monument. We're riding back on the *Alaskan Eagle* with our vehicles and gear. If you mean how did I get into the Corps, I'm an engineer. I took ROTC in school, and presto, a major after twelve years. How about you?"

Nick talked about the Juneau Coast Guard project and the *Eagle's* need for a temporary officer. "Next question for you. Your name is listed in the ship's log as Major A.N.G. Flowers. I assume the A is for Angie. It's unusual for someone to have two middle names."

"It didn't take you long to find me out," Angie said. "The quick explanation is that Aster is my first name. My middle names are Narcissus and Gladiola, hence ANG, or Angie. My mother liked flowers. Probably why she married my father."

"I'm panting more than you are," Nick said. "You must do a lot of running."

"I was a competitive runner in school, and have kept it up. You're doing okay for an old man."

"Ha!" Nick laughed. "You sure know how to hurt a guy. After my Navy training, I never stopped. Even ran a few marathons. Now, as an *'old man'*, I don't run as far, or as fast, or as frequent. But, I need to run. I need it for my head and for my body."

"What did you do in the Navy?"

"I was a SEAL."

"Ooh, neat. How long were you in?"

"About eight years."

"Why did you get out?"

"Another subject we won't discuss now. We seem to have a growing list. How much military training have you had in the Army?"

"Not much after ROTC and officer basic training, if that's what you mean. Why?"

"Just curious. As an Army Officer, don't you have yearly or periodic weapons refresher training?"

"Minimal. But as an officer, I do have a personal weapon at my duty station. I don't take it traveling—too difficult. This is more than idle curiosity. What's going on?"

"Oh, no, nothing. I have some weapons on board, but haven't had time to do any shooting lately. Maybe we could practice off the stern of the ship like we used to do at sea. Come to think of it, that might not be a good idea. I haven't checked it out with the Captain and we'd be close to a lot of islands. We could possibly do it in Ketchikan."

"Sure." Angie shrugged. "And the guys might like it."

"I shouldn't even have brought that up, without thinking it through, so I'd appreciate it if you'd forget the whole thing, and not mention it to anyone, for now."

Angie glanced over at Nick while shaking her head. "If we had had this conversation before the run, I might not have come along." She smiled.

"It seems like I've been told that too many times before," Nick replied, with a comical grimace.

CHAPTER SIXTEEN

October 20th—Juneau, 6pm

"*Okay, where are we?" Homer asked Ernie and Nick.* He didn't need to soften his words in this familiar and noisy bar.

"This morning's meeting at Coast Guard was nothing new, other than we should continue our holding pattern on the way to Ketchikan," Nick started. "They reiterated the need to get into one of the boxes so they can better understand what we really have here, what these people are doing, and why they're doing it. They need more information. So, over the next thirty-six hours, before we get to Ketchikan, we need to do it. At this point, the statement that they are suspected of several murders just hangs out there.

"We also discussed the Corps of Engineers group on board and how they could help us. I got an update on that about an hour ago. On their own volition, Coast Guard contacted Major Flowers' boss, and just received the go-ahead. We can use them as we see fit. He said they're army officers first, and engineers second. They cautioned, however, that they've had minimal training in combat, and with the use of weapons. We should not put them in harm's way. Major Flowers may have already been contacted for confirmation."

"Well, hell," Ernie said. "None of us wants to get into *harm's way*, but it's more personal for me and Homer, and we'll risk it."

"Yes, we will," Homer, agreed. "And we will not put any of these youngsters in a position to get hurt protecting Davy, someone they don't even know. If what we find in those boxes is a threat to the country, that's a different story, at least until we get back up from the government. I wouldn't want any of the kids to get hurt. Davy wouldn't want it either. Nick, did you get anything from them as to when they're going to end this? We're going to be in deep shit if the people on the yacht put a move on us on the way to Ketchikan, or on the way to Seattle. Once we're in Canadian waters, or off the lower forty-eight, I can't see the yacht people waiting till we get to Seattle."

"They stressed that they're not ready yet. Maybe in Ketchikan," Nick said.

"I'll be a son of a gun," Homer said, "That kid I met on the glacier, and again on the yacht, is sitting at the far end of the bar. Adams has him following us again. If you glance around, he's the one with the bandages."

"I spotted someone from Coast Guard," Nick said. "He nodded at me. It's good to know they're looking out for us. Coast Guard is recording their activities and photographing all the yacht people and their spies on the *Alaskan Eagle*. I wonder why this guy off the yacht is going out alone, particularly given what you've said about his limited English."

"I feel as if we're in the middle of a TV series," Ernie joked. "Hey, another surprise. Our own John Smith and John Brown are also here drinking. Is that your phone buzzing, Skipper?"

"Yeah, but I don't recognize the number." Homer rose to go outside. "Davy, is that you? Where you calling from? Is everything okay?"

"It's me, and I'm okay. It's the new phone, the extra one," Davy said. "I left my regular phone at home. It's one of those that you buy minutes for, as you use them."

"Good. How long have you had it?"

"I just got it."

"Where are you now?"

"Walking back to my car."

"Stay away from your car for a few minutes. Your phone may be clean, but that doesn't mean your car is. I've got some things to tell you. I told you about Nick Banner and his Coast Guard project. Well, his job for the Coast Guard is done and we'll have him and his gear going back on this trip. It seems that Nick is a former Navy SEAL and Coast Guard has enlisted his help. We're no longer in this alone." Homer told Davy the details, including the vicious and threatening aspects. "So, old friend, although we've got help, the danger to all of us, particularly to you and Maddy, is still real. They've bugged everything, your phone, house and car."

"Holy shit," Davy said.

"That's why you need to use the throwaway phone when talking to me, but use it away from the house and car. You can use your regular house phone and your other cell for your daily needs. Supposedly, there are still two guys monitoring your conversations and your every move. Your police friend, I assume it's Jim Larson, has been contacted by Coast Guard, but only him, because he's the head lieutenant, not anyone else at the police station. But he can't watch you and those guys continuously. He doesn't know that you know of his involvement. Better to keep it that way so we don't compromise his efforts. Davy, the danger is real and still there and seems to be worse than we could have imagined."

"Homer, I can't tell you how sorry I am for getting you into this."

"I know, Davy, but that's past us now. We have to solve the problems as they come up, just like aboard ship. I'm the one who should be apologizing to you. It's the *Eagle* that was targeted. You were just a way of getting to the *Eagle*. If you turned it down, they would have found another broker to handle the shipments using the *Eagle*. It's still a mess, Davy. I don't know when it'll be over. On one hand, I feel better with government support but the whole thing appears far more dangerous, more brutal, than we thought. Right now, with the cargo on the *Eagle*, we're somewhat safe. The minute that changes we'll have a problem."

"We're okay," Davy said. "They're leaving us alone. I don't know where they hang out. They can't just park and sit there. The neighbors would report it. I *have* noticed more police patrols in the area lately."

"Put Jim Larson's number in speed dial on both cells, and your home phone. And for God-sakes, Davy, carry your gun. You're licensed for it. But don't tell Maddy. That'll raise other problems. We had Coast Guard check out some of those hundred dollar bills. It's strange, but they're good. I wonder why. We'll find out, someday. Well, old buddy, I'm glad we have a safe way of talking, but you've got to be careful and on your guard all the time. With those guys breathing down your neck you're in danger, even more than we are. I've got your new number in my phone now. Whenever we're talking be sure to walk out of your house or away from your car."

"Damn it, Homer, I'm not a child, and I'm not senile."

"I know that, Davy, but you're family, 'nuff said."

Homer walked back into the bar and up to Ernie and Nick. He stood, leaning over the table to speak over the noise. "Let's get the fuck out of here. I don't like being spied on. But on the way out, let's say hello to all our friends. Shake them up a bit." Homer was told the name of the boy from the glacier, but couldn't remember it. He nodded at him, getting a big smile in response. He seemed to be alone, but probably brought by Smith and Brown.

Nick snapped his picture in case Coast Guard had missed him. Smith and Brown were as usual, Brown subdued while Smith was drinking.

Homer rarely placed restrictions on his crew in port. He required only that they perform their watches and duties and return to the ship with sufficient time to carry out their underway responsibilities. "Has Smith been drinking on board?" he asked Ernie as they were leaving the bar.

"I've had some reports indicating, yes, but he manages to complete his chores. No one in the crew has been able to get close to him. The feeling is mutual."

"We need to watch him," Homer said. "He's the loose cannon. Brown just follows."

"The whole crew knows that," Ernie agreed. "They steer clear of them, don't trust them."

"Adams must know this. He's no dummy. He probably encourages it. Keeps us busy watching Smith, so we don't think about other things. Sure different than our normal worst case scenario of the cops dropping off drunks, or some hot-heads, at the gangway."

CHAPTER SEVENTEEN

October 21st–6 am

"**W**e'll *be departing Juneau in a few minutes,*" Homer stated, at the start of his pre-departure meeting.

The crew was immediately aware of the lack of a jocular tone in Homer's voice.

"Our crew size is now twenty-one with the addition of a second mate, Nick Banner, and the loss of two officer trainees, called back to corporate headquarters. You might remember that we hauled Nick's equipment up to Juneau last year. In addition to Nick's gear, we've loaded more cargo. Some of Nick's gear will offload in Ketchikan, and some will go on to Seattle with the rest of our cargo. Our passenger list has increased to fourteen with the four Army Corps of Engineers surveyors who came aboard. Mr. McInnis will take over from here."

The small crowd all stared at him.

Homer held up his hand. "Wait a minute. Let me start this over again." He paused, and stood there for a moment looking down. When his head came up his demeanor looked somewhat more normal.

A few in the crew smiled.

"Gentlemen, and Ladies. We leave Juneau on this beautiful morning, heading for Ketchikan. The weather continues to be good. In the protected area on the way south to Ketchikan our only concern is fog." At six in the morning, the army surveyors and a few other passengers were around to observe the ritual. "Have you noticed the Army uniforms? Not to worry. There'll be no military exercises. The officers are, in fact, engineers. They'll be riding back to Seattle with their equipment. They made a smart choice to go back to Seattle aboard our comfortable *Eagle*. I was going to say beautiful and comfortable *Eagle*, but, although we love her, you can see for yourselves. The yacht that has been staying close to us since the Port of Homer, and is now parked nearby, will continue to accompany us for a while. We've agreed to help them out navigating part of the way to Ketchikan." Homer's mood now changed for the better.

While he talked, he, and others, noticed a commotion between one of the Corps of Engineers lieutenants and John Smith. "We got a problem back there?" Homer asked.

"I'm sorry, Captain," the lieutenant, said. "I keep moving away from this guy, but he keeps coming after me. I have no idea why."

"Mr. Smith, can I see you for a moment?"

"No. I told you we are in charge, not you."

John Brown, standing next to Smith, tried to calm him, but Smith shrugged him off.

Homer gestured to Ernie and a few of the senior crew to get him off the ship, which they did, while a stream of invectives, some in a foreign tongue, came from Smith.

"Pull in the gangway. Cast off the lines." The engines, already running, were in readiness. "Mr. McInnis, get the ship underway," Homer, commanded.

The crew immediately went to their stations, while the few passengers observing the meeting mulled around talking.

The lieutenant, accompanied by Major Flowers, came up to Homer. He started to apologize.

"Not your problem, son," Homer interrupted. "Without a brig on board, isn't that what would happen in the Navy or Army?"

"I guess it would," the lieutenant answered, smiling.

Homer walked away from the group with his phone out, waiting for it to ring.

"Captain Dixon," John Adams barked, "What do you think you are doing? You cannot interfere with my plans. I am warning you, Captain."

"Look, you are warning me every day with those people hanging over Davy and Maddy. And you do that to keep me in line. That's very clever of you. You know that without that, I would throw your ass to the Coast Guard!" Homer practically shouted.

"Calm down, Captain. You are correct, of course. We threaten you to keep you from doing something stupid. However, be careful not to carry your independence too far. It is a complicated plan I have developed, possibly too complicated. However, you can be assured that I have many contingency plans."

"I'm sure you do, Mr. Adams. I did what had to be done. The man was openly insubordinate. His remarks almost blew the cover on your whole operation. I should have him arrested. I guess you'll have to take him on board the yacht."

"Yes, I think so. I will wait until your ship is out of sight. However, Captain, I want him back on the *Alaskan Eagle* when we arrive in Ketchikan."

"If you expect to have him on your yacht, you'd better keep him below decks or my crew will wonder what the hell is going on."

"Yes, of course. I will need to discipline him severely. He will be very meek when you get him back in Ketchikan."

"I doubt that," Homer replied. "Are you sure you need him on the *Eagle*?"

"Yes, Captain, I need him on your ship."

Once underway, Homer got Ernie and Nick together on the bow. "Okay, I talked with Adams. He was on my ass about two minutes after we threw his spy off. Not only were we being watched, but both Smith and Brown must have called him. He'll take Smith on the yacht. Can we get Coast Guard to confirm that?" Homer looked over at Nick. "I told Adams that he'd better keep Smith out of sight, so none of our crew spots him. Now, the bad news. Adams wants him back on board the *Eagle* when we leave Ketchikan. Says he needs him. No discussion possible. Says he has plans for him. Doesn't look too good for what might happen south of Ketchikan. The leverage of Davy's safety came up." Homer was still panting, but less so.

"You did the right thing, Skipper." Ernie nodded his head. "Too bad, we couldn't just shoot him."

"Captain, just got another update from Coast Guard," Nick interjected. "They've been in contact with the Army to keep them aware of the situation and to let them know that to pull the four engineers off the *Eagle* at this point, might affect the balance of what Coast Guard is trying to accomplish. The Army is pushing to resolve this mess. They've been in touch with Major Flowers. We should be including the Major in our conversations."

"Ernie." Homer nodded his head at the first mate. "Find Major Flowers. Ask her to bring her lieutenants to meet with us in my stateroom."

Angie must have stayed nearby, expecting to be summoned. She approached the group with a tight smile, while looking at Nick. She nodded her head slightly, as they all made their way to the Captain's quarters.

"Major Flowers, I haven't had a chance to talk with you yet," Homer greeted, extending his hand.

"Please, Captain, it's Angie."

Homer and Nick proceeded to brief Angie. "We hope Coast Guard will resolve everything before we leave Ketchikan," Homer said. "If it goes beyond Ketchikan, we become more vulnerable.

They probably have an arsenal on board the yacht, compared with our limited supply of weapons. If a group of Navy SEALs, say, were to come aboard to help us, they might go ballistic. We don't know what they would do, and neither does the government, at this point. Our main task, which Nick will coordinate, is to find out what's in those boxes. That's key to our efforts over the next twenty-four hours. If the shit should hit the fan, I'm sorry, ma'am, I don't mean to offend."

"Captain, though I'm an engineer, I'm also an Army Major working with men and tough women every day. I've had a lot of shit hit fans in the last twelve years. Please continue."

"Okay." Homer smiled. "None of us knows what they have planned. Talking with this Mr. Adams every day I probably have the best idea what he's up to if I can strip away the bullshit and bravado. He might have a bunch of halfwits and muscle men working for him, but he's the one we need to be concerned about. I will continue to interface with him. I agree that Nick, with his background, should be on the lookout for and coordinate any rough stuff that might happen. My friend Davy and I are the only ones who are supposed to know of their smuggling. They did that on purpose, as we've told you."

All present seemed pensive when Homer paused to look at them.

"Their mastermind, John Adams, that's what he calls himself, is a clever, educated, and ruthless guy. He suspects that Ernie, Nick, and now the four of you are part of the effort to stop him. Frankly, I'm thankful that all of you are here. We've been winging it alone for the past week. But now that puts all of you in danger. Not just harm, but mortal danger. We'll let you know as soon as anything changes the status quo. Again, as for the next twenty-four hours, we must get into a few of the boxes. Nick will coordinate that, also. My immediate concern is to calm the crew and the passengers regarding what happened this morning." Homer glanced at Angie. "Welcome aboard. I'm sure you never expected this yesterday."

"No, we didn't, Captain. My Commanding General himself briefed me with the vague aspects of the situation, as he knows it. Coast Guard convinced him that because of extenuating circumstances, they could not move in as yet. He obviously did not know, or did not tell me, the details as you explained them, but indicated that new compelling information made it unlikely that it could even be stopped in Ketchikan—something about the threat of a dirty bomb."

Homer looked at Nick.

"I'll call them right now," Nick said.

CHAPTER EIGHTEEN

October 21st—En-Route Ketchikan

Homer bounded up to the bridge after making rounds of the ship, and after talking with passengers and crewmembers. He smiled and joked with the helmsman. Was it getting rid of John Smith, even temporarily, or was it getting underway closer to Seattle, closer to the end? He ignored the presence of the yacht. *Who am I kidding? This thing is never going to end. No way is the yacht going into Seattle. What the hell are they going to do?*

Nick's info from Coast Guard was a lot of crap. Some sort of veiled threat had come from, they don't know where, when, or how. The government targeted the *Alaskan Eagle,* the yacht, and dozens of other vessels and aircraft as suspects, because the areas threatened included Juneau, Ketchikan, Vancouver and Seattle. *It's a smoke screen. A clever way for them to get Coast Guard fragmented and over extended. It could backfire. No way is Coast Guard going to let the yacht or the Eagle out of Ketchikan without thorough searches. It doesn't change anything.*

"Captain, that damn yacht is too close to us," the bridge watch reported.

"I'll take a look."

The yacht had pulled abreast of the *Eagle,* about twenty yards off the starboard side—too close for maneuvering.

From the outer bridge railing, Homer could see their helmsman, but no one else. His gestures for the yacht to move away were ignored, as was his attempt to use the short-range radio provided by Adams. "Ease our speed," he instructed the bridge. "No, fuck it. Belay that. Pull up next to them. I don't care if they bounce off us. Yacht, *Mother's Love,*" he yelled through his bullhorn. "More like motherfucker," he said as an aside to Ernie and Nick, both called to the bridge when the charade began.

"What's he trying to do?" Nick wondered aloud.

"My apologies, Captain," Adams, yelled from the yacht. "I wanted to see how difficult it would be to receive help, if we should need it. We will pull back."

"That's his message," Homer informed Ernie and Nick, the three of them now alone. "They want to see how easy it would be for them to board us, pirate style. Nick, did you bring the passenger list? Have I met all of them?"

"Got it right here, Captain. Do you always have such a diverse and interesting group on board? In addition to the four Army engineers; we have a father with his twin sixteen-year-old sons, both Eagle Scouts, and a retired Mexican policeman with his wife and unmarried daughter, who's a nurse. Also, two couples traveling together, all seniors. That's fourteen of them. I'm told we might get more in Ketchikan."

"I wonder if we can talk some of them out of coming on board in Ketchikan or try to dump some of those we have," Homer said. "Not likely though. The problem is we'll have to protect them from what might happen—if anything should happen. I'm going to stay on the bridge most of the day. Is the bridge watch set for the next twenty-four hours?" he asked Ernie.

"John Brown is covered. He'll be on the bridge from noon to four and again, for the full mid-watch, from midnight to four."

"We'll do the scouting and planning during his day-watch, and break into the boxes at night," Nick said.

Homer's short-range radio buzzed. He motioned for Nick and Ernie to leave the area. "Mr. Adams," he said, "I thought you had abandoned this radio. I tried to get you a little while ago."

Ignoring the comment, John Adams said, "Captain, what are you planning? I think I will put two more men on board your ship. Also, why are you meeting so often with Mr. McInnis and Mr. Banner?"

"Mr. Adams, my planning involves how to get rid of you and your boxes in Seattle and put this nightmare behind me. The constant strain you have placed on me this past week is more than a year's worth of stress I go through on monthly trips between Seattle and Anchorage. I'm looking forward to the company decommissioning this ship and me walking away to live the rest of my life. In fact, I might ask them to relieve me in Ketchikan. I could walk away a week earlier."

"You do not have the option to leave the ship in Ketchikan, absolutely not. You should calm down, Captain, I did not think my comments would upset you so much."

"Well, they did. And my meetings with Ernie and Nick are routine ship's business. I could meet with them in my stateroom, but I'm never sure that I've discovered all of your bugs. And no, you cannot put two more spies on my ship. Coast Guard won't allow it and I will not permit it."

"In truth, I do not need anyone else on board, Captain. I have sufficient people watching you right now."

"John Brown is not people, Mr. Adams."

"Of course, Captain, John Brown is not people. Again, I have sufficient people on board. It was nice having this little talk with you, Captain. I look forward to our meeting in Ketchikan. Someone will pick you up at noon for the ride to my yacht."

He's fucking with me. That's what the son-of-a-bitch is doing. He's fucking with me again. Homer shut off the radio and stood for a while. He looked at the yacht and at the beautiful Islands beyond.

The water between two of the islands seemed to be frothing. He grabbed his binoculars. There were thousands of small fish bubbling on the surface. In a minute, the sky was full of small birds going after the fish. And soon, hundreds of eagles came out of the tall trees. Homer watched the eagles diving after the birds. When it looked like one of them was about to grab its prey, the bird would turn off on a tangent, leaving the eagle flying past, reminiscent of World War II aerial dog fights. *Who are we,* wondered Homer, *the birds or the fish—certainly not the eagles?*

CHAPTER NINETEEN

*A*t eleven in the morning Nick met with the four Army engineers in the passengers' dining area: Angie, First Lieutenant Luis Garcia, and Second Lieutenants Richard York and Sanford 'Sandy' Stevens. Nick kept them engaged in small talk, evaluating their interests and abilities as they ate. The other passengers occasionally glanced at them. From the expressions on the faces of the two Eagle Scouts, it was obvious the uniforms impressed them.

They sat there until the other passengers left. "What's the plan?" Angie asked, looking at Nick while she munched on a sandwich.

"At noon, when Ernie gives us confirmation that Brown is on the bridge, we start exploring. Ernie will join us. He knows every nut, bolt, and passageway on the ship. Our goal is to open two of the boxes, but it's not that simple." Nick gave them just enough background on the underlying threats to pique their interest and arouse their alarm. "So, we're defying these threats as well as others, by opening the boxes. But Coast Guard feels it's necessary particularly in light of the recent dirty bomb information, even though it's not given much credence based on the timing and the way it was received."

"Jesus, Major," Richard York, said. "What are we getting into?"

Nick broke in, "It took three days of meetings with Coast Guard for me to get the picture and help them out. I've been out of the Navy for a long time. I had a lot of questions. They, the bad guys, also indicated they know my daughter is going to college in San Diego. Not a good feeling. Ernie, Major Flowers, and I will brief the three of you extensively this afternoon. You cannot let others in the crew, or any of the passengers, know what's going on."

"And," Angie informed her group; "you cannot make calls to your family or anyone else until this gets resolved. Welcome to the war on terror."

The three officers sat there, looking a little surprised.

"I guess we're *in the Army now*," Sandy Stevens mused.

"Our planning this afternoon will show us how we'll need to proceed with our important tasks tonight, from midnight till four," Nick continued. "But let me say this, I will be the one who opens the boxes while you guys are at a safe distance breathing well ventilated outside air. I have some equipment to test the boxes for any explosives or toxic chemicals. If there is any indication we're at risk of an explosion or a release of toxic chemicals we stop right there and go to plan B, whatever that is. Here's Ernie. We can now start our little adventure."

"You guys look freaked out," Ernie observed, speaking softly.

They stared at Ernie with some apprehension.

"It's not you," Angie whispered quietly. "It's what Nick just told us about opening the boxes."

"I'm with you on that," Ernie said. "Nick will have to do his magic while we hold our collective breaths. Brown is on the bridge for the next four hours. Captain Dixon will make sure of that. First, we'll do an extensive tour of the ship to get you familiar with the layout. It's important that you know your way around in the dark. If anyone sees us, it will look innocent enough. If we get questioned, which we shouldn't, we're setting up for a test of the laser surveying equipment. A good cover suggested by Major Flowers.

"We have enough equipment to simulate a test without actually testing anything," Angie said.

"Then we'll pick a safe but secluded spot to operate on two of the boxes." Ernie continued. "We need an area that can't be seen by anyone on the yacht, but has a good flow of air. They shouldn't even see us setting up, or any of our activity in the hold or hauling the contraband boxes. In fact, no one can see us doing that. No passengers or crew. Someone might innocently mention it to John Brown. We're not even certain if there is or is not another spy on board as a passenger or part of the crew. We're flying blind."

The six of them sat there silently. "I've got few spots in mind, and we've only got 'til four this afternoon." Ernie kept the group within the interior of the ship, avoiding a possible sighting by the yacht and not taking a chance that Brown could see them from the *Eagle's* bridge. When they encountered any passengers or crew, Ernie went into his effusive tour guide cover.

After the tour, Ernie returned them to three locations: A passageway just under the bridge, the most secure based on limited access from unwanted passers-by; the large area in the hold, containing the seventy-six boxes, all of Nick's equipment, and most of the *Eagle's* cargo; and the third, a large athwartships passageway forward of the hold with hatches that could be opened on both the port and starboard sides of the ship.

The passageway under the bridge, although ideal from a security standpoint, was rejected because of possible danger and vulnerability to Homer and others on the bridge. The expanse of the large hold was also rejected because of security concerns and the lack of fresh air movement.

Ernie and Nick agreed on the athwartships passageway, although the danger of exposure for Nick was the highest. The four engineers would guard the two hatches, port and starboard, and the door openings to ladder stairways. Ernie would roam as necessary and keep an eye on Nick's progress—from a distance.

Nick spent the late afternoon, after four, casually inspecting all his equipment to locate the gear he needed.

John Brown, whose cabin was nearby, stared at Nick a few times, and no doubt made his calls to John Adams.

Nick was aware of the surveillance. He secured his gear, locked his trucks, and set the truck intrusion alarms.

Angie had asked Nick to come by before dinner to discuss details and answer some questions. She opened the door, wearing shorts and a loose cut-off tank top, greeting Nick with a grin. "Come in. Excuse the sweat. I was working out."

Uh oh, thought Nick, as he gazed at her nearly naked body. *I'd better get out of here.* "We can get together at dinner."

"No, no, come on in." She closed the door behind him, ignoring the protocol of leaving the door open when a male visits a female in her quarters. "I'll be finished in a minute. I have to do the last set of my push-ups, and shower."

Nick stared at her prone body effortlessly doing the push-ups. She looked muscular and well conditioned, not too big, not too small. Her bare breasts were totally exposed under her tank top. *She knows exactly what she's doing, knows exactly what she's showing. I'd like to fuck her brains out,* were the thoughts that came to his mind.

When she finished, she stood in front of him—with her tight abs and her nipples pushing her tank top out each time she breathed deeply. She looked up at Nick. "What do you think of my push-ups? Did you see enough to rate them?"

"A perfect ten, and you can never see enough." Nick got up. "Major, you're a sight for sore eyes, as the expression goes, but I've got to wash up also. I'll see you at dinner."

With a tight closed-mouth smile, and glee in her eyes, Angie replied, "Okay, Mr. Banner, and, thank you."

CHAPTER TWENTY

Oct. 21st—En-Route Ketchikan 11:45pm

Homer kept Ernie on the bridge waiting for John Brown. Ernie and Nick had briefed Homer earlier in the evening. "Will you be able to finish by four?" he asked again.

"Even taking it slow, considering all the safeguards, we should be able to do it," Ernie said. "We'll keep an open line with Coast Guard's Haz-Mat people. They'll also have bomb squad experts on the phone. If we run into something totally strange, we'll stop until we figure it out and get the go-ahead to continue."

"I don't want anyone to get hurt. If you're not finished at three-thirty, let me know. I'll keep Brown here doing busy work."

"Understood."

At a quarter to twelve, in accordance with standard procedure, John Brown showed up on the bridge. The extra fifteen minutes insures that the relief watch is on station and gives the watch stander being relieved time to complete any log entries.

"Well, I'm out of here—I need a night cap," Ernie announced.

"Have a good one," Homer said. "I'll have to wait for mine."

On the way to the hold, Ernie alerted Nick.

Nick rapped a signal knock on Angie's door and continued below deck.

Angie, in turn, knocked on Luis Garcia's door.

The covert procedure tended to prevent any crew or passengers seeing a crowd gathering. However, after a week of subterfuge and unusual activity by Homer and Ernie, some of the crew wondered what the hell was happening.

Newitt had even talked with Ernie earlier in the day. "I've been on too many trips with you and the Skipper not to see that there's something strange about this one. What is it Ernie?"

Ernie put him off with oblique statements about the company and the Captain, and asked him to try to suppress all discussions on the matter. "It'll all become clear in a few days," he said to Newitt. "Meanwhile, it's important to keep it low key. Any time you hear anything just play it down without making it an issue."

"We have to tell some of the senior crew," Ernie told Homer, later.

Ernie, Nick, and the four engineers met on the ledge at the stacked row of boxes. "Let's take the two boxes at the end," Nick said. "If something happens and we can't return them on time, there won't be gaps in the row that might be noticed, unless, of course, they count all the boxes, identifying them by number or label. I'm taking a picture of the exact position of the two boxes."

Ernie, Angie and Luis Garcia went ahead to secure the passageway. Ernie returned to give them the all clear.

Nick hauled some of his gear. York and Stevens followed him, carrying the boxes. He showed them where to set them down. The three of them went down to the hold for the rest of Nick's gear. The passageway was on the same level as the ledge.

The four engineers proceeded to their lookout posts after setting up bogus survey equipment to look like a test of high intensity lasers.

Ernie repeated the reason for closing the passageway; so all of them had the same story, that it could be dangerous or harmful to any passengers or crew.

Nick had his bag of equipment, supplies, sensing instruments, a trash container, portable lighting, and the communication and recording devices. He set up the lighting and established contact with the Coast Guard Station. From that point on, while he talked his way through the entire operation, Coast Guard would save the voice recording.

Nick started, "The box is taped one way at least a dozen times around all four sides, and across, around all four sides, providing double taping on the open top and bottom. I'm going to cut into a few layers of tape to unwind them."

"It's like opening Pandora's Box."

"It is," was the reply.

Because of the cross taping, it required continuous cutting and stripping. The tape was discarded in the trash bin. Ernie had supplied Nick with twelve new rolls of identical industrial tape.

"Do you see anything under the tape?" he was queried. "Any bumps that could be sensors?"

"Nothing yet."

Gradually, the layers were peeled down to the last few. "I'll have to be careful re-packing this. It's pretty exact. They must've had some sort of mechanical gadget to put it on. How am I doing on time?"

"It's one fifteen. You've got two and a half hours left."

"We might have to settle for opening only one box. I see some bumps under the last two layers of tape, four on the top of the box and four on the bottom. I get no signal or indication that it's anything electronic." Nick carefully peeled the last two layers. "They're staples. I can take them out, but we'll have to put it back together without the staples. Hopefully, they'll just cut the top off when they open it, without removing the tape. They should never notice the missing staples."

"Not to worry. If it even gets to Seattle we'll have customs cut the boxes open for inspection."

Nick checked his Haz-Mat suit and mask. He looked at the camera, and at Ernie, giving them both thumbs up.

"You okay, buddy?"

"Just fine, Ernie." Nick carefully removed the staples from the top of the box. The flaps lifted up slightly, unencumbered by tape. "I'm going to open it up. I've now got it open. I can see the survival suit material. No indication of any toxic substance or any unusual chemicals."

"Without a seal of some kind, the chemicals would have dissipated by now," came the response from Coast Guard.

"Well, at least we know this part is true, meaning they *are* shipping survival suits. Here goes. I'll pull the suit out. That was easy. It's tied tight, compressed with a tension-type buckle on a strap, similar to what truckers use to hold cargo from shifting on a flat bed. I'm turning it over, inspecting it. I can't see anything, only the suit."

"What's the problem?" asked the voice from the Coast Guard.

"I feel something hard in the center," Nick answered.

"Don't squeeze it or put any pressure on it. Try to ease up on the strap, releasing it slowly. Each time you slightly release it, stop to test for chemicals or an electronic signal. Take it slow, now."

"You're worrying me." Nick sighed. Sweat poured down his back as he gradually undid the strap and started to unfold the survival suit.

"You should be worried. Take it very slow, now," the voice cautioned.

"Bingo," Nick breathed out. "We've found the real cargo. It's a package, a little more than one foot cubed, encased in heavy dark green plastic. The plastic is thick, probably three to five millimeters, and sealed airtight. There's no easy way to open it, except to cut into it. And we'd have no way of sealing it shut."

"Hold on. Let's think about this. If there's any toxic substance within the box it would be in that sealed plastic. If so, there would be some chemical residue on the outer surface of the plastic. Check carefully with the sensor devices."

"I'm gradually going over all six surfaces. I get no indication of any chemicals."

"We're discussing this. Give us a minute. Here's what we'll do. Re-pack the survival suit in the box without the inner package. Bring the container tomorrow when you come to the Base in Ketchikan. We have the facility to open it safely. If it's a totally innocent item, we'll tell them what we did when you get to Seattle. But that's not likely. If it's contraband, or something lethal, we'll be impounding it."

"One problem," Nick replied. "The inner package weighs more than the suit. We'll have to find a substitute weight and repack a similar sized heavy box. Our First Mate, Ernie McInnis, said that while inspecting their cargo in Juneau they lifted some off the ledge, as if to weigh them."

"Fine. The fact that they did that indicates a lower probability of an active electronic device in the package. Do you get any readings?"

"No, none," Nick said.

"What if they should want to remove some or all of the boxes in Ketchikan?" the voice asked.

"I don't know. I'll ask Ernie. He's been on the other line."

Ernie responded immediately, "They can't do that. The cargo's been consigned to Seattle. It can't be removed. I'll find a small box we can use as a substitute. We can load it to weigh about the same. It will take me no more than ten or fifteen minutes."

"Okay, Ernie. I'll also need one to haul this package to Coast Guard."

"Good job, Nick," Harris said. "Wrap it up. You have less than two hours to finish. I'll meet you at the Base in Ketchikan. You can drive the container over in one of the trucks you're off-loading."

Ernie showed up with a few boxes, a scale, and some weights.

They used a metal container to hide the plastic package, sealing the container with tape.

At this point, Nick shed his mask and Haz-Mat suit. He took a moment to relax, wiping sweat from his face.

Ernie helped with repacking the large box, flipping it while Nick taped. They hauled both boxes back to the ledge.

"I'm placing the boxes back, in exactly the same spots."

"Good. You'd better leave, you're almost out of time."

"Ernie, tell the Captain to hold Brown for a few minutes. I've got to secure this thing and my gear in the truck."

"Good morning, Mr. Brown," Nick said, meeting him on his way out of the hold.

"You're awake early, Mr. Banner," John Brown said.

Nick was surprised at the statement from the normally reticent Brown.

"Yes," he replied. "I'm preparing some of my trucks for offloading to the Coast Guard Station in Ketchikan." *Shit, I should have just said yes, instead of fumbling a response.* He dragged himself back toward his quarters, passing Angie's cabin on the way. He stopped for a moment, then backtracked to knock on her door.

She answered sleepily, wearing a t-shirt held down to barely cover herself.

"I'm sorry to wake you. I wanted to thank you and the guys for giving up a night's sleep."

"That's okay, but I'm really beat—and you don't look too good."

"I know, and I feel as bad as I look."

"I guess the thank-you couldn't wait till morning," she said with a grin. "Here you caught me disheveled and ugly."

"Major; disheveled, maybe, but lookin' good."

"You have a charming way with words, Mr. Banner," she said smiling. "Going running tomorrow?"

"Yes, mid-morning, as soon as I get back from Coast Guard. I have a great route. Want to come?"

"I'd love to come," she said, releasing the grip on her t-shirt as the door closed.

CHAPTER TWENTY-ONE

October 22nd—Ketchikan, Alaska

Homer pulled himself back up to the bridge at seven** as the *Eagle* approached the dock. "I'm getting too old for this shit," he said to Ernie. "If not too old, then too tired. This trip is wearing me out."

"Maybe we're getting close to the end, Skipper."

"Don't believe it for a second. I'm edgy coming into Ketchikan. Something is going to happen here. What's the word from the crew?"

"Newitt came to see me again with, 'What the fuck's going on?' Some of these guys have been with us a long time. They know this trip is strange. They picked up on it when we were in Juneau. I put him off. Told him it'll be clear in a few days. I asked him not to discuss anything with anyone when either Smith or Brown is around. Smith is gone, he said. I told him Smith is coming back. That's when he looked at me with disgust and started walking away, shaking his head. I stopped him and asked him again to give us a couple of more days. He gave me a half-assed nod and left. We need to brief him and some of the senior crew, those we can trust."

"Let's hold them off until we leave Ketchikan," Homer said. "I was supposed to be the only one on board who knew. Now, there'll be ten or twelve of us. But that's good, as long as they keep it quiet. Okay, where are we? We won't know anything much until Nick gets back from Coast Guard, maybe not even then. The four engineers are going to help Nick move his trucks and equipment. They're all pretty beat."

"I saw Nick loading three of his trucks. He's getting ready to leave the ship," Ernie said. "He'll take his construction gear and the black box, but leave any gear that could be useful, or could be used as a weapon."

"Such as?"

"Some explosives, dive gear, communication and surveillance equipment, and a bunch of other stuff I know nothing about. It looks like we're preparing for a battle. Better to be ready than be caught by surprise. We might be ending our careers going out in a blaze of glory." Ernie smiled.

"What better way? The thought of it hops me up. No more doom and gloom. We have to take charge. We can't wait for Coast Guard. It's our asses on the line."

"Feel better now, Homer?"

"Much. Ernie, without you around, I'd be in sad shape. I wouldn't have anyone to open up to, to loosen up with. I'd go crazy being The Captain all the time. Remember, we're going to Sally's tonight. We haven't been there in a while. Do you think Sally is still around? She's a sweetheart. Remember how pissed off she pretended to be when we called it Sally's Boobs and Ass Place instead of Sally's Bluegrass Place?"

Ernie grinned.

"And," Homer added. "I'll need to relax after my meeting with Adams."

"What time is your meeting, and where is the *Mother's Love* tied up?"

"Someone will pick me up at noon. I don't know where it is. We'll have to be on the lookout for their spies, besides the one we have on board. The yacht couldn't get into this commercial yard, so they can't watch our deck and gangway. *Mother's Love.* It sure is a beautiful yacht. We should retire and just sail around in something like that, Ernie. Too bad you can't come with me to see the inside."

"It would be nice," Ernie said. "We could take out charters all summer and go south to Laguna or San Diego in the winter. It would be a stretch to reach Hawaii, but we could try. I wonder what the rental is? They'll probably stick some poor bastard with the bill for it. No way they'd use a good credit card."

"*Mother's Love.* It's a nice name. Makes you think. I miss the love of a woman, Sally's love. You see your Coast Guard squeeze twice a month in Juneau, but it's been too long for me. Let's definitely go to Sally's tonight. Tell Nick. We'll have a meeting there."

"Okay, skipper."

"I think it's time I let go of this ship, Ernie. She's been good to me, but she'll leave me soon anyway. She'll understand if I make the break first."

"She's been good to both of us, Homer."

"Growing up, we had a dog for fifteen years, a German Shepherd. She was like a member of the family. We loved her. When her body failed and the vet said 'it's time,' it took a while to accept it. I went with my Dad when we took her in. We sat in the car with her, saying goodbye. She wouldn't look us in the eye. I think she understood, but that didn't stop the pain and the tears. I'll never forget that."

"Homer, I've seen you hard-assed sometimes, but down deep you're a big softy."

"I guess so, and I guess I'll always be that way," Homer said, as they gazed down at the *Eagle* docking, and the setting-up of the truck ramp and gangway. "There go the three trucks. It's working out, having Nick with us. Shit. Here comes Smith. They didn't waste any time getting him over here. Go down on deck to see what happens."

Ernie walked down to the gangway area of the deck. The crew was securing lines to the dock and the gangway.

As soon as John Smith came aboard, he was beset with a verbal barrage from some of the crew. "What the fuck are you doing here, shit head, we already threw all your gear overboard!"

Ernie went over to intercede, but Smith himself was defusing the situation by calmly apologizing to the men. "I couldn't believe my ears," he told Homer later. "He probably got reamed out royally by Adams. He wants to talk with you."

"Send him to my cabin," Homer said.

The John Smith who entered Homer's stateroom was carefully controlled but far from contrite. "Captain Dixon, I was asked to remind you of your meeting with Mr. John Adams today, at noon. Mr. Adams has much to discuss with you. For myself, Captain, I will tell you that my actions may appear changed, but do not think I am a different person. I am not. I am the same person, and I am still in charge aboard this ship."

Homer smiled slightly, not with deference but with amusement. He felt pleased with himself for the way he reacted. "So, Mr. Smith, you kiss the asses of the crew to calm them, but you show me your true character. A poor choice of words, Mr. Smith. Don't you ever think I'm not in charge on my own ship. Do you understand what I am saying? I know English is not your native language."

John Smith's body stiffened somewhat, his face severe. He turned and walked out of the cabin.

CHAPTER TWENTY-TWO

October 22nd—9am

*N*ick introduced Angie to Frank Harris and to the Coast Guard Captain. Her three engineers had returned to the *Eagle*.

"Coast Guard thanks you for your willing support, Major," Harris said. "We've got an unusual situation here, unlike any we've faced before. I presume you've been fully briefed by Mr. Banner. Secrecy is very important. If this got out, these people would scatter to the winds. We need to get them all."

"We're happy to do it, sir, even without the arm twisting from our superiors in Washington. In fact, any leakage of this information would most likely come from the crowd back east."

"I know exactly what you're saying," Frank Harris said, smiling.

"I've hammered the secrecy issue into my guys," Angie said. "They should act correctly, but it's been a quick and sobering transition for a bunch of engineers used to doing surveys and inspections. As far as being fully briefed, Mr. Banner can best respond to that."

"I've passed on all I know." Nick said. "It's a lot for them to absorb in so short a time, however, their support has been extremely valuable. I don't think we could have gotten through last night without them. I, too, have stressed the need to keep this quiet. These Coast Guard meetings give us the perfect cover. I guess it's been tricky limiting information to the people here at the station, and up in Juneau."

"Yes, it has," Harris, said, nodding at the Captain.

"How long will it take to examine the package?" Nick asked.

"Let's go find out."

A few hours earlier, the Haz-Mat people had completed a procedure similar to Nick's. "No explosives or nasty chemicals detected," came a voice from the secure area. "We're ready to cut it open. Here goes. We've cut a small slit—nothing at all. I'll be damned. It's money, wrapped in clear plastic—one hundred dollar bills. Must be a million dollars."

"If that's their end game, it shouldn't be contaminated," Frank Harris said.

"We've cut off the plastic. The packs of bills are falling down. There are about twenty packs, each with about five hundred bills. What does that come to?"

"You're right," the Coast Guard Commander said. "That comes to a million dollars. If all the boxes are the same, that's seventy-six million. Could they be real?"

"I doubt it," Frank Harris said. "They must be bogus. We'll check them out. Is that it?"

"No," one of the Haz-Mat people responded, "The packs of bills are all banded, but open. You can see what they are. But one pack is completely wrapped and has a different shape. I think the other shoe has dropped. This is the unknown. We'll leave it untouched while we test for chemicals and x-ray it."

"You guys be careful," Frank Harris stressed. He turned to Nick and Angie. "This will take a while to set up. You want to come back later?"

"Yes, we'll do that." Nick said.

⟞⟝

Nick and Angie's run took them southeast along the water, through the downtown area of Ketchikan. "October is perfect," he observed. "We miss the summer crowds and it's still warm enough for a good run." He jabbered away about the town, his Alaska underwater survey jobs, Hannah's visits, and about why he left the Navy.

"You're showing me a new personality, Nick. What's up? Is it the experience of this threat, now more in the open, or is it that you dodged the bullet last night with that box, or what? Maybe it was the thoughts going through your head during the two visits you made to my cabin."

"You slipped that in very cleverly. That's a different subject to discuss. Let's finish the other topics first. I don't really know what's happened. I've gone through some rapid changes this last week, and the changes haven't stopped. Getting past that box opening was a relief. It's hard to believe, or remember, how tasks like that used to be routine in my Navy days. But I was young. It's not that I was foolish; it's just that I didn't fully realize the implications of the dangers, and the possible consequences for my family. And though I loved that whole scene, that's one of the reasons I got out."

"You're not hiding things any more, and you're not playing the game."

"What about you? How come you're not married, or don't have someone? Or do you?"

"Okay, I was almost married when I was too young, thought I was pregnant. I got out the relationship fast. I had fucked-up parents. The Army saved me. It gave me a family and a purpose. That's the story." Angie stopped their running and looked at Nick.

They were a mile or two out of town. The only noise on the quiet residential road was the rustling of the drying tree leaves. No cars had passed them for the last ten minutes.

"I don't come-on to everyone like I have with you," she admitted quietly.

The words didn't quite register with Nick. He was looking up the slope at a house he'd rented a few summers back, and he was remembering other things. A familiar screech distracted him. He turned to see an eagle staring at them. *I'll be damned. Is that you? How did you fly down from Juneau? You said it was too far and you're too old. Did you come to find me, to help me, to check up on me? You can tell I've evolved even more. I go through changes almost daily. It's as if I have no control. I don't know where it will take me, where I'm going to end up. Maybe we never stop changing. That's the way we should be. If we did, we'd stop living and just exist as we were. You're not advising me, you're not leading me—you're not my eagle, are you?*

"Nick, Nick," Angie said, her arms around him, her face close to his. "What's with that eagle? I could swear the eagle was nodding at you."

"Minnie?" Nick said.

"Who? It's Angie."

"Minnie?" Nick repeated, holding Angie's face in his hands.

Angie pulled away. "No, it's Angie," she said, her eyes watering.

"Oh, Angie. I thought I recognized that eagle from past runs. I used to stop and have thoughts of conversations with him. It actually helped clear my head."

"Those were more than thoughts. You were moving your lips." Angie backed away, staring at him, guiding him off the road as a pick-up truck sped past.

Nick turned to watch the eagle spread its wings and lift off the branch. He continued to watch as it flew out of sight. He turned to look at Angie.

"Nick, you certainly are different. I've never met anyone like you. You're alluring, infuriating, and crazy, all at the same time.

How did you keep the women away all these years? You really are special."

"So are you, Angie."

Angie paused briefly. "But I'm not *the* special one, am I?"

Nick didn't answer.

They finished the run mostly in silence. As they approached the ship someone yelled out, "Nick!"

Minnie was waiting at the top of the gangway. Seeing Angie, her face turned dour. "It's you," she said.

"Yes, it's me," Angie replied. "I was keeping him safe. How is your hand?"

"Much better, thanks. You guys have a good time?"

"A good run and a little shipboard excitement. Nick will tell you about it. Are you going to ride with us?"

"Yes, I think so."

"Hey, I'm here too. What do you mean you're riding with us? What did the doctor say?" Nick held her tight, as Angie walked away. "I'm sweaty."

"You sure are, and smelly too," Minnie said, backing away, but holding his face for a smooch in front of some of the crew and passengers. "I've got a few stitches, but the cuts aren't as bad as we thought. He'll take the stitches out when we get to Seattle. So, what's happening on board?"

Looking around, Nick took Minnie's arm leading her to his cabin. "I'll tell you," he whispered. "We need to keep this quiet. Let's go to our cabin."

They walked across the deck, into the passageway and up to the cabin. Nick stripped off his shirt and shorts. He remembered to use the surveillance gear for a quick check of the cabin.

Minnie sat on the bed with a smile on her face.

"What are you grinning at?" he said.

"I'm looking at you, your body. You fucking stud," she teased. "Go take your shower, so I can get close to you."

He shook his head and went into the bathroom.

"Your phone is ringing," Minnie yelled to Nick in the shower.

Nick spoke briefly to the caller. "We've got to ride over to the Coast Guard Base," he whispered in Minnie's ear. He made time for a quickie before he dressed.

"You owe me, Banner. I want more than that." Minnie teased.

On the drive over, he told Minnie what he knew. "You still want to come along? But no, I don't think you should come. You'll be in danger. It's not necessary. I don't want you to get hurt."

"I want to help you. I could help with the passengers, keeping them safe. Nick, please, I want to come. I want to help. Anyway, you need protection from that Major. I saw the way she looked at you. It wasn't casual and it wasn't professional. What happened between you two?"

"Minnie, I've told you everything."

"Bullshit, Banner. I can read you like a book. I can tell by your tone of voice."

Nick drove down a side street and parked. He pulled her close. His hands found a way through her clothes, so he could feel her skin from neck to thigh.

"Oh, God," she breathed sliding her hand inside his pants. They looked at each other, giggled, and pulled away.

"Listen," he gazed into her eyes. "You have *all* my love *all* the time. No one has ever made me defensive like this, and," he grabbed both her wrists, "It was my relationship with you that kept me from falling for her fuck-me advances."

"Ah-ha," Minnie shrieked, trying to get her arms free.

He stopped her mouth with his.

Slowly, her body relaxed. When he released her wrists, she socked him with an elbow, then wrapped her arms around him. They held each other for a few minutes before Nick sat back behind the wheel.

Frank Harris was near the entrance to the Coast Guard Base as they drove up. Nick introduced him to Minnie.

"I was reading your file," Harris said to Minnie. "It's fortuitous that you came with Nick. Could you lend us your skills while Nick and I talk? Are you okay with that?" He said, looking at the bandages on her hand.

"I'm fine. I'd be happy to help," she answered, tilting her head and smiling at Nick.

⇥ ⇤

"So, how did your computer work go?" Nick asked on the drive back to the ship.

"It was interesting. They don't know what it is."

"Don't know what *what* is? What did they have you doing?"

"It's that thing you found in the center of the box. They don't know what it is."

"That's what Frank Harris told me. They've x-rayed it, measured it and tried to analyze it. They think it's a part of a bigger device."

"What I discovered," Minnie said, "is that four of them can fit together to make a larger gadget, if that means anything at all. They've sent it to Washington for further study, and will send the item itself to some lab to be looked at. So, what happened at your meeting?"

"Captain Dixon will be at his wits end. He hoped it was going to end here in Ketchikan. Not so, according to Coast Guard. They don't see the benefit. I tried to tell Harris the danger and terror that Homer and his buddy Davy are under, and now, to a certain degree, the rest of us. What they did was load us down with more weapons. That's what's in the bags."

"Isn't that dangerous? What do they expect you to do? Have a naval battle? Isn't it shortsighted of them?"

"I think so, too. But they cited certain things, and other things they said I didn't need to know, as the reasons to keep going.

They're prepared to end it all in Bellingham, a Washington port before Seattle. We'll be guarded and monitored, even air surveillance. Homer is going to take this hard. I hope we make it back to the *Eagle* in time to see him before his noon meeting on the yacht."

"So, we'll be able to just relax and snuggle for the next few days, right?"

"Right."

CHAPTER TWENTY-THREE

A rental car approached the Eagle precisely at noon, parking near the ship but not near the gangway. The doors opened the moment the auto came to a stop. Two men exited. John Smith and John Brown were waiting for them on the dock. They nodded at the two men and escorted them up the gangway. To anyone interested, it was obvious that the cargo shippers were no longer concerned with concealing their association with Smith and Brown. They seemed not to care if the *Eagle's* crew knew this.

This brazen show of power and control was not lost on Homer and Ernie, or on the Coast Guard personnel, through hidden surveillance. Coast Guard could now identify ten of the adversaries, six on the yacht *Mother's Love,* two on the *Eagle,* and two monitoring the activities of Davy and Maddy in Kenai.

Homer stood on deck preparing to depart for his meeting with Adams.

Nick and Minnie drove up to the *Eagle,* parked the truck close to the bottom of the gangway, and hailed Homer on his way down. "Captain, have you met my friend Minnie? She may ride back with us."

Ignoring the waiting driver, Homer approached Nick and leaned into the truck. "Yes, I've met Minnie. Glad to have you on the trip. You'll be a welcome sight compared to all the ugly people we have on board." Continuing to look at Minnie, Homer lowered his voice. "Anything new, Nick?"

"They said everything is to continue as is, Captain. Nothing has changed for now. That's the word."

"Shit," Homer swore. "Pardon me, Minnie. Let's get together later on, Nick. And Nick, they're in the hold right now checking the boxes. Ernie is down there."

"That's interesting. I'll be here when you return, Captain."

"Good," Homer said. He walked over to the waiting car.

"I knew Homer would be pissed. I don't blame him. I wonder what he and John Adams talk about."

"Shouldn't you be at a meeting like that?"

"No," Nick whispered looking around. "I'll have to give you a full briefing. Homer is supposed to be the only person on board who knows what's going on. First, we'll go to our cabin for a while. After my meeting with the Captain, we'll go out somewhere and talk about what's happening." He drove down the loading ramp into the hold of the *Eagle*. The weapons cache was locked in secure cases inside his truck.

"How do we get to our cabin?" she asked.

"Let's sit here awhile. I want to see what they do."

"What are they doing?"

"These are the cargo shippers. They've come aboard in each port since the loading in Anchorage—to check their boxes."

"For what purpose?"

"None that I can tell. They just want to inspect them to see if they've been tampered with. Also, I think they want to flex their muscle and spread fear.

"Spread fear? What the hell are you talking about, Banner? What did they get you into? What's happened to you the last few days?"

Nick looked at Minnie. "A transformation. An epiphany that you started, and I welcome it completely," he said, as he grabbed her for a quick hug and kiss. "Let's get out of the truck. I need to see exactly what they're doing."

Two men, with the help of Smith and Brown, were counting the boxes and verifying each number. They chose some boxes, apparently at random, for a more detailed inspection, lifting them, turning them over, and by their own feel, judging them to weigh the same as the others. Satisfied with their charade, they stopped before getting to the last box, the one on the end.

God, I'm glad I took pains repacking that box, Nick thought.

After descending from the ledge, one of the two men, unknown to Nick, obviously the leader of the group, approached them near the truck. "Who are you? What are you doing here?" Brown whispered in his ear. "Ah, Mr. Banner, I've heard about you." He was surly, even more so than John Smith.

Nick saw no reason to comment.

"I will inspect these trucks," he announced.

"You can't do that," Ernie countered. "That's U. S. Coast Guard property. If you wish, I can ask the Coast Guard to come down to the ship to evaluate your request."

The man, referred to as Mr. Marshall by Smith and Brown, smiled slightly, glanced at the concerned look on Minnie's face, and gave her the once over. "Do not worry little lady, we will not harm you."

"Fuck-you, whoever you are," Minnie snapped back.

He stared at Minnie and Nick with what appeared to be anger and surprise—gradually recovering with a cunning grimace.

John Smith came forward to do battle, but was held back.

"I know what *fuck-you* says in your language," John Marshall responded. "It has two meanings. One is spoken as an unfriendly expression, and the other as a sexual invitation. I will remember you," he said, forcing a smile.

Minnie tried to back away, but Nick held her tight.

"That's all, gentlemen, you've inspected your cargo. I'll see you off the ship," Ernie stated, in a loud voice.

"Oh, boy," Minnie muttered as she and Nick followed the group up to the main deck. "What kind of assholes did you get involved with?"

"That's the picture," Nick said.

Ernie came up to them after the crowd dispersed. "Minnie, I like your spirit. Glad to have you back. How is your hand?"

"Much, much better, thank you."

"I hope you're gonna ride with us? Your buddy here needs some protection from unnamed parties."

"Oh, yes, I can take care of that. And, if you and the Captain want me, Nick is outnumbered and out ranked."

Nick shook his head, wistfully. "Ernie, who is that guy?"

"He's not the John Adams that Homer talks with. His name is John Marshall. They seem to enjoy using American history in their intrigue."

"Is this ship the *Alaskan Eagle?*" shouted a voice from the dock.

Ernie, seeing no deck watch, said, "Nick, would you handle this, I've got some things happening," as he walked away.

"Sure, Ernie." Nick turned to Minnie. "Can I meet you in the cabin, darling? Will you be okay? Be ready."

"I'm okay, and I'll be ready. But hurry."

Nick walked over to the gangway.

A woman with some luggage was standing on the dock.

"Hi, can I help you?"

"Is this ship the *Alaskan Eagle?*"

"Yes, it is."

"I have a ticket to go to Seattle. Could someone help me with the bags?

"I can do that," Nick said, as he walked down the gangway. I'm the Second Mate. Do you know what cabin you're in?"

"Yes, it's right here on the ticket. Thank you so much."

"It's no problem at all." Nick started up the gangway with the two bags. He glanced back. She was having difficulty following him. She wore a muumuu type dress, but he could see she was very large. "Your cabin is one deck down. I'll take the bags and be back to help you."

She had made it almost to the top of the gangway when Nick returned. She hesitated before taking the step onto the deck.

"Let me help you."

"Normally, this would be a piece of cake for me, but I've been under the weather."

Too much cake, thought Nick. "Let me help you," he offered again. "The deck can be slippery, and we have to descend a ladder."

"Thank you," she panted.

The narrow width of the ladder stairway required Nick to back down in front of her. He supported one arm, while she held the ladder rail with the other hand. Brushing against her, he realized her bulk was due to pregnancy, advanced pregnancy. He settled her into a chair and arranged the two bags. "Should you be making this trip?"

"Oh, I'll be fine. I'm Matilda Burke." She forced a smile and offered her hand. "Thank you."

Nick studied her closely. "Nick Banner," he said, shaking her hand.

She paled and gasped slightly.

"Are you sure you'll be okay," Nick asked, with concern in his voice.

She nodded, looking away. She seemed very young—not much older than Hannah. The puffiness of her face hid her good looks.

"This ship is not built for comfort. It rocks and rolls a lot, and chow is one deck up. Did Alaska Airlines turn you down?"

She said nothing for a few moments. Her resolve collapsed into tears streaming down her face. "Yes, and so did the Alaska State Ferry, and there are no more cruise ships, and the doctor said I should go to Seattle. I was waiting for my husband, he must be in Seattle, he is in Seattle," she sobbed.

Nick felt discombobulated. He brought a handful of tissues from the bathroom and sat down on the bed. "What month are you in?"

"Seventh," she replied, with hesitation.

He grimaced as if to say, *I know it's probably the eighth or ninth.* "Has it been difficult; any problems?"

"No," she whispered, "I'm healthy. What I need is a friend."

"I'll be your friend," he offered, as he rose.

"Please don't tell anyone?" she pleaded.

"I'm sure you have strong reasons to get to Seattle, or wherever. Can I help you with anything right now?"

She tried to smile, taking in a deep breath. "No, thank you." Tears formed in her eyes.

⇥⇤

"What happened?" Minnie asked, as Nick entered his cabin. She was lying on the bed in her underwear, smiling. "I was about to take things into my own hands."

"I'll take over with my hands," he promised, undressing. "You seem to have recovered from the confrontation."

"Oh, I've had to deal with lots of men like that. So, what happened?"

"I'll tell you later. She's pregnant. I'm worried about having to care for her on board. We don't know what's ahead of us. She's very young. She's got thin arms and legs and is probably pretty, but has gained a ton of weight. I had to help her down the ladder."

"So, you felt her up, you letch."

"I didn't have to. It was easy to see the big belly, not like this one." He removed Minnie's pants and bra. He ran his hands over every mound and curve, burying his face in her stomach.

"I want all of you," Minnie purred, as she started to undulate her hips. "I hope I never get tired of this. You make my whole body tingle, right down to my feet. Look at the way my toes are spread apart. Do you think I'm a nymph?"

"You're perfect. Look at this body. Don't you ever change, nymph. Yow!" he howled, when she bit him.

Minnie's eyes were shut. A pleased look passed across her face, as Nick slowly navigated his way over her body. He took care not to touch her hand. Her emotions gradually built to a satisfied moan. "I love you, Nick Banner, I love you," she whispered.

They lay there smiling and panting. "My god, it's only been a few days," Nick whispered, "I've missed you. I'm glad you came back. Never leave me again."

"You mean that Major with the perfect body you've been cavorting with hasn't satisfied you?"

"You can't get satisfied unless you get it off. You saw how it went off."

"Nick, do you think we should use protection?"

"There is no protection for the things we do, my love," he joked.

"You dunce. I meant I could end up pregnant like your new girlfriend."

"However you end up, sweetheart, I'll be right there with you."

"We've rarely have relaxed moments like this," she said. "It's nice."

"I know, but my new job, and this situation we're in, will have its tense moments. We don't know what's going to happen. Our new passenger has me worried. I'm going back to speak with her, try to talk her out of staying on board. In fact, I might approach some of our other passengers as well."

"You go ahead, limp one," she teased as she pulled the blanket up. "I'm gonna rest, shower and unpack."

"Limp one?" he faked outrage. "You didn't feel that way a few minutes ago."

"It is what it is," Minnie said, with a smile.

Nick knocked on Matilda's door. "Who is it?" came the reply.

"It's Nick Banner, the Second Mate. I helped you come aboard."

"Oh, come in. The door should be open."

"Are you okay?" he asked.

She smiled and nodded.

"The procedure calls for a passport or some official ID information. I could only find your name and the reservation you made."

She opened her handbag to retrieve her driver's license.

"You're very young," he said, looking at her. "Is this your married name?"

"I'm not officially married. I'm going to find my boyfriend."

"Are your parents aware of your situation?"

"What situation?"

"That you're about to give birth."

She paused. "I've still got a while to go, but the airline said no."

"Do your parents know?" Nick asked again.

"I don't have parents," she whimpered, starting to cry again. "My mother died when I was young," she sobbed. "My father remarried. I haven't seen him in years. I just need a friend."

Nick felt confused. He wished Minnie had come with him. He sat in the chair, close to her. "Don't you know people in Ketchikan? What did you do?"

"I've only been here for two years. I decided to stay when my friend went back to school. We were both barmaids at Sally's Place."

Nick smiled. "I know Sally's Place. I went in there last winter while in Ketchikan."

She looked over at him. "Did you used to have a beard?"

"I did," Nick said, a little startled. "I grow one when I'm not diving."

"I think I remember you."

CHAPTER TWENTY-FOUR

October 22nd—12:15pm

*T*he yacht was tied up near downtown Ketchikan—at the far end of the cruise ship dock. Homer recognized the route taken by the driver. The area was open for anyone to observe. *Adams must be pissed at this location,* Homer thought.

Adams was sitting in the lounge with a drink in hand appearing to have already had a few. He gestured for Homer to sit. "And so, Captain, our last port until we reach Seattle," he said in an abrupt manner, less casual than their previous meeting and conversations.

"Yes, Mr. Adams. And again, I need assurance from you that Captain Davy Masters and his wife Madeline are safe and will not be hurt," Homer said, still standing. "Your leverage against me is their safety, and the threat that they will be harmed if I do not follow your instructions. Well, mine against you is similar, in that if they are not kept safe and sound, I will blow your venture apart, and take my chances." Homer exploded these words, almost out of breath.

"Captain, Captain. You have to trust my word. Your friends Davy and his wife are fine. I urge you to call them every hour to assure yourself." Adams appeared more alert as a result of the exchange. "Now, please, sit, have a drink and some lunch and then I will show you this fine yacht, as I promised."

Homer sat down. He took a long swig of the beer he requested. They were both quiet for a moment.

"So, Captain Dixon, you have discovered our listening devices and destroyed them, much to my consternation," Adams said, in a casual manner. "How were you able to find them? We need to monitor what is happening on your ship."

Homer was still animated from his outburst. "I can't live under those conditions. You can hear every time I fart, for Christ's sake."

"So, you are a religious person, Captain?" Adams asked quietly.

Homer, frowning at the quick changes in demeanor, responded, "Not as much as I would like to be."

"I have heard the expression, for 'Christ's sake'. I was making a joke, as you say."

Again, both men sat in silence, sipping their drinks.

"We must talk business, Captain. We are at a critical time in our venture. The U.S. Coast Guard came aboard this morning to examine our papers and passports. I trust you were not aware of this or made it happen. Of course, all of our papers were in order. Their mannerisms and expressions were unusual. They were very casual, even when they inspected the boat."

Shit, Homer thought, *I hope they didn't fuck things up. Either they should end things here in Ketchikan or stay away.* "I get the same thing when they inspect the *Alaskan Eagle*."

"Has the Coast Guard inspected you since leaving Anchorage?" Adams asked.

"With your surveillance and on-board spies I'm sure you know the answer to that. No, they have not inspected us on this trip. Since we're a regular commercial ship and come through here twice a month, they rarely inspect us."

Adams smiled. "That is one of the reasons we chose the *Alaskan Eagle*. The other reason was you, Captain, and your friendship with Captain Davy. But we misjudged you. You are more combative than we expected. You have become an enigma. We cannot tolerate this, Captain."

"You know, Mr. Adams, your research on me must have portrayed a self-effacing type of character. Well, it's not true. I give that impression because I want to convey that image. I'm comfortable that way, friendly and informal. But, if you scratch the surface, or cross me, a whole new temperament emerges."

"Yes, I have seen that, Captain," Adams stated, in a condescending way. "However, you must contain yourself. We cannot have any irrational actions. We are too close to completing the journey."

"I can say the same thing to you, Mr. Adams." Homer wondered why he was portraying his own image so accurately. It came out in a self-demeaning way.

The condescending look remained on Adams' face.

Though he hadn't meant to expose himself as such, Homer thought it could work to his advantage.

As if it had become a pattern, they both sat quietly once again, eating and drinking.

"Captain, I'm concerned about some things happening on your ship. Mr. Banner made a number of visits to the Coast Guard Station in Juneau, and again here in Ketchikan, and has even unloaded some of his trucks. What is happening?"

"I will have to keep your men, Smith and Brown, a little busier. They seem to be spending too much of their time tracking nonsense. I thought we discussed this a few days ago, Mr. Adams. Nick Banner has just completed a project in Juneau to install a security and surveillance system at the Coast Guard Station. This is all public information. You should be able to find it on the Internet, so I'm not giving away any government secrets by telling you this."

Adams smiled. "The only place in the world this could happen."

"Well, the project was so successful that Coast Guard extended the contract to include a similar system at the Ketchikan Coast Guard Base."

"Without competition from other bidders?"

Homer stared at Adams. "How would you know this is unusual?"

"I have much knowledge of the workings of your government."

"I see that you do. So, Nick has been told he will be awarded the Ketchikan project. That should explain his trips over there."

"Why is one Coast Guard facility called a base and another a station?"

"A base is generally larger, with more services, aircraft and ships. It may also have to do with the rank of the commanding officer," Homer replied.

"When I try to research this on a computer, much of the information is blocked, requiring a password to obtain. Do you have a password?"

"No, the dealings I have with the Coast Guard are not classified. Information that could compromise the safety and security of the facility requires passwords. I do not need that information."

"Thank you, Captain, for the civics lesson. This is a good time for a quick tour of my fine yacht. Bring your drink. My man will clean up and have coffee for us on our return."

The layout was as Homer surmised; a large owner's suite and six to eight smaller staterooms, including crew's quarters and a sizeable storage area located below deck. Homer was shown only one of the staterooms. Other than the steward waiting on them in the lounge, none of the crew was about the yacht. The bridge looked roomy, with up-to-date navigation and communications gear.

"Now, Captain Dixon, back to business. About the four military people who came aboard in Juneau? Occasionally, they wear their uniforms. Their presence on the ship is disturbing. I had not planned on them. Who are they and what are they doing on your ship?"

"I'm certain we discussed them before."

"Please, Captain, humor me by telling me again."

"They made a last minute reservation on the *Alaskan Eagle*. The Corps of Engineers is part of the Army."

"That means they are military people. They are soldiers."

"That's correct. But their function is engineering, mostly civil engineering. They build things."

"I know what civil engineers do. I do not know what they are doing on your ship at this time."

"Mr. Adams, all I know is that they finished their inspection and surveying project of various U. S. Government facilities in the Juneau area and decided to ride the *Alaskan Eagle*, with their equipment, back to Seattle. It's more comfortable than the Alaska State Ferries, and the cruise ships are gone for the season."

"I see that the female military engineer, Major Flowers and Mr. Banner are very friendly. They go running together and spend social time. He spends considerable time in her cabin."

"Your Mr. Smith and Mr. Brown are certainly observant," Homer countered. "How can they possibly see what happens on the passenger and officer deck? I'll ask Mr. McInnis to keep them more occupied with ship's duties."

"Our Mr. Brown observes many things on his trips to and from his duties on the bridge. Do you not have a moral code on your ship, Captain? Are you not a moral person?"

Homer glared at Adams. "I have a personal moral code, yes. I do not judge another's morals unless it becomes evident that their actions are hurting someone. But all societies, cultures, countries, and religions have different views of morality. Wouldn't you agree, Mr. Adams?"

"You are correct there, Captain. That is why it is difficult to judge those out of our own society."

"Ah, but we can still judge abhorrent behavior, particularly of those who want to come here and inflict their codes on us. It is interesting that you speak of morals when you've threatened to kill someone if your shipment is not delivered as you specify."

"I do not intend to harm anyone, Captain. A threat is merely a threat. Let us get back to Mr. Banner and his many visits to the Coast Guard."

"Look, Nick's projects are valuable to the Coast Guard. We need these safeguards to keep out people like you, who wish to do us harm."

"Now, now, Captain, I have told you that this is a business venture for financial profit. I do not wish you or your country harm. Doing that might prevent me from future financial ventures here."

"Why do I have a hard time believing that?"

Adams smiled. "You are a strange people living in a fairyland—the most unique land in the world. You are so innocent and naïve, an amusement to other countries. It is amazing how you manage to prosper. Can you explain that?"

"As we discussed before, it's that our people have the most freedom, with the least intervention from our government, of any place on earth. These freedoms are guaranteed by our Constitution and Bill of Rights, and if any of our temporary leaders mess with this, they are voted out of office."

"I have read your Constitution, 'We the People, etc.' yet, your freedoms and openness are also your weaknesses. At one time, your two oceans and two friendly borders shielded you from the evils of the world. Millions of people came here to be citizens and became loyal Americans. It is not so anymore. One can now enter to study and work here, as I did, and as millions of others do, with no loyalty toward your country. A certain number of these people learn how to take advantage of you, as I am doing. Others, like myself, are using more insidious methods of undermining your society. You must wake up or your country and your freedoms will cease to exist. You must wake up, Captain. It would be sad to see this happen. You must wake up from the stupor that has reduced you to blind and pathetic sheep."

"My goodness, Mr. Adams, you impress me. You've learned much from the writings of your pseudonym, John Adams. Why don't you quit this nonsense, come here and run for public office? How did you come to pick the name John Adams?"

"The history I have read shows him to be one of the most influential men at the time of your Declaration of Independence."

"And that same history shows him to be morally incorruptible. Is that you, Mr. Adams? Shows him to be single-minded to the point of neglecting his family, as well as dictatorial and uncompromising, which affected his ability to lead. Is that you? And finally, for much of his career, without the council of his wife, he groped for the proper action or decision."

"Enough, Captain, you are reading too much into my name. Say what you will, I still plan to have other business ventures such as this. It is interesting that you are the only person with whom I have shared many of these thoughts."

"You seem quite relaxed, even happy, Mr. Adams. I take it you are pleased with the way we have done your bidding and succumbed to your intimidations and threats."

"My, my, Captain, we seem to be bitter today. It is true that I am pleased with the progress of our venture. My planning has been successful, and my choice of Captain Masters, the *Alaskan Eagle*, and you, have all proven to be brilliant."

"I agree. You planned this well by choosing decent people who care about the welfare of their friends and loved ones, and would do anything, almost anything, to protect them. It was clever, though nasty, when you poisoned Maddy's dog to scare them, and let them know that you know where their daughter's family lives."

"We had to show them how serious we were. I am glad they deduced it was us who sent the message. A dog is merely a dog. It can be replaced. It is not a human family member. The pain of losing the dog will subside, but the memory of the incident, and the thought that it could have been a daughter or granddaughter are powerful and force one into total submission. Yes, it is despicable, but obviously effective. It imparts fear and collapses the will to fight back. By contrast, had we killed a family member or a friend, the blind rage could have endangered our venture."

"It's sickening how you can talk of killing people for monetary gain. I read such things in the news, of people who randomly kill. It's possible they think the same way you do."

"What is important to you, Captain? What do you yearn for? Is wealth a goal for you?"

"Wealth? I've never craved money, as such. To me, it's not what's important in life. What would I do with it? I have what I want and what I need. The desire for more money would have put me behind a desk in the role of a manager of some kind. Why? I love my work and what I do as the captain of a working ship. It's real. I've achieved the status I need and want. I'm the boss, in charge, and I have full responsibility, with no one to second-guess me—most of the time. I'm faced with confrontations and decisions, daily. What sort of satisfaction would I get sitting behind a desk? More money? For what? No, I've had the opportunity and I'm glad I stayed where I knew I would be happy."

"I can see you are quite passionate about your status, Captain. I am pleased for you. Knowing you as we know you now, I do not think we will look to use you on our next venture. What will you do with your share of the fifty thousand dollars?"

"I don't know. I don't know. Tell me, why did you choose this method of smuggling your contraband into our country? It would seem there are so many other ways, and how did you get it into Alaska?"

"Now, now, Captain, the less you know, the safer it is for you."

"It's only natural, Mr. Adams, that these and other questions go through my head. Let me speculate. Except for occasional fishermen and commercial ships, the coast of Alaska is clear, more or less, if you avoid the May through September tourist season. In contrast, the west coast of the U. S. from Canada to Mexico is busy the year round. The coast of Canada would be a possibility but you'd have to cross the border into the U. S. By sending your goods on a large container ship there is a small possibility that your particular container could be inspected. Also, I have the feeling that you want to stay near your valuable cargo."

"Captain, we are shipping safety suits, nothing else."

"Mr. Adams, you insult my intelligence by saying that."

"Well, our conversation seems to have altered course somewhat. We leave soon for the final part of our journey. We must get back to serious business. There was an incident in the hold of your ship this afternoon, after my people inspected our boxes," Adams said, leaning toward Homer.

"What sort of incident?" Homer asked, tensing.

"You should hear about it when you return to the ship. It involved our John Marshall and a young lady. Mr. Marshall is my brother and can be a hothead. The woman is Mr. Banner's lady, I believe."

"What sort of incident are we talking about?"

"I do not know the details, Captain. When I talk with Mr. Marshall, and you speak to your people, I am certain the account I hear will be somewhat different from the report you get. I will decide then if I should be concerned or not."

"It's interesting how the description of an incident can vary," Homer said. "It's similar to studying history, and how history books covering the same period, about the same occurrences, even written the same year in the same country, will be dissimilar."

"I have discovered the same thing. As a result of my observations, I have come to an identical conclusion, that all history, oral or recorded, is flawed. It seems we do agree on some things, Captain Dixon."

"I guess we do, Mr. Adams. Well, I must get back to my ship, there is much to do," Homer said, rising.

"Yes, you must get back to your home," Adams retorted, dismissively.

"It *is* my home and in many respects also my family, and has been for many, many years. But, a ship can also be a prison to some people. I've been fortunate."

"Why do you not have your own wife and family, Captain?"

Homer smiled. "As I said, I do have my shipboard family. Are you married, Mr. Adams?"

"Yes."

"Do you have children?"

"Adams paused. "Yes, I have a son."

"Does he know how you earn your income?"

Adams shifted in his chair. He gazed out through the spacious yacht window, toward the mountain hovering over downtown Ketchikan. "I would like to come here one day and climb that hill."

"I climbed it a few years ago. It's about three thousand feet high, not too difficult, and on a clear day like today, offers a spectacular view."

"I have often wondered why Americans travel the world to view scenery when many of your states offer similar or even better sights. Most likely to observe different cultures and see age-old structures. In my travels around your country and now with my son..." Adams halted.

"Your son is in this country?"

Adams stood to refill his wine glass. "I have been foolish in my conversations with you, Captain. It shows that I, too, have weaknesses. The people I bring with me to conduct these business ventures have limited intellectual interests, including my own brother. As a result, sometimes I yearn for discussions on topics other than business and the tactics to achieve their success. That is why I discuss other topics with you after discerning that you are an honorable man who will keep to an agreement. Remember, you are complicit in this undertaking; you and your friend, Captain Masters."

I'll be a son-of-a-bitch, Homer thought. *I've got him on the ropes.*

"My son is at a university in your country. Of course, I will not tell you where."

"Will you see him while you're here?"

Pausing, Adams replied, "It is possible."

"Does he have a slight accent when he speaks English, as you do?"

"No, he does not. At least to my ear, he does not. We learn English in our schools and he is very conscious of his speech."

"What country in Eastern Europe do you come from, Mr. Adams?"

Adams smiled. "It is a small country, of no consequence. Too much of our country is involved in international crime. Not terrorism, if that is what you are thinking."

"It reminds me of an incident about thirty-five years ago," Homer reminisced. "I remember sitting next to someone on a flight, with a similar accent. Did your country support the Germans during the war?"

"From my father, I learned that too many in our country were Nazi sympathizers. Unfortunately, our people and our government have not fought for a free society. I will relocate my family elsewhere. Since my wife died, what I do is for my son. We treasure our children. It is your loss that you do not have a family, Captain. In a less than perfect world, your children, and your grandchildren would give you an ever-expanding outlet for the human instinct to care for them and to love them. Just like animals in the wild, we birth them, raise them and protect them, then send them off to do the same. It is our instinct, our duty, and our pleasure to do so. Do I surprise you, Captain?"

"Yes you do, Mr. Adams, very much. Well, Mr. Adams, I look forward to seeing you in Seattle."

"One final thing, Captain. Circumstances dictate that I must remove some of my boxes before we get to Seattle."

"What? Can't be done. You know that."

"I realize I cannot remove them here in Ketchikan, however, I need some of them soon. I would like to make arrangements to perform an at sea transfer about halfway to Seattle, off the coast of Canada."

"Mr. Adams, the shipment has been consigned from Anchorage to Seattle. Legally, I can't release it." Homer repeated, his voice rising.

"Very well, Captain. Do not get yourself excited."

Homer glared at him. *What the fuck are you trying to pull now? Just after you soften me up with your smooth talk, you pull a stunt like this. What do you think you're doing, you lying piece of shit?* "We'll be leaving in the morning, at first light. Have a good trip, Mr. Adams. We may get some fog for a few days."

"Thank you, Captain. As usual, we will stay close to you. Bon voyage."

Homer's mind raced on the way back to the *Eagle*, laying it all out. Planning and execution, it's what I'm good at. "Planning and execution," he said to himself again, like a mantra. All of a sudden, he felt good. The numbness of the past week was lifting. Adams' final words cleared Homer's head, stripping away all uncertainties. "I'm going to make it happen," he muttered.

The day looked unusually clear and calm for October, with a full sun lifting the midday temperature to the sixties. Glancing up, he could see the top of Deer Mountain, and blue sky. *God, I love this part of the country. I climbed the glacier in Juneau; maybe I'll have time for another climb this afternoon. If not, definitely the next time I come back.*

Homer nodded appreciation to the driver and bounded up the gangway.

Nick and Ernie were among a group of crewmembers hanging around on deck. He stopped by them. "All-hands meeting tomorrow morning, at six." He gestured for Nick and Ernie to follow him, indicating no questions. Once in his quarters, he wrote a note to Nick asking him to check for bugs on him and inside the cabin. As Homer suspected, Nick found one in the space inside his cap. "Motherfuckers," he mumbled under his breath. "They must have planted it while I was touring the yacht with Adams. Nick, would you call Coast Guard and ask them to conduct a surprise inspection of our safety and lifeboat equipment. It's important that they do it here, this afternoon. Ask them also if their left hand doesn't know what their right hand is doing. Why did they inspect the yacht this morning while all this is going on?"

"That was dumb," Nick said. "I'm sure it was routine and unintentional."

"Ask them to do a serious and thorough inspection. It might keep Adams from going ballistic," Homer grumbled.

"Will do, Captain."

"Again, it's important."

Ernie looked at Homer. "What's up, Skipper?"

Homer shook his head. "Also, Nick, what kind of containers would plastic explosives be shipped in?"

"They're usually shipped in wooden crates. In fact, I've got some with my gear—very safe stuff to transport. Why do you ask?"

"I saw some empty wooden boxes in their storage area, with C-4 printed on them."

CHAPTER TWENTY-FIVE

*T*hey *walked into Sally's Place about the time the hard-driving Bluegrass Band started.*

"It looks about the same as always," Homer said.

"It's been the same for twenty years," Ernie agreed, "Except that Sally gets older and the girls get younger, or seem to."

"You two bums, where have you been?" Sally yelled. "I know you come through here twice a month. Where the hell have you been?" She gave Ernie a big lip smooch, and grabbed Homer for a full body hug and kiss.

"Hello Sally. It's good to see you," Homer greeted, "And, it's only been about six weeks. We got swamped with end of summer cargo and passengers."

"I thought that rust bucket of yours must've sunk. I even checked with Coast Guard. I got pissed at you for not coming by. Or are you getting too old for lovin'?"

"Sally," Homer said, while they were still locked in a full body clutch, "You never get too old for lovin'. You never lose the thoughts and longing. The good news is that you have a wider range of women who turn you on. The bad news is that the equipment doesn't work as well as it used to."

"I don't care about the efficiency of the equipment. That's only a small part of lovin' anyway. No pun intended, hon." She gave Homer another kiss and tight hug and led them both to a booth.

"How about this one, Sally?" Ernie suggested a larger booth. "We're expecting a few others. This gives us a good view of everything."

"Ernie, I never know what you're thinking. I won't even bother to ask," she replied, patting him on the behind. "I'll get someone to bring your drinks."

"Thanks, Sally." Homer smiled at her, as the band got up to full volume.

"When did Nick say he'd be here, Ernie?"

"Right about now. Maybe that young lady is keeping him busy. All right Homer, what's going through your head? I know you too well not to see that you've been back at full strength since you left that yacht this afternoon. What happened?"

"Nothing too different." He ran through the conversations and experience he had had with Adams, and ended up by saying, "Adams wants to remove some of the boxes before Seattle—like hell, he wants them all," Homer said, "that's why he was practicing coming alongside the other day. That's been his plan all along—in case Coast Guard or someone else got too close. He figured if someone became concerned about the boxes they'd be gone, that is, he'd make them be gone by the time we got to Seattle."

"And this all came out during the meeting?"

"No, this all came to me on the ride back from the yacht."

"That's what the inspection party wanted to do this afternoon," Ernie said. "I told them, no dice. What else is going through your head, Homer? What should we do? Hey, here's Nick and Minnie. They see us."

Minnie grinned at them, as she and Nick sat down. "I don't know everything that's happening." She leaned toward Homer and Ernie. "But Coast Guard filled me in a little when I was there yesterday. I want to let you know that if I can help in any way, I'd be happy to do so."

"She's a dynamo, as you might have figured out, and she's also a whiz on the computer," Nick added.

"Well," Homer said, looking at them, "we expect thick fog about a half a day south as we enter Canadian waters, and our communication sources are limited if we can't connect with the city of Prince Rupert. It would be good to maintain satellite connections for weather, GPS, and communications. Problem is that our ship's computers are old and out of date."

"Both Minnie and I have new laptops," Nick offered.

"Good," Homer replied, "Keep them dry."

Ernie looked like he was about to question that, when Sally came up.

"Is that you, Nick? You look a hell of a lot better without all that hair on your face, love. And who do you belong to?" She looked at Minnie. "Are you Nick's daughter?"

Minnie grimaced. She was about to respond when Nick beat her to it. "Sally, how have you been? This is my very good friend, Minnie. I wanted to answer before she did because she doesn't know that's just your way of talking."

"Child," Sally said, taking Minnie's hand, "I give my friends hell, and I don't give the others the time of day. I meant that, if you're not attached, I could always use another young, pretty waitress."

Minnie glanced over at Nick, and grinned.

"Sally, you are good," Nick joked. "I wanted to say that she belongs to me but I would have suffered a bruised shin."

"Nick, that's more words than I heard you say *all* last winter. Honey, you've got him to open up!" she said to Minnie. "Did my little girl, Tilly, show up at your ship? She's desperate to get to Seattle to have those twins she's carrying and she's too far gone to be traveling."

"She's on board," Nick said. "We'll take care of her."

"I hope you do," Sally said, wagging a finger at Nick. "She was always a little sweet on you."

"Ouch," Nick cried, grabbing his leg.

"Oh, boy," Ernie said, looking at Homer. "Can we give him back to Coast Guard?"

"Shit, I'm out of here," Sally muttered. "I always talk too much."

"Sally, you're as lovely and as unpredictable as always," Homer said. "Come back to join us."

"Homer, the band is playing old folks' music, just right for us. Come on, dance with me."

Homer got up looking back at the table. "Be back soon, guys."

Sally took Homer's hand, leading him to the dance floor where she wrapped her arms around his neck. "Where have you been? I was worried about you, and you didn't make contact."

"I never stopped thinking about you, Sal. I've missed you, darling. I've been a horse's ass."

"I've missed you, too, my love." She put a hand on Homer's cheek. "You seem more tender, more vulnerable than you've been recently. Your expression reminds me of years ago." Sally signaled the three-piece band to play extra soft, slow, dance music.

Homer held Sally close. They barely moved to the music. He whispered in her ear, "I've really missed you, Sal."

"You've missed me or the lovin'?" She gave him a peck on the lips.

"It's all part of the same package," Homer replied. "But I've missed you. I've missed *Sally*."

They danced quietly for a few minutes. "Why didn't we get married years ago, Homer? Why were we both so stupid, me with this bar and you with your ship?"

"It's not too late, is it?" Homer said.

Sally pulled her head back and looked into Homer's eyes trying to judge his sincerity. "No, it's not too late," she answered hoarsely.

"Good, let's do it," he said.

Sally held Homer tight as they danced, her chest heaving.

"Hi, Edna." Homer greeted Sally's second in command.

Sally kept her head wedged against Homer's neck.

"Homer, what are you doing to Sally?" Edna teased.

"Everything is good," Sally said, still clutching Homer.

"I can't remember the last time I saw you cry, Sal,"

Sally pulled her head up. She looked at Edna with a weak smile. "Everything is good, Eddy, *really* good."

As she walked away, Edna stared at Homer, shaking her finger, warning him to be nice.

"We leave for Seattle in the morning," Homer told Sally. "When we get there, I'll fly right back."

She nodded. "What about your trip north?"

"I think this might be my last ferry job, north or south."

She looked at him, puzzled. "Does this have anything to do with what's going on?"

"What do you mean?"

"Some of your guys are regulars here, you know that."

"What have they said?"

"They said there seems to be serious problems with two of the crew and with the people shipping boxes to Seattle. That's all they said."

"I knew there was no way we could keep all this quiet."

"What's going on, Homer?"

"It's too convoluted to explain. I'll tell you the whole story next week. I'd better get back to the table. We're discussing that very problem." Homer took Sally's face in his hands. "I'm happy. I'm glad we had this conversation. We'll make up for the past twenty years. I'll make it happen."

"So will I," she promised.

At the table, Homer looked somber. "Let's get serious."

Ernie started, "Looked like you were getting serious out there on the dance floor, Skipper."

Homer waved away that discussion.

"Okay," Ernie continued, "Coast Guard gave us a marginal passing grade for our lifeboats and safety inspection. Said they would notify Seattle of the results, stating that everything must be improved before the *Eagle* takes to sea again. Three of our four lifeboats are okay but two of the launching mechanisms are shot and may not do the job. Fortunately, our blow-up Zodiacs are in good shape, as are the inflating systems."

"We could work on the lifeboats tomorrow," Nick suggested.

"No," Homer disagreed. "John Adams is so skittish he might misconstrue what we're doing and freak out." Looking at Nick and Minnie, he said, "Things could get dicey in the next few days. I don't want you or anyone on board to get hurt. I feel that they think the *Alaskan Eagle* and Davy have served their purpose, so I don't trust what they might do at this point. Would you check out all the passengers first thing in the morning? Appraise what their physical limitations might be and any other handicaps they might have. For example, I know we have three Mexican citizens on board as passengers. How well do they speak and understand English? You might want to ask one of the engineers, Lieutenant Garcia, to go with you to talk with them," he paused, as if thinking of the whole list.

They sat—staring at him.

"Also, check out the conditions of the life jackets in all the cabins. Above certain latitudes, Coast Guard requires survival suits on some types of vessels. We do have Adams' survival suits in those boxes. I won't hesitate to use them. I don't know the specific requirements for their use because we've never been told we needed them, but the water temperature here is pretty cold, only in the forties. Ernie will do the same for the crew. He'll ask Major Flowers and her people to help."

"Captain, everything seems changed, seems to be headed toward a conclusion," Nick said, stating the obvious.

"Nothing's different, Nick, except that my head has cleared. Contingency plans are being formed, just in case."

CHAPTER TWENTY-SIX

October 23rd—6am

Homer watched the crew gathering. He waited for a nod from Ernie. *What the hell do I tell them? What am I doing to them? What am I getting them into?* His character was not that of Captain Homer Dixon. He tried to mask it with a fixed smile.

As usual, some of the passengers were present, including Major Flowers and her group.

Homer assumed Smith or Brown had notified the yacht of their earlier departure and that they would be leaving before first light. "Gentlemen, and Gentle Ladies," he began. "If you've had the feeling that this trip has been a little different, a little disjointed, you are right." He could see he had their attention.

Not only did Ernie have a concerned, *what now*, look on his face, so did Smith and Brown, who were fingering their cell phones. Newitt and some other senior crew stood together, nodding almost in unison. The other crew and passengers looked on with amused, questioning expressions.

"Two things." His mind raced back to what Davy had said to him a week ago, there's two things I have to tell you. Well, his two things would be different. "First, I'm in love." When the laughter subsided, and he again had their attention, he continued. "But for those of you who have been with me for many years, you know I've been in love before," eliciting more laughter from the small gathering.

"Now the second thing."

Ernie and Nick glanced at each other.

"About twenty years ago, I was on an Alaska Airlines flight. The plane was decked out with streamers and party things. When we got near Seattle, the pilot was given permission to buzz the runway at SeaTac Airport, something I'd never seen before or since. Well, we don't have party streamers, or the ability to buzz Puget Sound, but we can still be merry. Just like that retiring pilot, chances are this will be my last trip."

They were surprised, some murmuring amongst themselves. "No, don't say that, Captain!" The response came from a few of the crew.

"Mr. McInnis will tell you about more important issues and the chances for fog the next few days. God bless you all, be well, and have a fine trip."

"You, too, Captain."

At six-forty, Homer stood on the port side of the outer bridge tapping his hand on the railing in cadence with the thumping of the *Eagle's* drive shaft and propeller. They headed southeast in the channel past downtown Ketchikan and past the *Mother's Love*, still at its berth. He could see the crew scurrying to ready the yacht for sea. Even at a hundred yards and in semi-darkness he saw a scowling John Adams, binoculars in hand, looking at the *Eagle*, and no doubt at Homer.

"Homer, what's going on?" Ernie asked, walking out.

"I'm there, Ernie. I know where I'm going and what I have to do."

"Skipper, I can see you're on a high now, but I'm concerned about the course you're taking."

"I'm going to do what has to be done. I've been shocked, as if hit by lightening," Homer explained, but didn't offer any details.

Ernie shook his head in disapproval. "You've never held out on me before, Skipper."

"Ernie, when you think back on your life, what do you remember?"

"Homer, the end is not near. Don't take a fatalistic attitude on things."

"Not at all, it's just the opposite. I'm coming out of a fright that I'll always remember. What things do you remember, Ernie? I can recall the first time I had a birthday party, my first sexual experience, and significant incidents with my parents. What was one of the shock memories for you, Ernie?"

"Oh, boy" Ernie sighed, "What now?"

"Did you know that a Warrant Officer in the Navy is at a grade higher than a Chief Petty Officer, but lower than an Ensign? It's an enlisted sailor who has been promoted to officer status."

"Yes, I know that, Captain."

"Well, the accent that our antagonists here have reminds me of a memory that goes back to my cadet days. I don't think I've ever told you this one. I was returning from a summer training course at Barking Sands, a Navy facility on the west coast of Kauai, in Hawaii. Sitting next to me on the flight to San Francisco was a Warrant Officer retiring after thirty years in the Navy. If you remember what years I was at the Maritime Academy, go back thirty years from that, you realize that he was in the Navy during World War II and chances are he spent most of his career in the Pacific, though he could have been involved in D-Day or other invasions of Europe or North Africa. Well, he started talking about the war. I can remember nothing of the conversation except his remark that the Germans only wanted Lebensraum. I looked at him. He said, you know, 'living space'. I was stunned. As a youngster, I didn't know what to say, either to comment on it or challenge it. But I've never forgotten it."

"Is that it?" Ernie asked. "What made you think of it?"

"I've told you. It's the accent that John Adams and his crew have. I remember that this Navy guy told me his name. I don't remember the name, but recognized it as a region that our friends on the yacht probably come from."

"What are you going to do, Homer? You're planning something. What is it?"

"I don't know yet. I'll have to see what happens. When the time comes, I'll know it and I'll know what to do."

"Damn, Homer, you're scaring the shit out of me. But, promise me one thing?"

"What's that, Ernie?

"Whatever you decide to do, tell me. Let me work with you. Let me help you."

"Will do, Ernie."

They stared at each other for a moment. Ernie nodded as he left the bridge.

CHAPTER TWENTY-SEVEN

Minnie *followed Nick down to Tilly's cabin.* "You'd better go in first," Nick said. "She might not be dressed."

"What difference does it make?" Minnie quipped, poking at him. "You've already felt her up."

After a number of light knocks, the door opened and Tilly peeked out. "Yes? Oh, Nick, it's you. Thank you for coming. The ship seems to be moving. I don't feel so good," she said, in a squeaky voice while holding her robe tight with one hand and maintaining her balance with the other, appearing like a child imitating an old woman.

Minnie rushed in to help her withstand the sharp rocking of the *Eagle.* They walked back toward the bed.

"Wait," Tilly said, "I need to use the bathroom."

Nick looked around the room while Minnie was in the bathroom with Tilly. He could see no evidence of food or drinks among the mess of clothes and personal items. *It's going to be a long few days before we get to Seattle.* He watched with amusement as Minnie helped Tilly back into bed.

"Have you eaten since you came aboard?" Minnie asked.

"Just a few candy bars."

"We'll get you some food and drinks."

"Is it possible to get hot chocolate and maybe some toast and jam? I don't know if my stomach can take much. I hate to bother you, but I don't think I could make it up the stairs to the dining room. All of a sudden, I feel so wobbly."

"It's the life on a small ship. It's not designed for comfort," Nick explained. "Everyone feels like that the first few days underway, but in your condition it's more so. I'll have them bring some tea and soda and a bunch of saltines. You might like that."

Minnie gave Nick a hard glance. She took Tilly's hand. "Don't you worry, we'll take care of you.

"Are you Nick's girlfriend?" Tilly asked.

Minnie smiled, "Yes, I guess I am."

"Oh," Tilly muttered.

"That poor girl is in love with you," Minnie said, as they headed for the mess hall and galley area. "What did you do to her?"

"Is she a poor girl because of her condition, or because I had a few drinks with her a year ago at Sally's Place?"

"Nick Banner," Minnie scolded. She stopped in the passageway, stared at him and smiled. "If I had a mirror, you could see the sheepish guilty look on your face. How come I never saw you so unguarded these past months?" She hugged him tight. "It's a good thing I love you," she said, as she turned to continue walking.

Nick took a deep breath and rolled his eyes.

The galley was located between the crews' mess and the passengers' lounge. They arranged for Tilly's food, then picked a small table in the lounge.

After ordering breakfast, Nick whispered, "I'm going to have a quick chat with some of the passengers." It was customary for passengers to choose a table at the beginning of a voyage and eat there during the entire trip. He'd joined Homer and Ernie, in either the lounge or with the crew, the few times they ate out of their own quarters. He approached a table with three people who were chatting in Spanish. "Mr. Sanchez?" he inquired.

"Yes, I am Senor Sanchez," the gentleman said, as he rose to greet Nick.

"I'm Nick Banner, Second Mate on the ship. I came aboard a few days ago in Juneau. I apologize for not introducing myself sooner. I'll be conducting a follow up safety inspection required by the Coast Guard. May I visit your cabin sometime this morning?"

"Please excuse me," Mr. Sanchez said. He spoke briefly in Spanish to the young woman at his table.

She responded to him in length then gazed up at Nick. "I'm Maria Sanchez. My father can speak only limited English. He welcomes your visit to our cabin."

"Please, can you both eat with us?" Mr. Sanchez looked over at Minnie. "My daughter needs a companion."

"I'm fine, really." Maria smiled politely. "But my father feels he should look after me. Please join us?"

Minnie had been watching them from a few tables away.

Nick motioned for her to come over. "We've been invited to have breakfast with the Sanchez family."

"I heard, and I understood most of the conversation in Spanish," she said, smiling at Maria and Mrs. Sanchez.

"We have enjoyed the voyage," Mr. Sanchez added. "It is not as nice or as luxurious as a cruise liner, but it is more real. We have a small boat in Acapulco. I like the feel of the ocean. My daughter, Maria, is not very happy. We get pleasure having her with us. On a big tourist ship, we would never see her. She works in San Diego as a nurse. I no longer work, but it is a long distance from Acapulco to San Diego for a visit."

Mrs. Sanchez, quiet up to this point, but seeing the expression on Maria's face, spoke to him rapidly in Spanish.

Mr. Sanchez threw up his hands in mock despair.

Maria grinned at Nick and Minnie. "My mother does not understand English, but knowing my father's penchant for talking, decided that enough is enough. It pains him that I am so far away, and he worries that I am not under the watchful eye of an elder family member."

"Why did you move to San Diego?" Minnie asked.

"I attended schools in Southern California and now work in a San Diego hospital while continuing my studies. Eventually, I plan to return to Mexico to make use of my education."

"In what specialty?" Minnie asked.

"The women of Mexico are sorely limited in the area of health conditions that affect mostly, or exclusively, women."

Minnie gave Nick a knowing look.

They both nodded at Maria, who was distracted, as the four Corp of Engineers' officers came into the breakfast area.

Nick rose to talk with them.

Luis Garcia stopped to greet the Sanchez family in Spanish.

Mrs. Sanchez and Maria smiled, but Mr. Sanchez didn't look thrilled after watching Maria greet Luis.

"I'll see you guys after breakfast," Nick informed the engineers, and nodded politely at Angie when she smiled at him.

Maria and her mother, noting the grimace on Minnie's face, gazed at each other with raised eyebrows.

"I must excuse myself," Nick announced. "I need to talk with the father of those two boys, and to the engineers. Do you want to join me?" he asked Minnie.

"I think I'll stay with Mr. and Mrs. Sanchez and practice my Spanish."

"Good morning, Mr. Marsden," Nick greeted, looking at his list of passengers. "I'm the Second Mate, Nick Banner, and you guys must be Jacob and Jonas. I won't even try to tell you apart." He smiled at the twins.

"Name's Peter." Mr. Marsden rose to shake Nick's hand. "And I still have the same problem. They even get identical haircuts and dress alike to fool everyone."

"You might have noticed the Coast Guard people performing a routine inspection of the ship yesterday afternoon," Nick said. "As a follow up, they asked us to document that all personal safety gear is up to current Coast Guard safety requirements; life vests with whistle and light attachments, thermal wet suits, and such. I'd like to check the gear in your cabin later."

"Sounds good," Peter nodded. "What about survival suits? We had them on the fishing boat we chartered out of Seward. They told us about requirements for their use above a certain latitude where water temperatures are somewhat lethal. Do we have them on board?"

"Our type of commercial vessel, even carrying passengers, is not required to have them, but if you've been down to the hold, those seventy-six boxes on the ledge all have survival suits in them."

"We have been down to the hold," said Jacob or Jonas. "We noticed the dive gear in your trucks. We've done some shallow water scuba and snorkeling, but they won't let us do any serious diving until we're eighteen. Two more years."

"It's a sensible requirement," Nick said. "I'd be happy to show you my gear any time."

"Is that a Navy SEAL emblem on one of your trucks?"

"It sure is. I was a SEAL when I was in the Navy." Nick smiled.

"Oh, man!" Both boys said in unison.

"They became Eagle Scouts a few months ago," Peter said. "Their specialty was water related; boats, and marine activities. This trip is their surprise reward for that achievement."

"Isn't this the middle of a school term?"

"Yes, but their school started early. This is their fall break."

"Well," Nick said. "I've got to find my last two sets of passengers, the Wilsons and the Talbots, our senior citizen contingent."

"We talked with them at the crew meeting," Peter said. "They're going to be out on deck watching the sunrise and will be playing cards when the fog rolls in."

Smiling at the boys, Nick said, "Let's get together later to check out the dive gear."

On the way out of the lounge, Nick stopped and leaned into the group of army engineers. "Don't any of you look at your watches when I say this. The Captain wants a meeting of all of us in his stateroom at ten, about an hour from now. He expects things to heat up today." He saw the twinkle in Angie's eyes, as he walked away.

So did Minnie and Maria.

"Good morning, again," he said to the Sanchez family. "We should have some good sightseeing this sunny morning before we encounter fog."

Maria translated for her parents.

"Minnie, let's complete our safety inspection tour."

As they left the lounge, Minnie leaned in close to Nick. "Banner, you're pissing me off. You and your fucking women. How did you restrain yourself all those months on the job? How come you're not looking to spread Maria's legs?"

"You saw, she's got eyes for Lieutenant Garcia," Nick said, unlocking the door to their cabin.

"So, if not, you'd fuck her, too," Minnie snarled, swinging at Nick.

When they entered their cabin he caught both her arms, joining them behind her back with one hand. With his other hand, he ripped some of her clothes off, enough of them. His mouth stopped her lips from ranting. Her fighting spirit gradually subsided. Lately, this was new for them, quick and violent.

A little while later, they both lay there, gasping for breath. "Holy shit," Nick exclaimed. "We've got fifteen minutes to get to the Captain's cabin."

Minnie rolled on top of him, pinning him to the bed. "Banner," she whispered in his ear, "I don't want you to get hurt. Promise me you won't take foolish risks."

"I promise," he said, extracting himself from under her. His hand pushed hair from her face, as he leaned close to her. "I'm glad I waited all those years to fall in love again."

"I'm glad I did, too. You go to the meeting. I'll see you after. I'm going to keep you so busy, you won't even want to look at other women."

CHAPTER TWENTY-EIGHT

"*Are we clean, Nick?*" *Homer asked.*

"Looks good, Captain, no bugs."

"Hopefully, this will be the last time we'll have to do that. Just had another call from the enemy. We're back to calling them that based on the latest subtle and not so subtle signals they've given us. It's difficult for me to explain my thinking on this, but trust me— God, I hate that expression—I've had two long meetings with him on his yacht, and about twenty phone conversations. I've seen him change his goal, or possibly it was his goal all along. You probably can't follow my concerns here. I'm having a hard time myself."

"Captain, how does this affect us, and/or how can we assist you—in any way?"

"Thank you, Major Flowers, for trying to get me back to reality. We're heading into a pretty thick fog bank. Not to worry. We've been through this hundreds of times before. We'll slow down to a crawl, if necessary. In daylight, we'll always have some visibility, with course charting done by our Global Positioning System, GPS, plus our two radars."

"What'd you do before GPS, Captain?" Lieutenant Stevens asked.

"We had LORAN, Long Range Navigation, to guide us if we were close enough to get a signal. In fact, we still have a LORAN receiver on board. To get archaic, we used sextants and slide rules, no GPS, computers or calculators. For our nighttime transit through fog, we'll have two tools, GPS and radar, but no visibility except for an occasional lighthouse." Homer paused for a moment and smiled. "One summer when I was at the Maritime Academy we were on a cruise in the Sea of Japan. I had the mid-watch duty, midnight to four in the morning, for you non-sailors. No fog, just the opposite."

"Captain," Ernie interjected.

"I know, Ernie, this'll only take a minute. We had no GPS, no charts of value to keep us in the designated ship channel, no reliable depth soundings, and no LORAN. What we had was a useless radar screen full of too many blips. The only navigational aides we could use were visual, lights, but there were hundreds of lights from ships, mostly from fishing boats. They masked the lights we needed, from lighthouses. Our charts showed a few lighthouses, each with a different signal. When we finally narrowed down our location based on the lights, we were about a mile off course. We were lucky we didn't go aground or hit one of the yet-to-be cleared mines before we got back into the channel."

Those in the room listened, some nodding their heads.

"All right, I'll stop my story telling. Ernie's heard them all and he's having a fit. One navigational aide I left out is our depth sounder, backed by accurate depth readings on our navigation charts. We'll make use of that in the fog."

Homer paused to change the tone of the meeting. "I need your help. It was a good thing for us that you chose the *Eagle*." He gazed at Major Flowers and the other engineers. "I'm concerned about what devious plans a Mr. John Adams has with his group on the yacht, and the two we have here on the *Eagle*. The seven of us, plus Mr. Banner's friend Minnie, are the only ones on board who are aware of the circumstances." Homer paused.

"Yet supposedly, they think I'm the only one who knows about the boxes, and they don't have a clue that Coast Guard is aware of anything. I doubt all that," Homer said. "I think they, or at least their leader that calls himself John Adams, strongly suspects that some of you and even the Coast Guard knows what's going on. I think that this Adams has been holding his breath for us to get out of Ketchikan—so he's back in control. Why haven't I done anything to force Coast Guard to move in on them, or to blast it apart?" Homer paused again. "I've got selfish reasons. A close friend of mine, and his wife, are under a death threat up in Alaska if they, or I, do anything foolish. Adams' men keep them under surveillance. So, here's where I need your help." Homer stared at them, as he sighed.

The room was quiet, as they listened.

"John Smith and John Brown in my crew are with the yacht people—planted here by Adams. They need to be watched around the clock. If I put them off the ship, or lock them up, my friends will be killed and Coast Guard would have to move in before they're ready. If we do anything while we're at sea, the yacht people will come aboard with guns blazing and signal their men up north to kill my friends. Why didn't Coast Guard end it in Ketchikan, you ask? They said they needed to be certain they are able to round up all these people, including shore-based collaborators, if any. There's the matter of the unknown piece of metal in the center of the boxes. So, now we need to put together two teams; one to watch Smith and one to watch Brown, and do it in such a way that they don't know they're being watched. Mr. McInnis will give the teams specific work assignments, to start at noon today."

The group nodded and glanced at each other.

"These guys need to be watched at their workstations and, more risky, on the way to and from work, and during their leisure time. We can't raise suspicion by significantly changing their routine. The easiest time will be when they're in their cabin for the night, except for Brown's night watch on the bridge. But they're unpredictable and dangerous, particularly Smith. Know this—they certainly have weapons. That's it." Homer was quiet while the four engineers absorbed the situation. "Please talk it over, but let me know quickly, so I can devise a different plan if necessary."

"Captain," Angie said, "We're under the same commitment as regular Army officers and under the same orders from our superiors, just as we were when we assisted with opening the box. We follow the orders we've been given. This is not an ethical or moral situation, but a possible public threat—a threat against our country—for which we have been, again, ordered to provide assistance. That's been made clear to us. When we went through boot camp, in our case the Army's Officer Candidate School or ROTC at college, we were not engineers; we were trained to be military officers. This is an unusual situation, in that our immediate, or day-to-day, orders do not come from a military source, but if you go higher than the Joint Chiefs of Staff to the Secretary of the Army, they're all civilians. That being said, we're at your disposal." Angie smiled at Homer and Nick, while her officers nodded their heads, albeit somewhat confused.

"Thank you, Major, I appreciate your support." Homer nodded. "This is not one that you'll ever find in the textbooks. Now, the four of you coordinate your efforts with Nick and Ernie, while I answer this damn phone. It's been shaking in my hand. It's either my friend Davy, up in Kenai, or John Adams. Also, I need to get up to the bridge."

It was both of them. He listened to Davy's message, saying that he and Maddy would be out of touch part of the day. The call came from Davy's new phone. He wished that he could have talked with Davy and that the yacht would be the one out of touch, out of contact—and, no message from Adams. *Good. He'll call back.*

The visibility was still good. He waved at the Talbots and Stewarts, energetically walking laps out on the main deck. It was unusual for any passengers or crew to be older than him.

"Well, Mr. Brown, you're quite early for your watch," Homer noted with a raised brow.

"Yes, Captain, I am. I wish to observe what activities are happening on the ship."

"And you are very good at that."

"Excuse me, Captain, I do not understand your meaning."

"No matter. I was just making pleasant conversation. The yacht is not yet in sight. They are usually right with us."

"I received a message from Mr. Adams a few minutes ago," John Brown said. "They are having a problem with the engine. They will proceed using the extra engine."

"Auxiliary propulsion," Homer guessed.

"Yes, auxiliary propulsion. The problem with the main engine will be repaired soon. Mr. Adams tried to telephone you, but you did not answer."

"I was unable to answer the phone just as he did not answer when I called him back," Homer said, groping for words that would be in Brown's English vocabulary.

"Mr. Adams asks that you proceed more slowly and wait for them."

"I can't do that. I have a schedule to maintain and we need to travel as far as we can with this good visibility. When we get into the fog, we will slow down, losing valuable time. Do you understand what I am saying?"

"Yes, I understand. Mr. Adams said you were told that the cargo is to be transferred to his ship. He said it would be easy to do during the day."

Homer stared at Brown. *So, the truth comes out. I'm sure Adams didn't word it like that. Well, it makes it easier for me.* "I told Mr. Adams I am not permitted to do that." Homer busied himself studying their location and course on the charts until Brown walked away. "Newitt," he called to the bridge watch, "Make as much headway as we can. Let's take advantage of the good visibility. Pass that on to your relief."

"Aye, Captain."

Homer returned to the chart table, his jaw tightening. *They give me no choice.*

CHAPTER TWENTY-NINE

October 23rd—1:10pm

"*The surveillance is set up,*" *Ernie told Homer.* "The Engineers seem like a capable group. But, they're different than they were when they first came aboard. They're more like professional soldiers. First, that night with the box, and now, all this. And that Major. She's a tiger. She's quiet but alert and wary."

"What do you think, Nick?" Homer asked.

"I agree, Captain. They've been transformed. It's like what happens to you in combat when you come off a landing craft onto the beach, or you're part of a parachute air drop. If you survive, you're a different person than you were an hour before, and certainly different than you were a week or year before." Nick wore a rueful smile. "And that experience will change you, and stay with you for the rest of your life."

They stared at Nick, looking surprised. "Good analogy," Homer said. "We've all had similar experiences, but not in a life or death situation. What did you find out about the passengers?"

"They're all somewhat as they appear. The only extreme condition, if I can call it that, is Matilda Shepherd. Sally summed it up last night. Tilly is probably too far along with her pregnancy to be traveling, and certainly to be traveling on a ship like the *Eagle*. I hope we won't need a doctor. As back up, though, we could ask Maria Sanchez to help. She's a registered nurse."

Homer grimaced. "In my 'hundred' years at sea, we've had some births and dozens of accidents and conditions requiring medical assistance. The Coast Guard, both U.S. and Canadian, have come to our rescue. We're in a different situation here." Homer stood up and looked out at the sea. "We've also had four deaths. I'm actually surprised there haven't been more. One overboard, one accident off a passageway ladder, and two with medical conditions."

Ernie nodded. "The crew is relatively clean. If we get into a catastrophic situation, our only handicap will be the few who have a difficult time with English, but we have enough people on board who are bi-lingual. Here's the plan and schedule we worked out for the surveillance—regular four hour assignments to coincide with the crew's shifts."

"Okay, guys, let's see what happens now," Homer said.

A few minutes after the group left, Homer answered the phone supplied by Adams.

"Captain Dixon, what do you think you are doing? You must stop at once and wait for us. You have been told about our engine problems, yet you keep speeding ahead. What are you up to? What do you think you are doing?"

"Mr. Adams, we can't just stop the ship and stay still. The ship channels between and around these islands are narrow. Maneuvering is tricky. If we stop or go too slow the currents and eddies and tides are going to ground the ship for certain. When we're in open waters, off the Canadian coast, we can stop. We can even anchor and wait for you. But if we anchor in the fog around these small islands, some cargo ship will run us over."

"You are talking nonsense, Captain, and you know it. What I want to know is what are you up to? What plans do you have that will surely doom you? Is it worth the sacrifice of your friend Davy and his wife? You have gone mad. I need my property now and I will take it by any means. Do you understand, Captain?"

"I understand you very well, Mr. Adams. Your message makes things very clear to me. Goodbye, Mr. Adams, and good luck."

"And good luck to you, Captain, and to your ship full of people, and to your friend Davy. Good luck."

Homer stood for a moment, glaring at the phone in his hand, then shouted, "What the fuck are you going to do, you sadistic bastard!" He threw the phone as far as he could into the still waters. He watched it plop. It looked as if it bounced back up, with a cone and a spray rising about a foot, then settling quickly down into calm. He turned to watch the spot as the ship moved, straightening up to see through the fog, and gradually releasing his hold on the rail.

CHAPTER THIRTY

October 23rd—3:15pm

Nick checked the bridge where Lieutenant Garcia was loafing around—keeping an eye on Brown. He wandered out on deck and down an outside ladder, looking for Angie's surveillance of Smith. He spotted the work crew aft, replacing stanchion chain along the gunwale, at the edge of the deck. The chain had been removed during cargo loading in Ketchikan. When Nick was about twenty feet away, Angie spun around on instinct and faced him with a coy smile. *Oh shit, if Minnie sees us, I'm dead.* He didn't stop, giving her a slight negative shake of his head as he passed by.

Later on, when Nick had his truck open, showing Peter Marsden and his sons some of his dive gear, he saw Lieutenant York walk up with a concerned expression. "What's up Richard?"

"Can I speak with you for a minute, Mr. Banner?"

Nick walked away from the group.

"We can't find Major Flowers and Luis Garcia. I went to relieve her, but couldn't find her. Mr. McInnis said John Smith is off duty somewhere."

"Where is Mr. McInnis?"

"He was looking for you. He said he was going to find the Captain."

Nick turned to the Marsdens. "Sorry, I've got to lock up the truck. Something to tend to."

"Anything wrong?" Peter Marsden asked, looking between Nick and Richard.

"Don't know yet," Nick gave a short reply.

Nick and Richard raced along the passageway and up the ladder. "Where did you see Ernie last?"

"He was heading for the bridge to see the Captain."

"Where are your guys?"

"Sandy is looking for Luis Garcia. He was supposed to be watching John Brown."

"Hold up a second," Nick said. He checked his cabin for Minnie, not there. He looked at his watch as they headed for the lounge. Minnie was sitting with the Sanchez family. The only missing passengers were the three Marsdens and the two engineers. He strolled around the room offering his greetings to Mr. and Mrs. Sanchez and Maria. The lieutenants sat alone. With his hands on Minnie's shoulders, Nick whispered, "Minnie, can I have a word with you. We have some things to take care of," he informed the table.

"Is there a problem?" Mr. Sanchez asked.

Nick hesitated. "We don't know. The Captain asked us to meet with him concerning our tasks during the time we are in the fog." He gave the lieutenants a head motion to follow him. When they were in the passageway, he said, "First, we need to find the Captain and Mr. McInnis."

"What's going on?" Minnie asked.

"Two of the engineers are missing."

"What do you mean, missing?"

"We don't know. We have to find the Captain and Ernie."

"Mr. McInnis gave us walkie-talkies, to be used in an emergency," Sandy piped in. They have four separate channels." He handed the phone to Nick.

"What channel is Ernie on?" Nick asked.

"He's on one, and the two people on watch have channels two and three. We hand it off when we relieve the watch. Right now, Major Flowers and Luis Garcia have two and three. This is number four, the extra phone."

"Ernie, over," Nick spoke into the phone.

"Where are you?" came the immediate response.

"We're looking for you and the Captain."

"Come to the Captain's stateroom."

"Good," Ernie said, when they entered Homer's quarters. "You've got two of them."

"Let's get everyone's story," Homer said, staring at the two lieutenants.

Richard York started, "Lieutenant Garcia relieved me on the bridge just as Brown was going off his watch. I went to my cabin, and to the lounge to wait for Major Flowers. I called Major Flowers about four-twenty to find her location. I couldn't get an answer. I looked around the ship, including the hidden spot we were to use near Smith and Brown's cabin. I called Mr. McInnis to tell him, and then found Mr. Banner in the hold."

"Okay, time is critical, very critical," Homer, said. "I'm turning the ship around. I don't think they went overboard but I have to do it."

"Captain." Nick said, concerned. "I'm not saying that your action is wrong, I would do the same thing, but you realize that survival is not possible after ten or fifteen minutes in water this cold?"

"Yes, I know that, Nick, but I must do it. Now, Ernie, find out where Smith and Brown are. I'd like to confirm that they are in their cabin. Ask Newitt to get his usual crew to conduct a routine stowaway search of the ship. I've seen them do it in thirty minutes.

Make sure they know the seriousness of this one. It has to be fast but very thorough. If they ask, tell them that the two are missing and that we can't rule out foul play. The fact that Major Flowers is an attractive woman could be a reason. Now, this is important. If they see Smith or Brown around the ship, they are not to do anything, but have Newitt notify us. I'll be on the bridge. And, they must skip Smith and Brown's cabin."

"Not go into it at all?" Ernie asked.

"Right, not go into it and don't even knock on the door. If your guys are at chow, pull them out. They can eat later. You two," Homer said, looking at the lieutenants, "go to the location used to watch Smith and Brown's cabin. If you see either one go in or out, call us immediately."

"Yes sir, Captain."

"Nick, would you and Minnie come up to the bridge with me? I'm going to backtrack on our course for a few hours. We'll set up overboard lights. If Ernie and Newitt and the others come up blank, our search has to be in the water. Minnie, please bring your computer to check our equipment."

They'd barely laid out the charts on the bridge when Ernie called.

CHAPTER THIRTY-ONE

October 23rd—5:50pm

"What is it, Ernie?" Homer asked.

"We found Garcia."

"Found him, where? Is he okay?"

"He's in the rope locker. He's tied up and taped."

"Is he okay, or what, Ernie? Tell me."

"He's, wait a second, he's moving. We didn't know if he was dead or alive. Newitt called me. He's been banged up a bit. I think they left him for dead. His head and face are bloody. He hasn't said anything yet."

"Take him to sick bay and find Doc."

"I think this is way beyond what our Corpsman can handle," Ernie said.

"Okay, but take him there anyway. We'll see if the nurse will help us out. Ernie, did they complete the search?"

"Almost. We started aft and swept forward to the bow. I guess they figured we wouldn't be using the rope locker until we get into port."

"Any sign of Major Flowers?"

"Nothing. No clues at all. If we can get Garcia to talk, that's the first thing I'll ask him. He doesn't look good. He's out completely, but he's breathing."

"Be careful with him. Get a stretcher or something to move him with. Watch his neck. No, wait. Don't move him. Get Doc to look at him first and we'll get the nurse." Homer turned to Nick and Minnie. They'd been listening to Homer's side of the conversation. "It's Lieutenant Garcia. They found him in the rope locker. He's been beat up pretty bad. He's unconscious. Do you think Maria Sanchez would look at him?"

"I'm sure she will," Minnie answered.

"We'll go find her and take her down," Nick said.

Nick and Minnie raced to the lounge. "They'll be here or in their cabin," Nick said.

"What's wrong?" Maria asked, watching them head for her table. "I can see it on your faces."

"Maria, can you help us? There's been an accident and there's no doctor on board," Nick said.

"Yes, of course." She explained the situation to her parents.

Mr. Sanchez looked at Nick. "What kind of accident? Who has been hurt?"

"Lieutenant Garcia. He needs help."

Maria gasped. "What happened?" Mrs. Sanchez, hearing the name, surmised the incident. Maria spoke rapidly in Spanish to her parents.

"Maria cannot nurse to a man," Mr. Sanchez argued.

Maria stood up staring at her father. She talked to him in Spanish, at which point, her mother joined in. Shrugging at Nick and Minnie, she said, "It's hard for him to accept that I must tend to men as well as women."

"We will come with you," Mr. Sanchez offered.

"It's too difficult for you to climb down to that area of the ship," Nick said.

Minnie spoke to him carefully in Spanish. "I will escort Maria, and watch Maria. Please, the man is hurt. We must go."

Maria flushed somewhat, as her father nodded acceptance and her mother crossed herself. "Please, tell me what happened," she said to Nick, as they walked out.

"We don't know. We received word that he was hurt just a few minutes ago. We didn't want to move him until someone examined him. He may have fallen."

They climbed down into the rope locker. Newitt and his crew had left the rope locker with Ernie to complete searching the *Eagle*. Luis was still lying among the used and tattered ropes, as if he'd been tossed in. The ship's Corpsman was standing there shaking his head.

"Oh, my God," Maria muttered. They parted to let her get close. She wiped tears from her eyes, as she started to examine him.

Looking at Maria, Minnie started weeping softly. She knelt down to assist her.

Maria proceeded to check his vital signs; breathing, pulse, blood pressure and eyes, and, as well as she could discern, his limbs and neck. "This did not happen when he fell in. He's been attacked with a club and knocked unconscious. I've seen many such injuries in the ER," she said, as she cleaned his head and face wounds with wipes provided by the Corpsman. She sat looking at Minnie and up at Nick with a grim expression. "All his vital signs look good, but we need to check him with medical instruments. He might have a slight concussion. I don't know about internal bleeding. Let's get him off these ropes and onto the stretcher, but first carefully put the head and neck brace on," she instructed the Corpsman.

Nick knelt to help move Luis. The four of them rolled him over.

"Where did that blood come from?" Maria pulled away his shirt. "My God, I think he's been shot. He moaned when I touched the spot. A good sign."

Nick examined Luis also. "It looks like a bullet grazed his side."

"Yes," Maria agreed, trying to compose herself.

"There were a few shots," Nick said, picking up some spent bullets and casings. From their location, he could tell they came straight down from the opening above the rope locker—after he was dumped. "Bastards." He glanced at the Corpsman. "Get some hands to help get him to sick bay, and someone to operate the hoist. Tell them that he just fell in here. We don't want to panic anyone." To Minnie and Maria he said, "I've got to find Captain Dixon."

Nick and Ernie met going into Homer's stateroom. "Major Flowers is not anywhere," Ernie informed them. "The only place we haven't looked is in their cabin. Let's hope she's there. God forbid, she went overboard."

Nick briefed them about Luis Garcia. "They're taking him to sick bay. Maria will keep tending to him. Fuckers figured they'd just be sure with a few extra shots. Don't know how they could have missed, even with the ship rolling. They were standing right over him, about eight feet up."

"We've got to stop them, Captain," Ernie said.

"Yes, we do. Let's get ready."

CHAPTER THIRTY-TWO

October 23rd—7:10pm

"**I**'*m taking a pistol and a short barrel shotgun,*" *Ernie said.* "Why the shotgun?"

"That's if we have a problem. You don't have to aim much. When they see it they'll know that. What about you, Homer?"

"I've got two Glocks. The clips hold 12 rounds each and they're semi-automatic. They don't have safety switches, so I've got to be careful. You too, Ernie, and remember to keep a tight grip on the gun. We haven't been shooting in a while, have we?" Homer took in a deep breath. "Goddamn, Ernie, this is a first for us."

"Do you think we'll actually have to use them?"

"I hope not, but we have to be ready. Just showing them should be enough, but that Smith is crazy. We can't tell what he'll do. I wonder if they've got that girl, or what they've done with her? Garcia still hasn't said anything. That they meant to kill him is warning enough. Ernie; remember, you'll be standing behind me showing the shotgun."

They left Homer's quarters with the pistols concealed and the shotgun shrouded under a towel. They passed Nick and Lieutenants York and Stevens keeping an eye on the door to Smith and Brown's cabin. Nick was armed. He gave each lieutenant a pistol to hold, just in case. He would not let Minnie come with them even after she told him of her experience with guns.

"Nick," Homer whispered, "I know you're more experienced at this than we are but I want you to stay off to the side, out of the line of fire. This is our fight. I don't want you to get hurt. Once the situation is under control, or if we go down, you move in to take over."

"What if the door is locked?" Nick asked. "You can't knock. That would give them time for whatever."

"Ernie has a pass key." Homer and Ernie silently walked up to the door. There was no hotel-type peephole. Ernie carefully inserted the key in case it was locked. He reached in with one hand on the key and the other on the shotgun. Homer placed his hand on the door latch. The engine and propeller noise, more prevalent in this part of the ship, masked any sounds they made. Homer turned to Ernie and nodded. They both acted in concert, Ernie with the key and Homer on the door handle. The door didn't budge. "They've rigged a safety bolt," Homer said. "Open up!" He yelled, banging on the door. "Open the door."

"Who is at the door?"

"You know damn well who it is. It's the Captain. Open up or we'll break it down. Nowhere for them to go," he whispered to Ernie. These cabins had no connecting rooms, and were outfitted with portholes, not windows. The latch clicked and the door opened slowly. Homer tensed.

John Brown stood there staring at Homer with a frightened expression.

"What do you want with us?" John Smith snarled from an easy chair. Two pistols lay on a desk near him. Following Homer's eyes, Smith glanced at them and back at Homer.

"Where are they?" Homer demanded.

"What are you talking about?"

"We're looking for the Army Major and Lieutenant. They were down here inspecting their gear about an hour ago. Where are they?"

"We did not see anyone."

"You were seen talking with them."

"Ah, yes, the military people," Smith replied. "We did talk with them for a few minutes. We do not know where they are now. The ship is moving slow. Maybe they went swimming." Smith stood up. He moved slightly toward the desk.

Ernie came out from behind Homer, showing the shotgun. "Don't even think about it!" he yelled.

Homer paused. "And maybe you're going swimming after them," he said, bringing his pistol out. "Stop fucking around. We found the lieutenant. You killed him. What did you do with the girl? Where's the girl?"

Brown had been standing in the middle of the room, glaring at Homer. He turned his head slightly to Smith and said something, the tone of which sounded like—*what the fuck do we do now?*

"You killed that soldier, now where's the girl!" Homer shouted.

As the ship rocked while turning, Smith, crouching like a full-back, lunged at Brown. hurling him toward Homer. He grabbed the two pistols and immediately started shooting, all in one motion. He was adept at handling the guns.

To Homer it was a blur, as if in slow motion. He hadn't expected it to come to this. The bullets from Smith's guns started spraying all over. Homer regained his footing and started firing in the direction of John Smith as soon as he could. Once committed, his anger at this man and the whole incident of hijacking his ship turned to fury.

Both he and Smith fired wildly, neither setting their stance for proper aiming.

John Brown suffered the most. One or two of the bullets from Smith's guns hit him in the back. He went down.

Smith paused, as Brown dropped to the floor. Smith was now exposed to Ernie.

Ernie bent over, with his head down and legs parted.

Smith swung toward him, his pistols barking and echoing in the confined cabin space.

Ernie stood his ground. He hesitated for an instant, then fired the shotgun directly into Smith's chest.

Homer watched Smith go down. He held his pistols ready. All was quiet. "Holy shit," he said, starting to breathe again. "You killed him."

They looked at the two men lying there. Smith was obviously dead. Brown stared at them with a frightened and pleading expression. For some reason, Homer's mind went to a scene from an old John Wayne movie where one of the bad guys he was holding stabbed the other. John Wayne's dispassionate response was, 'Your friend killed you'.

"You okay?" Ernie asked Homer.

"I'm okay. What about you?" Homer looked around. "Is everyone all right?"

"I think he nicked me," Ernie said, holding his side. Blood seeped between his fingers.

"Ernie, Goddamn it, where?"

Nick came up. "You took both of them down, Captain."

"No, Smith started shooting wildly before he got in position. He hit Brown in the back. Then Ernie fired on him. Ernie's hurt. We need that nurse."

"I'm fine," Ernie grunted. "It just grazed my skin."

"No, I want the nurse to look at it," Homer shouted.

"Sit down, Ernie," Nick said, "I'll take a look at it."

The lieutenants came down from their lookout post; their mouths open in disbelief.

Nick sent one of them to get Maria. "She's tending to Garcia in sickbay," he said.

A moan came from the cabin. Brown was moving on the floor, his eyes open.

"Captain," Ernie called out, "we've got to find that girl."

Terror showed on Brown's face.

Homer knelt beside him. "Mr. Brown, you were shot by Mr. Smith. We do not have a doctor on board. We have a passenger who is a very good nurse, but before I get her, I need some information. If you cooperate, you may still live. Can you speak?"

"What do you want to know?" John Brown asked.

"How many people does John Adams have? Are they all here on the yacht? Are any more still in Alaska? Are Davy and Maddy okay? Are there any people in Seattle? Is there poison in those boxes? You can start talking."

Minnie had followed Nick down, even after he told her to stay away. When she heard the shots, she rushed up to him.

"I'm okay," he assured her. "Everyone is okay, except the two guys. They're down, but Ernie was hit. I sent for Maria."

"Do you hear me Mr. Brown?" Homer yelled. "I'm waiting."

Brown coughed up some blood, becoming more terrified. "The boxes are not dangerous; only money and a piece of metal in the center. I don't know how many on the yacht, six or eight. I don't know of others."

"And where is the girl? Where is Major Flowers?"

Brown turned his head gesturing toward the closet.

Minnie opened the door. Angie lay sprawled on the floor with tape across her mouth. Her hands and feet were tied to a pipe.

"Oh, my God!" Minnie exclaimed. "What did they do to her?"

Nick removed the tape and cut her free.

Minnie cradled her shoulders and pulled her out on the cabin floor. She sat on the floor holding her.

Angie opened her eyes. She looked at Nick and Minnie, and started to weep.

"It's okay," Minnie said. "Everything is all right."

"You did good Mr. Brown by telling us where she is," Homer said. "What happened to her? What happened to her?"

"We did nothing but tie her up. He said he had plans for her."

"You're hurt bad, Mr. Brown. I will call the Coast Guard to come take you to a hospital, but not until I get more information."

Brown became more agitated. "The other one is with the ropes."

"Yes," Homer said, "we found him in the rope locker. You beat him up pretty bad."

"Smith did that," Brown said, becoming frantic.

"That's what I figured," Homer said. "Now, what can you tell me that I don't know? What are your friends on the yacht going to do? How are Davy and Maddy?"

Brown remained silent.

"I'm not calling the Coast Guard until you talk. Don't be afraid of John Adams or anyone else, because you'll never see them again. You're bleeding pretty bad, Mr. Brown."

"They will attack soon. They want the boxes. They will destroy your ship. They *will* kill."

"What about Davy and Maddy?"

"They have told the men near their house to kill them."

"Oh, shit!" Homer panicked. "Oh, shit." He rushed out of the cabin, leaving Brown on the floor. He stopped near Ernie to watch Maria as she examined him. "How is he?" Homer asked Maria.

"It's a flesh wound, similar to Luis Garcia's, but deeper into the flesh. Mr. McInnis has more flesh," Maria answered, smiling at Ernie. "I'll treat it and bandage it. It should be fine, but will be somewhat painful. Are any others hurt?"

"Thank you," Homer said. "But you can't do anything for the other two. I'd appreciate it if you just take Ernie to sick bay and treat him."

"What are you going to do, Homer?" Ernie asked, standing up.

"I've got to contact Davy. We're out of cell phone range. I'll use Nick's satellite phone or the marine radio."

Nick covered John Smith's body with a blanket and placed one on John Brown.

He put a pillow under Brown's head. Brown had passed out. He didn't look good. There was considerable blood on the floor.

Minnie continued to hold and stroke Angie. "It's okay," she whispered. "You're safe now. Everything is fine. Did they hurt you?"

Who is this woman? Nick mused, staring at Minnie. *Where did she come from?*

"No, they didn't hurt me," Angie answered, while sitting up. "The other asshole roughed me up a little and was going to rape me, but this one yelled at him, so he just felt me and tied me. Where is the other one?"

"Under the blanket," Nick said.

"Is he dead?"

Nick nodded.

"Good, the prick," Angie said. "Where is Luis? They took him."

"We found him. They banged him up a bit but he should be okay," Nick said. "One of the passengers, Maria Sanchez, is looking after him. She's a nurse."

Angie smiled. "They've been ogling each other. Can we get out of here? All this blood."

"Come on," Minnie said, helping her up and out of the cabin.

Angie smiled at her two lieutenants. "I'm okay," she assured them.

Homer told Newitt to clear out a few of the crew who had gathered. "Let's cordon off the area and start our deceased passenger procedure. This one's a little different, more unusual, though. Set someone up to keep people out of here, particularly passengers."

CHAPTER THIRTY-THREE

*H*omer followed Ernie up to sickbay. "What are you going to do, Homer? What an experience. I never thought it would come to that."

"I gave the bridge instructions to turn back south and put on more speed. They questioned it, in this fog, but they cranked it up a bit. We've got to get past these islands so we're in open sea. I don't know if we can outrun them though, those high priced yachts are built for speed. I can't get hold of Davy. If he's in the house, either he can't or won't answer the phone or he's not picking up his cell phone. His new phone doesn't have message service."

"Call his daughter," Ernie suggested. "She might have one of his neighbor's phone numbers."

"I can't, without telling her what's going on, and I can't do that."

"You've got to do something, Homer. They'll be sitting ducks. They might already be hostages. Call the police. Tell them you were talking to them at home and heard a thump and the line

186

went dead. Ask them to check it out. Everyone knows Davy and Maddy in that community."

Homer tried Davy's daughter in Carlsbad. "Uncle Homer, is that you?" Lorraine asked. "I can't get hold of Mom or Dad and I'm worried. I've been trying all day."

"Lorraine," Homer said. "I was calling to see if you've talked with them."

"Are they all right? Have you talked with them, Uncle Homer? Are they okay?"

"I've been trying them also. Listen, Lorraine, can you keep calling their new cell phone while I contact the police to go check their house? If you get them, and they're out somewhere, tell them to stay away from their house—not to go into their house until the police come."

"Why not? What's going on?"

"I can't tell you right now, Lorraine, but you must tell them that there's a serious problem at their house."

"What problem? What has happened, Uncle Homer? You're frightening me."

"Lorraine, please do this. I can't explain right now, but you have to do it—and keep trying until you get hold of them. I'm up to my eyeballs with a disastrous problem on the ship. Will you do that, Lorraine, and please try to call me after you get hold of them. I'm not certain you'll be able to get through to me because of telephone reception where we're at, but try."

"Okay, Uncle Homer, I will. You be safe on that old ship."

"Thank you, sweetheart."

Homer contacted the police in Kenai. "Hey, this is Captain Homer Dixon, a friend of Captain Davy Masters. I'm worried about some strange sounds I heard when I was cut off from him before, and I can't get him back. Do you know Captain Masters?"

"I remember you, Captain Dixon. This is Jim. We played poker last year at Davy's house. I'll go check on him myself."

"I'd appreciate it," Homer said.

━✠ ✠━

Davy was driving with Maddy on the street, approaching their house. "Your phone is vibrating," Maddy said.

"Damn," Davy swore. "I forgot to put the ringer back on."

Maddy picked up the phone. "Hi, Honey, how are you, what? Davy, stop the car."

"What do you mean, stop the car, there's our house. I'll pull into the driveway."

"No," Maddy yelled. "You have to stop here. Lorraine said you must stop. She has to tell you something." Maddy passed the phone to Davy.

"Dad, thank God I got hold of you. I just talked with Uncle Homer. He found out something and said, absolutely, do not go into the house. The police are on the way."

Davy stared at the house. Someone was standing at his kitchen window. A man looked out, then backed away. The front door of Davy's house opened. The man held a gun in his hand.

"Who is that?" Maddy yelled. "Is that a gun?"

The man looked up the street at Davy. He pointed the gun at them, lowered it, and sprinted to a car that was moving slowly from the other end of the street.

Maddy gasped.

Davy sat motionless, then reacted. "Talk to your mother, Lorraine," Davy said into the phone. "I've got to drive." He tossed the phone to Maddy, swung the car around, and headed away from his house.

"Lorraine, oh my God, oh my God, a man just came out of our house with a gun. They've started following us." Maddy started to sob.

"Mom, I heard. Tell Dad to get away fast. Uncle Homer said he was calling the police. How did he know about them? What's going on? Are you getting away?"

"We were getting away, but now they're catching up. I think your father knows more about this than he's told me."

Davy headed for the populated area near Sterling Highway but suddenly turned off on an unlit dirt road leading to the cliffs that overlook the beach.

"Davy, what are you doing? Where are we going?"

"I'm doing what has to be done."

Maddy put the phone on speaker. "Dad, Uncle Homer said the police were coming."

"Well, they're not here. We can't wait for them while these guys have their way."

"What do you mean, have their way? What are they going to do?" Maddy asked, her voice rising in panic.

"Quiet, now, both of you," Davy commanded. The dust rose off the road. It clouded the visibility behind them. Davy couldn't tell where the other car was.

"Davy, this road ends."

"I know it ends. Can you see how far back they are?"

"Mom, what's happening? Mom? Mom?"

"Davy, they're right on top of us. They've moved alongside. I see their gun."

"Good, good!" Davy nodded his head.

"What do you mean, good?" Maddy shrieked. "Their car hit us. They bumped us. They hit us again. Davy, what's happening?"

"Mom, Dad!" Lorraine screamed on the phone.

Maddy looked terrified, paralyzed with fear. She breathed in shallow gasps. They were broadsided again, right where Maddy was sitting. She screamed as the two cars scraped and slid against each other, metal tearing and glass breaking.

Davy lurched to the right, bounced off the other car, turned left and jammed on his brakes. The car skidded out of control, spun around on the gravel and climbed backwards up a small slope. It gradually stopped thirty yards from where the road ended.

The stillness was broken by Maddy's moans, sobs from Lorraine, and a crash followed by an explosion.

"Good," Davy gasped, trying to catch his breath. He eased the car down the slope and to the broken fence at the end of the road. He peered down the cliff at a car burning on the rocks.

Maddy sat there in shock, her body shaking, tears streaming down her face.

Davy put his arms around her and spoke with surprising calm, "I'm sorry, my love, I'm sorry. It's all over. Everything is fine." A problem solved, a burden lifted. He was transported back to his command days, on the bridge of his ship.

"Daddy, are you there?"

Davy picked up the phone. "Everything is fine, honey. The guys are gone and a police car has just pulled up. Let me call you back, sweetheart." Davy kissed Maddy and got out of the car.

His buddy Jim stood shaking his head near the edge of the abyss, peering down at the burning site. "Davy, what the hell happened here? I just called this in. We'll have a crowd here soon. Is Maddy all right? We got a call from your friend, Homer Dixon. I was heading out to your house and saw you being pursued by another car. The dust you guys were throwing up blinded me. I had to slow down, but I did see the bumping back and forth. I thought you were both going off that cliff. Listen, Davy, before that crowd gets here, will you tell me what just happened?"

Gazing down the hill, Davy paused—glancing at Jim he cleared his throat. "I don't know who they are. I saw them at my house. One of them aimed a gun at me as I drove up. I turned around as he jumped into a car to come after us. There was another guy driving."

"What were you doing on this road? Why didn't you come to the station in town?"

"I was trying to lose them on the back roads, but couldn't do it. They broadsided us, probably trying to make us stop. Then we went out of control."

The Police Lieutenant studied Davy's face. "What I saw were the lights of two cars banging into each other, then you putting on your brakes."

"Jim, all I know is what I've told you. I was out of control most of the time. I couldn't stop with them waving guns. I had to brake, I knew the road ended."

"And, obviously, they didn't know that," Jim said. "They realized it just before the fence and tried to stop, but it was too late. We'll leave it at that for now. Davy, I wasn't supposed to tell you this. They told me not to tell you. Coast Guard contacted me about a week ago. If those are the two guys I was told to keep an eye on, this is a problem. I'd better call the Coast Guard. And, Davy, don't go back to your house until I get a police unit to check it out."

＝┥ ┝＝

Davy's phone rang when they arrived home that evening. "Davy, where the hell have you been?" Homer shouted. "Where are you? Don't go back to your house! Did you talk with Lorraine?"

"Okay, calm down. We're back in our house. I got rid of the bastards, Homer. We have two less bandits to worry about. They're dead, both of them. Here's what happened." Davy and Homer exchanged details of their day's encounters. "You're still in deep shit," Davy said. "What're you going to do? What's Coast Guard going to do?"

"I don't know, Davy. I've got some ideas, but I can't tell you on the phone. It's a good thing, what you did. From what I found out, they were supposed to get rid of you, kill you, fly to Ketchikan, charter a boat and meet us here. Now that you're a little safer up there, we can talk more often. I'll keep you up-to-date. Call Lorraine to tell her you talked with me. I didn't tell her anything about what's going on here. This is a strange one, Davy, and it's not over yet."

Davy maintained his same story during follow-up interrogations. Coast Guard interceded to put the incident at rest. Davy's neighbors identified the automobile as one that had been seen numerous times on the quiet street the past couple of weeks. The car was rented at the airport in Anchorage, charged to a John Adams, who proved to be untraceable—his address and phone number could not be validated, although the credit card charges were accepted.

It was difficult for Davy to explain the situation to Maddy.

She railed against him until she was exhausted. She finally relented and admitted that his silence had shielded her from herself, protecting her from unbearable daily terror.

CHAPTER THIRTY-FOUR

October 23rd—11:30pm

October 23rd—11:30pm

Homer was sitting on the bridge dozing in his Captain's chair when he heard two things—a thump that emanated from the bowels of the ship, then a significant lack of background noise.

Anyone who has ever been to sea on a small ship will notice and expect a certain amount of vibration and background noise when the ship is underway. It's the norm. If this noise stops or changes, day or night, it will be evident immediately to almost all on board, and be of concern to those with at-sea experience.

"Captain, we've lost steering control and power," the helmsman shouted.

Ernie reached the bridge a few seconds later. He seemed pale, and was panting. "What happened?"

The speakerphone from the engine room lit up. "Bridge, we've had a main engine failure."

"What about the steering control?" Homer asked.

"I'll be damned," was the response. "The rudder control mechanism is smoking. It's on fire. Some oil is leaking out and it's burning."

"Sound the ship's alarm," Homer ordered. "Ernie, head for the engine room. Emergency station personnel will be on their way. Give me an assessment of the damage. Goddamn old ship, and Goddamn a company that won't pay for maintenance. Attention, all passengers," Homer announced on the PA system, "we've had a main engine failure. We'll be adrift until the problem is corrected. Regulations require that you prepare for lifeboats, but you should stay in your cabins until the notice is given to proceed to your life-boat station. Sea conditions are good, the best possible." He put the PA back. "Keep charting our position," Homer instructed the bridge watch. "I'm going down to the engine room. If I'm not back in fifteen minutes, repeat that message to the passengers."

Engine room smoke was permeating the lower deck passage-ways and the hold. "I can't see a fucking thing in here. Ernie, where are you?"

"Over here, Skipper. Put on this mask and goggles. Damn stuff burns your eyes."

"What happened?"

"When we cranked up the engines for more speed, they started heating up—not above normal limits, though. Engine room watch said he noticed some dirt on the deck near the engines but fig-ured it came from someone's shoes. With everything that's been going on it's possible that someone dumped sand or dirt in with the engine oil. Normally, that would destroy the engine in no time, but as old as they are, the clearance between the pistons and the cylinder walls is loose, so it took some time for the damage to build up. It was probably done earlier today when we were well south of Ketchikan."

"When was Smith's watch in the engine room?"

"Noon to four. Same as Brown's on the bridge."

"Well, we're adrift," Homer said. "What's the Chief Engineer's evaluation?"

"He can't give us one until we get things cleaned up from the fire and vent the smoke out of here."

"Adrift with no power, and no steering even if we had power," Homer said, summing it all up. "When was the last time we checked the mechanical steering override, meant for just such a situation?"

"Don't know, Captain," Ernie said, "But we can find out from the engine room logs. Sort of a moot point without ship's power. Remember, they never even responded to our request to install independently powered thrusters. I guess they didn't want to throw money away on a fifty-year-old rust bucket."

"I guess not, Ernie. Why don't you round up Nick and meet me on the bridge. We've got to take steps to protect the crew and passengers."

"Aye, Captain."

Not exactly what I'd planned, thought Homer on the way to the bridge. *I've got to re-evaluate.*

The three of them stood over the chart table. "We're drifting in the direction of these rock shoals." Homer pointed at the chart. "We've passed them hundreds of times but always at a safe distance. We could be lucky and miss them. If we do miss them, and if the wind and seas stay the same to keep our drifting constant, we'll have about fifteen hours before we hit beaches on a nearby island. The hull of this ship hasn't gone up a beach since World War II. I researched it once. It was in the South Pacific. It's been through a lot. What a history. Now it's going to end."

"What's the plan, Skipper?"

"Okay, Ernie. The hull has deteriorated to a thin piece of rusty crap, riddled with holes. That's why we have to keep the bilge pumps going around the clock, even in port. Whether we hit the rocky shoals or a smooth sandy beach, the bottom will rip out like tissue paper. At least on a beach we could just walk ashore. If we go aground on the shoal rocks, the ship won't last long. We'd have to use the lifeboats to take us to one of the islands. In either case you'll end up losing your trucks and equipment, Nick."

"Not a problem, Captain. It's all insured, and most of it was offloaded in Ketchikan."

"What *is* a problem," Homer said, hesitating, "is the safety of the passengers and crew, particularly if we have to go to lifeboats. I'll need you to take the lead on that, Nick. Ernie and I will be up to our asses with everything else."

"I'm already on it," Nick assured him. "I'll assign a mix of passenger and crew to the lifeboats and the inflatable life rafts. We'll use experienced seamen to run the lifeboat engines. I'll ask Major Flowers and her two able lieutenants to assist. Garcia is still recovering. We might even get the Marsden Eagle Scouts to help. I'm less worried about Garcia than I am about Matilda Burke. She's going to be a handful, but Minnie will be with her, as will Maria Sanchez."

"Good. Try to calm the passengers. Before that, get the deck crew to work over the lifeboats and rafts. They should start up all the engines, top off fuel and load supplies. The inspection that the Coast Guard did was perfunctory. I don't trust those boats. They haven't been in the water in ages."

"Aye, Captain, I'm off to it."

"Well, what do you think, Ernie?"

"I think we should kill Smith and Brown all over again. Sons-a-bitches. And I think we're lucky the company pulled those officer trainees off and we got Nick instead. Can you imagine having two company spies on board while this is going on? They'd have second-guessed us and recorded our every move. Brown wasn't a bad guy. I don't know how he got mixed up with the others. Too bad, he didn't make it." Ernie said, as he rambled on, "he did try to help us out. That Smith was a snake."

"You'll never meet Adams, Ernie. He's different from all his people. He's smart, smooth and devious. Even after all the conversations I've had with him, I still can't figure him out. There's something driving him. Some reason he's doing this. It's more than the money. This was his back-up plan all along. That's why he didn't just wait and meet the shipment in Seattle. Now there's a crack in his well-planned venture. If Davy and Maddy are really safe, and he has no one on the beach to do them harm, he's lost the hammer he's had over our heads. Now he won't trust us at all. So, he put Plan B into effect, and Plan B makes us sitting ducks." Homer paused and shook his head.

"My last conversation with him was before Davy eliminated his threat, and before we dispatched ours on board. He has to know that his two guys in Kenai are dead. He hasn't had any reports from them and he can't contact them. But, he must have seen something on the Internet or CNN or other news outlets about the accident, and heard Davy's name. No doubt about it. And he can't get hold of Smith or Brown. I keep both their radiophones in my pocket. That they both keep ringing means he doesn't have another 'plant' on board, another spy to keep him informed. I've wondered about that. He must be frantic at this point. We're a big target on his radar—a familiar target. When he showed me the bridge on the yacht, I saw two new sophisticated radars."

"And you've been studying our radar screens for hours," Ernie said.

"Ours are old, but they still work. I can recognize their radar blip."

"I can, too," Ernie said. "And so can most of the men on the bridge."

"What we have to do is keep someone on the radar around the clock. We've got to know when they're getting close. The timing of the engine room sabotage will throw them off. They won't know exactly when our engines went bad. And, there's no one to call them with the report. Even if they knew, I don't know if they're smart enough to track our drift based on the wind and sea conditions."

"This radar screen is flickering," Ernie said. "And so is the other one—and the lights are dimming."

"Bridge, engine room," came a call from below.

"Engine room, this is the Captain."

"Captain, we're losing the generators. We've switched from our normal units to back-ups, but they've all been tampered with. And because we have these back-up units on board, we don't have equipment for generator repairs."

"What about the gas-powered portable unit?"

"I'm heading for it now. It's kept pretty much stored away. We've rarely started it except during shipyard overhauls. I found it, Captain. Whoever screwed up the other equipment probably overlooked it. It looks like an outboard motor."

"See if you can get it working."

"Aye, Captain, but it can't power the needs of the ship."

"We only need it for electronics, and some lights. No heat or galley use. Can that be done?"

"I think so, Captain, yes sir."

"Ernie," Homer said, "If we can't spot them before they get here we may be in deep shit. Even with a constant radar watch, we need a lookout on the bridge around the clock, an extra man to do nothing but scan the sea for the motherfuckers. Their phones have stopped ringing. They know the score. With the fog lifting, we make a big target. If they sneak up on us we're in trouble."

"I'll get someone up here on the double, Skipper."

"Ernie, you look like hell. Sometimes your face is beet red and other times you're white as a sheet. What's happening?"

"I haven't had much sleep, and it's getting to me."

"What about your wound?"

"I'm taking so much pain killer I don't feel a thing. That medicine could be part of the problem. I'll ask the nurse about it."

CHAPTER THIRTY-FIVE

October 24ᵗʰ—3:30am

*N*ick entered an empty lounge, not expecting to find passengers. The galley was feeding breakfast to a few in the crew's mess up for the four to eight watch, and others up to deal with the engine room problems. If any of the passengers were awakened during the night, they went back to their rooms. *Good, no panic to deal with.* Luis Garcia and Doc were asleep in sickbay. He wanted to check on Tilly, but decided to wait until Minnie could go with him. *I'll let her get some sleep.* He took a cup of coffee out on deck.

Peter Marsden stood at the port side rail. "You're up early," he said to Nick.

"And so are you, Peter. We have some mechanical problems."

"I've noticed. Is our drift out of control or can we give it any power to keep a heading?"

"Are you a seaman, Peter?"

"I've spent some time at sea. I heard the noise below decks, probably the engine room, then a loss of engine and propeller noise. The boys slept right through it. Am I right?"

"You're right on, Peter, that's what happened. We're in an uncontrolled drift. There are some rocky shoals ahead. If we miss that, and our drift stays steady, we'll end up on a sandy beach island about thirty miles beyond."

"And if we hit the shoals?" Peter asked.

"We'll have to use the lifeboats. And if that happens, I may need you and your sons to help out. Are you willing to do that?"

"Absolutely, Nick. We'll help in any way we can. If the sea stays as calm as it is now, we should be in good shape. I was on a cruise ship in the North Atlantic many years ago—terrible sea conditions. One of the main engines blew up. We were at lifeboat stations for about six hours while they cleaned up the engine room and got the other engine on line. The ship was rolling about forty degrees until we had the power to head us into the seas. The captain told us the next day that he came very close to issuing an abandon ship order. Fortunately, the ship's rolling was so bad we couldn't have gotten the lifeboats in the water anyway. I couldn't imagine being in a lifeboat in those sea conditions."

"That must have been hairy," Nick said. "Even if the sea picks up when the fog lifts, and it has started to lift, we're close enough to islands and the mainland shore line, that we should still be okay. We *will* get some wind, choppy seas and swells, but nothing our boats can't handle. And that's where I'll need your help, Peter. We've got sixteen passengers, counting my friend Minnie, and nineteen in the crew. That's thirty-five total. We've got four lifeboats, but only three I'd trust. We've got four inflatable life rafts. The First Mate and his crew have checked them out."

"Yes, I was watching them. They're still at it."

"They'll evaluate the lifeboats, fuel them and start the engines. Then inflate the others, check them out, and if all the out-board engines work, we're okay. If we can get six boats in the water—that'll be about six in each boat. The problem is boat drivers. I don't have enough coxswains with experience. Will your sons run one boat each?"

Peter Marsden's mouth tightened as he pondered the question. "Nick, I've seen what my boys can do and I'd trust them over anyone else. There are two things. The danger of what we'll be doing—but even so, I'd rather have Jacob and Jonas at the helm. The important thing would be their judgment. They're only sixteen. They don't have the experience factor. That's why I'm hesitating."

"We'll have all the boats in tandem or attached abeam," Nick said. "I would not let any one boat go off alone. I know what you mean by the experience factor. When I went through dive school, I was picked by the instructor to work with him on an exercise in about thirty feet of water. We were in hard-hat gear, full suit, weighted belt, heavy shoes, and all. I was lowered to the bottom and waited. After a while I got tired of waiting so I added air to my suit, enough to inflate it and raise me back to the surface. Wrong move, and I was a lot older than sixteen. It was strictly a no-no. You can lose control of your dive. Your arms can expand with air to where you can't reach your control valves. Boy, did I catch hell for that. That being said, what do you think?"

Peter chuckled. "I remember going through similar dumb things. Tell you what. I'll go with one of my boys, and if you could let my other son drive the boat you're in, it's a deal."

"Thanks, Peter. That'll be a great help."

"Nick, I'd like to ask you another question. What was all that shooting about? I also know guns."

Nick hesitated. "Do you remember that seaman we escorted off the ship in Juneau during the morning all-hands meeting? He was drunk and belligerent. He met us in Ketchikan and asked forgiveness. The Captain relented. He acted up again. We heard from his buddy that he had guns. When he was confronted in his cabin, he literally came up shooting. It was lucky for the Captain and First Mate that he was drunk again and the ship was rolling. His wild shots killed his friend and hit the First Mate on his side. Ernie got off a shotgun blast that put him away."

"Jesus. How's the First Mate doing?"

"He's hobbling, but he should be okay."

"And the engineer who fell into the rope locker? This is a small ship, Nick. You hear things."

"He's also doing fine."

Peter seemed to study Nick for a few moments. "Nick, I'm only concerned about the safety of my boys."

"So am I Peter, believe me, for the three of you and for all the others on-board."

Nick headed for his cabin to wake Minnie. She was sleeping on her back, purring slightly. He lifted off the covers and gently pulled her nightshirt up to her neck. *Damn, I'm a lucky guy.* He watched as one of her hands started roaming her body. He took both her hands in his. She woke, grabbed his neck and pulled him down to her. He kissed her then pulled away. "We don't have time for this. I never thought I'd say that. The ship's got problems. We've got lots to do. We need to check on Tilly Burke and make the rounds of the other passengers."

Minnie held on to Nick's neck, wearing a mock pout on her lips.

He pulled back, lifting her up and out of bed. "Go wash up." Watching her as she walked away, he smiled, "you have the most perfect ass."

"Lot of good it does you now," she said, sticking her tongue out at him.

After Minnie dressed, they headed for Tilly's cabin.

They had difficulty getting a response from Tilly. After a number of knocks and inquiries, Nick used his passkey.

Tilly lay in bed moaning slightly. The cabin felt steaming hot. She was sweating. "Something's happening," she said. "I don't feel so good."

"You stay with her," Nick instructed Minnie. "I'll get Maria."

Maria arrived a few minutes later. After examining Tilly, she was concerned. "Tilly has started to dilate. I'll have to stay with her.

Could you ask my mother to come here?" Maria said to Minnie. "She'll be able to bring me some things and get us food."

"Damn," Nick exclaimed, walking out with Minnie. "That will really complicate things. You get Mrs. Sanchez while I continue my rounds of the passengers."

Nick caught the Talbots and Wilsons in the lounge and asked if he could join them. As the oldest on board, he needed to evaluate how they would approach the ship's situation. Their breakfast conversation put him at ease. Both couples had had the experiences that gave them the self-confidence to question, and accept and function in an emergency situation.

As he finished breakfast, Angie and Lieutenants York and Stevens came in to eat. "Morning guys," Nick greeted, smiling at all three.

Angie smiled back at Nick, not flirtatiously but more thankfully. "Minnie here?" she asked. Overnight, it seemed, she and Minnie had become friends.

"Minnie and Maria are tending to Tilly. How is Luis this morning?" Nick realized that with everything that had gone on in the short time since leaving Juneau, all of them had bonded. It's good for what they might have to face soon.

"He's a tough guy," York responded. "Should be up and around pretty soon."

"Just like Major Flowers," Sandy Stevens added, looking at Angie. "She's a tough guy, too."

Angie nodded her head and smiled. Her eyes watering a bit.

Nick gave her a quick hug.

Maria and Minnie came in with Mr. and Mrs. Sanchez. Minnie went over to sit with Angie. "Tilly is very close to giving birth. I'll have to stay with her," Maria said.

"Maria?" Nick asked, "Has Minnie explained the situation we have with the ship's power, and if so, could you tell your parents and let them know we may have to abandon ship into lifeboats?"

"Minnie has told me." Maria nodded. "My father will understand and my mother will accept what my father says and what I say.

However, as you probably know by now, my father will want to ask many questions. I may need your help."

"Anytime—just let me know."

"At my hospital, we have an emergency helicopter landing spot on the roof. Does the Canadian Coast Guard have helicopters for this purpose? I'm worried about Tilly."

"Absolutely. They should have the same services as the U. S. Coast Guard. We'll try to contact them. At present, a low hanging fog complicates that scenario. When the fog dissipates, our plan will be for the Coast Guard not only to rescue Tilly but the rest of us as well. There's a good chance, though, that we'll have to transfer Tilly to a lifeboat."

"I may need a lot of help." Maria sighed.

"You'll have it, Maria. The Corpsmen and Minnie will help and, if you need them, there are two women in the crew."

"I will also need medical supplies," Maria added.

"I was about to mention that. Please get together with Doc as soon as you can. Empty out all of the stores in sickbay that could be of use, not only for Tilly but also for everyone else on board. I'll talk with Doc, also. It's important to do it quickly. We don't know how soon an emergency will overtake us."

Nick left the lower decks and found Homer with Ernie on the bridge.

"Good," Homer greeted him. "Let's have a three way swap of status reports. I'll start. Here it is mid-morning. No sign of the yacht yet. Every once in a while, Smith or Brown's phone rings. They must be getting frantic, but they'll find us. It's only a matter of time. We can forget about the main engine. We don't have equipment on board to open it and make repairs. Our generators are gone also, as you've found out if you tried to get serious food from the galley. We're down to a single propane stove for coffee, eggs and such. The electric ovens are out. They've got the emergency gas generator working. It'll power some of the electronics on the bridge, including one of the radars. As if that isn't enough, the bad news is that we're drifting straight for the rocky shoals." He shook his head and gazed out through the port window.

Homer continued, "I'd estimate about four or five more hours. At least it'll be daylight when it happens. So, we have that much time for preparations and abandon ship requirements. I even thought about putting all the lifeboats in the water using them to try to pull us slightly off our present course, so we'd miss the shoals. But I don't think it'll work and we'd waste gas we might need. Also, we don't want to take the chance of smashing any of the boats on the rocks. Okay, Ernie, your turn."

"All of the crew have been briefed, including some who have a difficult time with English. I took a few of them up to sickbay so Luis Garcia could help out. We have six boats ready to go in the water, three lifeboats and three Zodiacs. The Zodiacs have been inflated. The motors on all six boats are working and gassed up. We had enough gas tanks to put a spare on each boat. The crew knows their emergency boat stations, but Nick and I will need to coordinate who goes in each boat. We'll have a mix of passengers and crew in each boat. If and when we have to go to the boats it would be best, of course, to do it in daylight. We can't count on any shipboard light. Our flashlights will have to do."

"High tide will happen between six and midnight," Homer added. "We may even pass over the shoal rocks. That would be good. If the rocks do put us aground in high tide, we'll be high and dry on top of the rocks in low tide."

"In that case," Ernie said, "We'll need to launch all the boats at maximum high tide. They'll be able to find good water between the rocks."

"So," Homer concluded, "We need to go to lifeboat stations two hours from now. Lots of preparations plus food, water and supplies."

"And survival suits," Nick said. "I'll use the two second lieutenants to help me cut open the boxes. We'll haul the suits up to the main deck at the port side gangway. Everyone on board will need to wear one, even if no one gets wet."

Ernie added, "If the ship maintains its present heading and the port side hits the shoals first, and if we have clear water beside the ship, we'll lower each boat with its driver, then we should be able to board the boats using the gangway."

"Sounds good, Ernie. Nick," Homer said, "Pile up all that phony money before we totally abandon ship. We'll dump it overboard after all the boats are clear. If not, the yacht people will come aboard, gather it all and continue with business as usual."

"Captain, I think we should burn it. If we dump it, it'll be floating all over the ocean and some will go ashore."

"Good point. Set up a simple system for me to torch it just before I leave the ship. That'll keep them, and anyone coming aboard after that, from roaming the ship to collect souvenirs."

"Some other things, Captain," Nick said. "We need to pack those nuggets of metal, or whatever, from the center of each box. Coast Guard will want them. I think we'll find one in each box, or something just as strange. I'll use the Army Engineers to help me. They have minimal personal gear and all their work equipment is Government Issue, all easily replaceable."

"So," Homer seemed pensive now. "I assume all the passengers have been briefed?"

"That's right, Captain, except for Tilly Burke. When and if we have to move her, she should be okay."

"Thank you, guys." Homer spoke, in a tense, almost emotional, way. "We've got a full schedule over the next few hours. If any of us should think of anything else, or if the parameters change, let the others know."

"Captain," the radar watch shouted, "I see something!"

CHAPTER THIRTY-SIX

October 24th—Noon

Homer, Ernie and Nick went to the radar.
"It sure looks like their blip," Homer said. "Good work," he said to the seaman. "They seem to be about sixteen miles away. I'm going to plot their position. We should know in about fifteen minutes if they're closing in on us, or haven't picked us up and are continuing on the route to Seattle, searching for us. We can't send out a Mayday to the Canadian Coast Guard or even call by satellite phone. Adams' crew would pick up the return messages we'd receive. They'd head right for us and probably beat the Coast Guard. We're between a rock and a hard place. You heard what Brown said, that they'll come aboard and kill. At some point, they will realize they've passed us by. Before we dispatched Smith and Brown, they must have fed Adams our location at least every hour."

"It looks like the distance is widening," Ernie said.

"I'll be damned!" Homer looked surprised. "If that is them, it's about eighteen miles. Okay, I'm going to keep monitoring this screen. I'll let you know if I see another similar blip, or if this one turns and heads for us. You two begin the countdown planning we discussed."

Nick and Ernie started to leave the bridge. "I could get some people to give you a hand," Ernie said to Nick.

"The only things I need are some sharp knives or razor cutters and a lot of big plastic garbage bags. We'll use the Army Engineers. No one should see that money and certainly not the prize in the center of each box. We'll cut out the exposure suits, seventy-six for the people left on board. Hopefully, the suits will be in various sizes, because we'll need them. We should take all of them on the boats, just in case."

"Ernie, you look like you're dragging," Homer noted, with concern. "You've got to take it easy."

"I am dragging, Skipper. It's hell to get old, and this scratch that Smith gave me doesn't help any."

"None of us got any sleep last night," Homer said. "That can't do you any good."

Ernie glanced at Homer. "How about you, Skipper? Can I get you any help?"

Homer peered at Ernie closely. With everything happening, he'd neglected to think about Ernie's wounds, assuming he was okay. "Thanks anyway, Ernie. I want to stay on top of it until we know what our course of action will be. We won't take Smith and Brown with us. I'd just as soon they disappear. We'll work on that problem later."

"It looks like you've got everything worked out, Captain," Ernie said.

"Not everything. Not nearly everything. You look like shit, Ernie. Is that new blood, or the remains of the wound? Get Maria to check you out again, and change your clothes."

"I'm a big boy, Captain," Ernie responded, forcefully, unlike his usual controlled responses as a subordinate, and as a friend.

Homer stared at him for a moment, and at Nick, who was listening to the exchange. He looked as if wanted to respond, but just shook his head and gazed back down at the radar screen.

"I'll get you the box cutters and plastic bags," Ernie told Nick. "Let me know if you need other help."

"Once we get the suits topside, and if you're ready, we should have an all-hands meeting, well prior to approaching the shoals," Nick suggested.

Nick left the bridge. He located and briefed Minnie, Maria, and the three engineers. Angie said she was able to help. Nick told Maria that right after his work in the hold they would bring Tilly up on deck and prepare one of the boats for her. It took them ninety minutes to cut open the boxes, haul the suits aside, bundle the money, and package the nuggets in a few boxes. All the nuggets in one box made too heavy a load.

During that time, Homer came down to tell Nick and Ernie, that sure enough, the yacht had changed course and was heading for them. "It depends on what we encounter at the shoals," Homer explained. "Latest calculation has us there about three pm and they should get there about two to three hours later—after dark. In some respects, it's safer for us to be high and dry on the rocks, so they can't get too close, or they risk sinking the yacht. Since they've spotted us, I've sent a few messages to the Canadian Coast Guard citing our location and problems, and stressing the need to notify the U. S. Coast Guard because of the type of cargo we're hauling. Others could have picked up the SOS messages. The lingering fog and about fourteen hours of nighttime darkness will complicate any rescue attempt." *Sinking the yacht,* Homer mused.

"What if we miss the shoals and avoid getting grounded?" Ernie asked.

"We'll be sitting ducks for half a day, drifting where the weather takes us. If it stays constant we'll hit an island, a much bigger landing site than the shoals." Homer took Nick aside while Ernie's crew hauled the suits up on deck.

Nick studied Homer, trying to judge the seriousness of the questions he was being asked. "It can be done," Nick, said.

"Can it be done safely?"

"It can be done," Nick repeated.

⇒+ +⇐

The loudspeaker blared a call for all hands, crew and passengers, to proceed out on deck, no exceptions. "We are an exception," Maria told Tilly in her cabin.

"I'm Captain Homer Dixon," Homer announced, standing on deck. "You've been briefed either by First Mate McInnis or Second Mate Banner about the mechanical problems we're having in the engine room and the possible need to abandon ship." Homer paused to allow his statement to sink in and to let some others get the information translated.

He didn't mention the malicious damage done in the engine room, though most of the crew knew of it. "The Canadian Coast Guard has been contacted. Other nearby ships may have heard the call for help. Using our hand held GPS units, we know exactly where we are. We are fortunate that the weather and the seas are calm, but continued fog, although breaking up somewhat, will hamper rescue efforts." Homer paused again.

The passengers murmured to each other, as they waited for him to continue.

As with his routine pre-sail meetings, he could judge the reaction to what he was saying by observing the consternation in the faces of some of the passengers and crew. *Years ago, I wouldn't have been able to judge anything.* "We're drifting very slowly, but out of control. If we should hit anything, even moving this way, it could damage the ship. If the damage is severe we'd need to go to lifeboats. We will do that only as a last resort. I'll let Mr. McInnis and

Mr. Banner discuss these procedures. Let me mention an incident we had on board last night. Two in the crew were drunk in their cabin. Things must have gotten out of control. With the illegal firearms they had on board, they ended up killing each other. Very sad."

Some of those who knew the actual events grimaced and nodded.

"I see many of you are looking at the survival suits. There are twice as many suits as there are people on board. They are a precaution for general exposure. We don't expect anyone to get wet. If we do go to lifeboats, everyone must wear one. They are waterproof and will protect against hypothermia, as in freezing." Homer smiled. "This is not the Titanic. Don't even think about making the comparison. Remember; be careful always, we don't want anyone to get hurt. Be well, and God bless you all."

"You too, Captain."

His casual, confident talk calmed almost all. Those not fully convinced or not fully cognizant of the situation would hang on to the coattails of others.

Luis Garcia was sitting in a chair with Doc assigned to look after him.

Angie looked somewhat recovered from her ordeal, but seemed more subdued than usual.

Tilly would be briefed and handled separately.

Homer departed, signaling his bridge quartermaster to follow.

Ernie repeated the lifeboat drill that each of the passengers and crew had been through. This time they all seemed more interested.

"For the crew, you have no routine work to do, at this point, except care for yourselves, unless otherwise instructed by a leading petty officer, myself, Nick, or the Captain. We'll need to load water, food, ropes, tools, walkie-talkies, supplies, etc. on the boats."

Nick took over at this point. "The first and most important thing each of you, passengers and crew, must do, is find a survival suit that fits. Do it now. Try them on so you know how. You will need to be wearing a suit before you get into a lifeboat. Mr. McInnis and I will assist you. I'm putting mine on now so you can see how it's done. Once you find one that fits, take it off and hold on to it. It's better to find one that's a little big on you than to not be able to close it securely."

They listened intently.

"We've got other things to cover now. Please listen. Go to your cabins. Get any valuables and medicines you may have. Get your lifejackets and other lifesaving equipment. Adjust them, so they'll fit over your survival suits. The suits have buoyancy, but the life-jackets will add to it. The suits have large pockets. Fill them up. You may take a backpack, belly bag, or small carry-on bag. I'm sorry, but the boats will not have room for suitcases. If any of you, crew or passengers, have something large that you feel could not possibly be left behind, ask Mr. McInnis or me. But please, it must be something that is not replaceable."

CHAPTER THIRTY-SEVEN

October 24ᵗʰ—3pm

Homer paced back and forth from the radar screen on the bridge, **to the outer bridge deck,** trying to spot the rocky shoals. He switched the radar from the close-in range to spot the rocks—and to see if the rocks would even show up on the radar, then switch the radar to a greater range to plot the progress of the *Mother's Love* yacht. He stationed two of the crew with binoculars as high as possible on the *Eagle* to scan the sea for the mass of shoal rocks barely above the surface of the water. There was no doubt of the yacht's pursuit. They were still two to three hours away. Less, if the *Eagle* were to get stopped by the rocks. The limited range walkie-talkie radios he took from Smith and Brown still rang from time to time. At some point, he would answer them.

If the GPS and charts were accurate, they should almost be on the rocks. As the time for high tide neared, most of the rocks would be hidden below the surface of the water. *I've got to announce it now.* "Listen up, everyone on board. You must all sit down and hold on. We may be hitting submerged rocks soon. If so, the ship will lurch. Hold on. Do it now." Homer raced out on deck.

The two lookouts were yelling for him.

Staring over the port side, Homer saw the rocks. "Don't try to come down yet," he yelled at them. "Just hold on." He went back inside the bridge. "Everyone hold on now," he announced. He felt the first subtle scrape. The noise built to a roar. The *Eagle* screamed and writhed, as if convulsing in violent death throes, then grew quiet and calm.

As soon as the *Eagle* stopped shaking, Ernie dragged himself up to the bridge.

"Ernie, get your damage control crew down to the hold.

"All hands, including passengers, report any injuries," Homer announced. He stood there, breathing deeply, with a hand over his closed eyes, shaking his head. "Well, old girl, we've come a long way. I didn't think it was going to end like this."

The two men on the bridge looked at Homer, and at each other.

After a few minutes, Smith or Brown's walkie-talkie radio vibrated in his pocket. Homer looked at it and nodded. He let it ring. *They know the Eagle is dead in the water.* When the second radio vibrated he picked it up. "Well, Mr. Adams, you've accomplished what you wanted. We're powerless and up on the rocks."

"I told you I would get my way, Captain."

"Yes, you did. What are you going to do with us?"

Ignoring the question, Adams asked, "What have you done with my two men?"

"They're indisposed."

"As you are going to be. You may have dispatched my two men in Alaska, and the two on your ship, but I still know where your friend Davy's daughter and granddaughter live."

"You harm either of them and I'll make it my life's work to pursue you to the ends of the earth and gut you like a chicken," Homer shouted, gesturing for his bridge people to go below deck.

"My, my, Captain, you talk big for a man out of options."

"I'm never out of options, Mr. Adams," Homer said, calming. "You should know that by now."

"We will see, we will see. Prepare your ship for boarding. I expect your men to assist me with off-loading the boxes. No one will get hurt if you cooperate."

"Why do I have a problem believing you, Mr. Adams?"

"Be sensible. I cannot kill everyone on board, and if I harmed anyone, you would have the Coast Guard after me."

"When do you expect to be here, Mr. Adams?"

"You can judge that from your radar, Captain, as I am certain you have been doing up to now."

"My radar is erratic due to limited power. Your Mr. Smith did a good job of destroying my generators as well as the main engine."

"I'm glad he was able to do his job before he became indisposed. We will see you soon, Captain." Adams signed off.

Homer gazed at his watch. About an hour of daylight remained. "For everyone," he announced, "proceed on deck and prepare to board lifeboats. Wait until directed by Mr. McInnis or Mr. Banner."

Ernie and Nick came up to the bridge. Ernie looked ashen and seemed out of breath. "...and the bilge is flooded. The bottom appears to be ripped open. There's some water in the hold. We'll ship more water until high tide starts ebbing. By morning, in low tide, we'll be high and dry on the rocks."

"We've got a lot to do before dark, Ernie. Rearrange the boat plan. I'm going to need the smallest Zodiac left back for my use."

Ernie and Nick looked at Homer.

"What the fuck are you talking about, Homer? You're not going down with this ship."

"I don't intend to, that's why I need the boat."

"If you're staying back to deal with those motherfuckers, I'm staying with you," Ernie shouted, "And don't pull that shit about, *you're the Captain and I have to do like you say*, crap."

"Thanks, Ernie, but what about your injuries? You're hobbling. I thought you only got hit on the side."

"I got nicked on the leg, too. No big deal."

"I want the nurse to look at you and tell me you're okay," Homer ordered.

"You're both crazy," Nick said, before Ernie left. "You've had your gun fight. You can't take on a whole bunch of madmen, and you don't know what they've got to fight with."

"We're not going to fight them," Homer confided after Ernie had gone. "I've got to prepare the *Eagle* for burial. Nick, how much C-4 do you have in your truck?

"Not much, but enough for anything you might have in mind."

"Is that the same stuff you'll use for the other job?"

"No. I've got other pre-made devices for that."

"You've got to set it up for me, Nick, and you've got to give me the know-how to do the job. Are you okay with that, Nick, and will you have time to do it before you leave with the boats?"

"Yes, I'm okay with that. Homer, I was trained to recognize and destroy the bad guys. I've been away from it for many years, but the intensity of that training stays with you. I'll make sure I can get it done before I take off with the boats. I'll get on it right after I check with Ernie and talk to Minnie. Come down in about an hour, and even if I'm not done, we'll go over it while I finish."

CHAPTER THIRTY-EIGHT

October 24ᵗʰ—4:30pm

*E*veryone gathered for boarding the boats.
Nick re-assigned personnel loading—setting aside Homer's boat, while Ernie directed the handling of water, food, and necessary equipment.

Maria and Minnie brought a frightened Tilly topside. They put on her survival suit, placed her on a mattress in a lifeboat, and stayed with her. The boat was swung out and lowered by the davits.

The plan was for all the others to use the gangway or a rope ladder to get on their boat. The gangway was lowered until it just touched the water. This let the boats come close enough for personnel and equipment loading. Ernie had tried to vary the process to the more unsafe procedure of lowering people from the deck while sitting in their boat. It did not work well.

Once Tilly's boat was in the water, Minnie climbed back on deck, wondering where Nick was. She found him in the hold with the Captain. They were discussing explosives as she approached. "What's going on?" she asked, startling both of them.

"What are you doing here?" Nick asked. "I'm showing the Captain some things."

Minnie just stared at him, her expression intense.

"Oh, God," Nick said to Homer. "She has the uncanny ability to see right through me."

"Fucking-A, Banner, I do. What's going on?"

"Nick's showing me how to set off these charges on the *Eagle,*" Homer, said, "to keep the yacht people from taking what they want. So, is this all I need, Nick?"

"That's it, Captain."

"Thanks, Nick, I'm going up to the bridge. Be careful with that stuff and let me know the details."

"Will do, Captain."

Minnie looked at Nick with a fearful expression. "Be careful with what? Aren't those the same charges we used on the job? What are you going to do? And why do you have your dive suit out?"

"I've got some tasks to do."

"Does it involve diving?"

"Yes."

"Since when do you go diving alone, and at night, and in a treacherous place like this? You always told us no one dives alone, and that was in a safe place like the Coast Guard pier in Juneau." The pitch and intensity of her voice went up. Tears streamed down her face. "I'm coming with you, you motherfucker. Don't do this to me! Don't you do this to me," she wailed.

Nick embraced her, placing her head on his shoulder. "It's risky. I'm best doing it alone. I don't want to have to be concerned about you."

"I don't care what you're doing. I'm coming with you," she said, holding him tight. Gradually, she calmed. She pulled her head back to look at him. "I'm coming with you."

He stared back at her and smiled. "Okay, my love, okay. Get your gear out."

She kissed his face a few times.

He explained what they were going to do, as she prepared.

Nick checked each piece of equipment and each item they were taking. He confirmed their course of action to Minnie by starting again, this time speaking out loud as he re-checked item by item. *That's good,* he thought. *Had I been alone I probably wouldn't have done that.* Sure enough, the gauge on Minnie's air tank showed it was a little low on air. He added a dual breathing device to his tank, just in case. He didn't want them to have to swim back on the surface.

Minnie calmed slowly from their encounter, yet still breathed deeply, with an occasional sob erupting from her chest. She glanced over at Nick while they prepared for the dive. "You're pissed," she said.

Laying out their peripheral equipment, he paid no attention to her remark.

"Don't be pissed at me, I can't take it."

"I'm not pissed."

"You sure seem like it."

"I'm not." He looked at her, without emotion. "This is a complicated dive. I've got to be certain everything is perfect."

"You sure seem pissed. I've never seen you like this."

"Look, I think I should do this dive alone. I can't be worrying about you."

"Don't start that again," she said, beginning to emote.

"Okay," Nick said, not wanting her to get too worked up. "You've got to calm down, quickly. If not, I'll have to go alone. We don't have much time. What'll it be?"

"All right, all right. I'll be your partner, but don't expect any partnering after this is over."

Nick looked at her with a more relaxed smile. He went over, putting his arms around her again. He held her tight until she calmed, then pulled back.

She put her arms around him; kissed his neck, and said, "don't try that again."

It was dark on deck when they completed their preparations. All the boats were in the water, with everyone wearing a survival suit. Most of them took a spare suit to wear, or to use as a blanket, pillow, or whatever. The crew continued to load water, food and supplies in each boat. Unlike cruise ship lifeboats, these had no provisions.

Nick and Minnie climbed down to the lead boat. Jacob Marsden was getting familiar with the engine controls and steering mechanism.

Ernie relayed orders from Homer to test only one boat engine at a time. Homer didn't want to alert the yacht, though the concerns about the yacht were known by only a few.

Others in the lead boat included the Talbots and one of the crew. Mr. and Mrs. Sanchez were with Maria and Tilly in the next boat.

The two Mexican women were in a nearby boat to assist Maria if necessary.

Doc was with Luis Garcia in the third lifeboat.

Peter, with Jonas Marsden as coxswain, was in one of the full size Zodiacs, with Angie and Richard York in the other.

The last boat, a smaller Zodiac, was outfitted for Homer and Ernie. The four hand-held GPS units were calibrated for use by the boats.

Nick stood up in his boat, holding a battery-powered lantern. "Everyone, please listen up. We're in the process of rigging the boats so we can tether them, that is tie them together on lines, once we get clear of the rocks. At that point, we should have calm seas until we get to an island's sandy beach, sometime tomorrow morning. We will continue to load supplies on each boat. It's still about two hours till maximum high tide, the ideal time for us to avoid the rocks. It was necessary to get into the boats early, for safety. That's because as high tide approaches the stability of the *Eagle* becomes uncertain. I'm going up to the bridge to talk with Captain Dixon. The Captain and First Mate McInnis will follow us in a few hours. As you can imagine, they have many ship related task to take care of, as do I. Lead Petty Officer Newitt will continue directing boat preparations."

"Where's your suit, Nick?" Someone yelled.

"That's one of the reasons I need to go back on board. Mr. McInnis has set up procedures with Newitt and the other petty officers for keeping the boats together, now, and when we take off. Let them know if you're okay and if your boat is okay."

Nick and Minnie raced up to the bridge.

Homer was out on deck. He watched the yacht approach. The yacht tried to edge close to the *Eagle*, but backed off after touching some rocks. Homer picked up his ringing walkie-talkie.

"You have us in quite a predicament, Captain," John Adams said. "We had planned on coming alongside."

"You mean as you practiced a few days ago before we got to Ketchikan," Homer said.

"Precisely, Captain," Adams, said, laughing.

"The fucker seems pleased. He thinks he has us over a barrel," Homer said, covering the phone. "He can't get closer than about fifty yards." He uncovered the receiver and spoke, "Do you plan on anchoring, Mr. Adams? Or just maintaining position?"

"I am not certain my crew is sufficiently skilled to do either, Captain."

"We could pass you a line, so you can hold position by slightly backing down against the current." *And that way you won't be able to see the port side of the Eagle*, Homer thought.

Adams fell silent for a moment. "It is pleasant that you are so cooperative. What are you up to?"

"Just trying to get the inevitable over with—while we wait for the fog to lift and have the Coast Guard rescue us."

"You have contacted the Coast Guard, Captain?"

"Of course, Mr. Adams. I'm responsible for thirty-five souls on this ship."

Adams paused again. He said, "how would you get the line to us?"

"I have a special gun that can shoot a thin line over your vessel. You haul that line in and then the heavier rope attached to it."

"Yes, do that, Captain."

Ernie poked at Homer, as Homer covered the radio. "What the hell are you doing, Homer? You're making it easier for them."

"No, Ernie, I'm making it easier for us. You'll see. Right now, have someone get the line-throwing gun. Rig it to a freewheeling reel of one-inch diameter nylon."

Ernie shook his head.

"Ernie," Nick whispered, "He's trying to secure the yacht, so we can reach it when we dive. That way it'll stay in position and the propeller will be turning slowly."

"What dive? I'm out of the loop here."

"Ernie, we need the line gun," Homer said. "Nick, get yourself ready. I'll let you know when to take off."

CHAPTER THIRTY-NINE

October 24th—6:10pm

*N*ick and Minnie went below to get into their thermal suits and *dive gear.* They put on single tanks. They took no acoustic communications gear, for fear the signals would interfere with the instruments and packages they were carrying.

Nick strapped other equipment to his belt and hoped the yacht had turned off its depth sounding devices. He explained all this to Minnie as they waited for Homer's go-ahead. Their surface bubbles would be masked by darkness and water turbulence near the rocks. They should not be visible a few feet under the surface. He wore his only pair of special night goggles developed years ago for the SEALs.

He rigged a tether between himself and Minnie. It would make maneuvering more cumbersome, but was necessary to keep Minnie from getting disoriented in the dark. She carried a low visibility flashlight to help Nick attach two magnetic devices to the metal hull near the stern of the yacht, but forward of the propeller.

If that section of the hull turned out to be plastic, or fiberglass, they would need to find a steel fitting or vent of some kind.

The dive in itself shouldn't be difficult, except for the darkness, the tether, the propeller and the concern about the explosives Nick was carrying which, once armed, and could be set off by the correct acoustic frequency. He considered rigging a longer tether to Minnie to keep her as far away from him as possible in case of an explosion, but knew the shock wave would kill anyone underwater in the vicinity.

They waited at a ladder near the stern of the *Eagle,* out of sight of the lifeboats and of the yacht. The time it took them to get ready closely matched Homer's rope hauling exercise.

Homer came down from the bridge to give Nick and Minnie the go-ahead and the location of the yacht, as best as he could determine.

Nick set his watch computer to get them near the yacht. Once in the water, they were somewhat hampered by darkness. The fifteen-foot tether to Minnie had a quick disconnect link at Nick's end. Their underwater lights needed to be dimmed to avoid detection from the surface. Nick's main concern was the yacht's turning propeller. He was fearful of Minnie getting hurt.

When they were clear of the *Eagle* and the rocks, Nick set the dive at twenty feet. At that depth, their flashlights would not be visible and their exhaust bubbles would be more disbursed at the surface. It would take a broad beam searchlight scanning the water to detect them. Without voice communications, they used a series of tether line pulls similar to signals used by hard-hat divers in years past.

God bless them, and God help me. What have I done, putting them in harm's way? Homer watched them slip into the water. He stared at the water for a few minutes, then went up to the bridge to scan the water surface between the *Eagle* and the yacht. There was no indication that divers were in the water. He couldn't see anything, or any activity on the yacht. He was too restless to go to his cabin to prepare his own gear or to start what he and Ernie would need to do in the hold.

After talking with passengers and crew at the lifeboats, and going to the bridge once more, he went back to wait at the dive ladder. Homer looked at his watch often. Nick told him fifteen minutes was possible but thirty minutes was more likely. Homer talked Nick out of pre-arming the devices, telling him it was not worth the risk. Nick said they could be armed and activated by two different underwater acoustic signals at a nearby distance, depending on the magnitude of the signal.

⊷ ⊶

Nick repeatedly checked his depth gauge, compass and watch. *Should have seen it by now. Where the fuck is it? We're running against the current, but should have seen it by now.* They swam for a few more minutes on a zigzag course. *Nothing! I must have missed it. I've got to risk going to the surface.* He edged up toward the surface, feeling some turbulence. Not knowing where it was coming from, he descended back down; pulling Minnie with him. He swam in a wide circle trying to orient his position. The current had maintained an easterly flow, due in part to the rising tide.

The wind, slack during the heavy fog, was now low, but erratic. The yacht's propeller turned in reverse, keeping a slight tension on the line to the *Eagle*. All these factors caused the yacht's position to shift slowly in an arc of about sixty degrees. As a result, Nick missed his target.

Minnie swam close to him with a palms-up gesture asking *what's happening?*

He signaled that he was going to the surface and Minnie was to stay down. It took only two seconds with his head out of the water for Nick to determine their position. They'd passed about twenty-five yards beyond the yacht's bow. They headed for it. Once under the boat, he was careful not to bump into it. They increased the intensity of the flashlight.

As he suspected, the hull was not steel. He found two exhaust fittings that were located near the stern of the yacht, but not too close to the turning propeller. Nick removed the first device attached to his belt. He stayed as motionless as possible. With Minnie holding the flashlight, he turned off the safety device, an action that gave him pause. It now needed two acoustic signals, one to arm it and another to set it off.

A steady green light indicated it was ready to arm. If the light started blinking, it was ready to receive the signal to set it off. A strong magnet held it to the steel fitting. A diver could shut it down by switching the safety back on, but it would be perilous to try to pull it off. After placing the second device, Nick indicated that they were heading back in a hurry.

Halfway back to the *Eagle*, Minnie yanked on the tether line a few times.

Nick turned back to her. He hesitated to use the flashlight, as they swam in more shallow water.

Indicating by hand signals that she was almost out of air, Minnie frantically tried to get to the surface.

Nick turned off the flashlight, as he followed her up.

"You gave me a defective tank, Banner!" Minnie yelled when she reached the surface.

"Quiet," Nick shushed her, "Sound carries over water. Sorry, love, it checked out okay. Turn around, I'm going to unhook your tank and drop it."

"How are we doing this?" Minnie asked, "swim on the surface or buddy breathe off your mouthpiece?"

"We need to get back underwater. I've got a dual mouthpiece coming off my tank. Put it in your mouth and clear it. Now turn around. We're going to spoon. I'll hold you under me. We can both use our flippers. You guide with your arms."

Minnie took out her mouthpiece for a moment. "Watch your hands, Banner."

"No fooling around now," Nick chided. "I want to get back and out of the water in case one of the units activates."

"How will they work?"

"I'll tell you later. Let's go now." Nick held Minnie with one arm, using the flashlight with the other. They circled the stern of the *Eagle,* past the silent propeller and up to the ladder, out of sight of the yacht.

⚌ ⚌

Homer's anxiety kept him at the ladder near the stern of the *Eagle,* waiting for them. He glanced at his watch. Forty minutes had passed. "Damn! Damn! Damn!" he said as he punched his fist into his palm. When he spotted them his expression showed both relief and concern. "Boy, am I glad to see you guys! That was quick, but it felt like an eternity. I didn't see any unusual activity on the yacht. So, how did it go?"

"We got it done, but I'm glad to be out of the water." Nick gasped for air as he and Minnie quickly climbed aboard. "Once we found the yacht and dealt with the pull of the propeller, it was okay. As we suspected, the hull is not made of steel, but we were able to find spots that were. The real anxiety came after we armed the units. So, we swam like hell to get back here. The current helped. I'm still out of breath. What's happening on the yacht?"

"They seem to be busy preparing both of their small inflatable boats. They've even practiced lowering their port side boat."

227

"Shit. I hope they didn't see our bubbles, or spot us when we came out of the water. It's possible that due to their own activity, we might've lucked out."

"I think what we do in the next hour or so will determine our luck. They'll be coming, by first light or before. What happened to Minnie's tank?"

"We dumped it when it ran out of air. She was so pissed at me, she sucked all the air out, but it was worth it riding the waves together on the way back."

Breathing deeply, with her hands on her hips, Minnie just smiled.

"More information than I needed," Homer said, smiling. He patted them. "The boats are ready to take off with you guys."

"We're ready, too. Most of the stuff we need is on the lifeboat. We'll just shed this gear and put on our survival suits. I want to be sure no one gets into the water for any reason until we're at least a few miles away. Homer," Nick said, staring directly at him, "why are you staying on board?"

Minnie stopped and looked into their faces.

Homer returned their stares, shaking his head. "It's not what you're thinking. We have our own personal stuff to take care of and other things on the ship that need to be done. And it will take me awhile to set up my goodbye surprise. But, we should have time to do it all. Chances are, they won't want to come aboard until daylight. I don't want to be here when they do. They'll be pissed at what we did with their money and that precious cargo in the center. I'm certain the loss of the survival suits will be of no concern to them."

"Captain, remember what Brown said before he died? They're going to kill."

"I remember, but I don't think so. Some of his people, maybe, but Adams isn't like that. Nick, I can't tell you how pleased I've been to have you aboard. We would have been in deep shit without you. Now, you keep all my people safe. I'll see you on that island a few hours after you get there."

Nick shook Homer's hand. "You be safe too, Captain."

Nick and Minnie went down to the trucks to shed their dive gear and gather personal items, plus other gear that would be difficult or almost impossible to replace.

"What's going to happen to the trucks and all your equipment?" Minnie asked.

"It's only equipment." Nick shrugged. "If insurance won't cover it, I'm sure the Coast Guard will. They won't want a lot of what's happened aboard the *Eagle* to go public. I've got an inventory of my equipment, although a lot of bits and pieces aren't in that inventory. It'll be a hassle replacing everything, but I have no choice."

They put on survival suits, and went to their cabin to stuff their pockets with personal items. Nick grabbed Minnie for a hug. "You did great on that dive, my love."

"Everything we do together is great, Banner, but I can't feel your body through our bulky suits."

"Once this is over, you'll have plenty of my body," he said, as they walked across the deck to the gangway. "I better put on my serious face."

"Mr. Banner!" Some of the people in the boats shouted, anxious to be on their way.

"How is she?" Nick asked Maria, referring to Tilly. "And how is Luis doing?"

"Both about the same," Maria replied. "Luis is recovering rapidly, but I'm worried about Tilly. Her spirit seems to be waning."

Nick stood up in the boat. "Please, everyone listen up. We're taking off now, but wait to start your engines till after we finish talking. High tide has come up to where we should miss most of the rocks, but not high enough to float the *Eagle*. Each coxswain should be on the lookout for any rocks you may encounter, that the boat ahead of you may miss. Once it's evident we've cleared the shoal rocks, we'll pick up speed. Weather, wind, sea conditions, and swells all continue to be favorable. These same wind and current conditions that landed the *Eagle*, without power, high and dry, will help us land on the beach. Unlike the *Eagle*, we have power. There are a few things that keep us from heading for the town of Prince Rupert or a known populated island. First, we have a young woman here, Matilda Burke, who's due to give birth very soon, so we need to get to where a helicopter can land safely."

There were some audible gasps from the few people on board who were unaware of this.

"Second, there's a chance that several of our boat engines will run out of gas. If that happens, the other boats will pull them. The Canadian Coast Guard knows we're in trouble. It would be easier for their helicopters to rescue us from a sandy beach than off a boat on the open sea. Any questions?"

"How long should it take us to get to the island?" Peter Marsden asked the question again.

"We hope to be there by daybreak. One last thing," Nick added, "no one should get into the water for any reason without letting me know first. The danger of rocks and other boat engines makes this very unwise." He paused to let this sink in.

"Okay, start your engines," Nick ordered. "We'll be heading due east from the port side. Coxswains, raise your hand when you're ready to go. Our boat will lead."

CHAPTER FORTY

October 24ᵗʰ—8:00pm

*H*omer stayed at the port side rail watching the boats slowly inch away from the Eagle.* The deafening noise of the outboard motors gradually decreased. Restrained by a line to a partner boat they bounced off each other, avoiding the rocks. "I hope Nick can control them," he yelled to Ernie.

"He may have to change the configuration when they get to open water," Ernie mumbled.

Homer turned to enter the bridge as the radio in his pocket buzzed. "You okay?" he asked Ernie. "You don't sound good."

"I'm all right. I'm just beat. We're too old for this shit, Homer. Answer that damn phone."

Homer looked out across the water at John Adams talking with two men on the deck of the yacht. Even at eighty yards, he could see them gesturing excitedly. "Mr. Adams," Homer said, answering the radio, "I guess you heard our boat engines warming up."

"Yes, I did, Captain. What do you think you are doing?"

"My ship is damaged and unstable. It could capsize or sink when we're at high tide. My crew and passengers need to be protected if that happens."

"I suppose they do. I notice that one of your starboard lifeboats is missing. Why do you not use the other one I see?"

"We may not need it," Homer said, staring at the damaged and unusable boat at the starboard rail.

"Fine. Put it in the water. I will use it for the transfer of my boxes. I will send some people over so they can learn how to operate the larger boat."

"Two problems with that, Mr. Adams. The rocks are pretty sharp, and near the surface here. Your soft-sided boat would get torn to pieces. The other problem is my crew. They are exhausted from trying to keep this ship afloat. They haven't slept the last two nights. I've told most of them to rest until first light in the morning. We can do it then."

"I see. You and Mr. McInnis do seem to be the only people around."

"So, you've had us under surveillance, Mr. Adams?"

"When your ship has been in sight of our yacht, one of my crew has been assigned to watch you. I have ordered that to be done day and night since we departed Anchorage, even when we were in port. In Ketchikan, when we could not dock close to you, I had a man nearby in a car reporting back to me. Of course, you knew that whenever you or Mr. McInnis were off the ship we had you followed."

"Didn't you trust me, Mr. Adams?"

"It is not a matter of trust. I must be careful and think of everything. You are an interesting American, Captain Dixon, but no, I cannot permit myself a careless relationship and allow myself to trust you. Possibly under other circumstances, but not this venture.

It is much too important to me, and you have shown yourself to be unpredictable."

"Thank you, Mr. Adams. It's nice that you recognize my abilities," Homer said, tiring of the banal exchange and anxious to get on with his tasks. "I'll expect you in the morning."

"Yes. Get some sleep, Captain."

Homer closed the radio. He walked in to check on Ernie. "Ernie, Ernie."

He looked pale.

Homer touched his shoulder.

Ernie jumped.

"You scared the shit out of me!" Homer said.

"I need some rest. I took more pain pills. They must've knocked me out."

"I've never seen you like this."

"That's because I've never been shot before."

"Goddamn it! You should've gone in the boat with the nurse. You'd be under her care and probably get to a hospital sooner."

"We've got work to do. I'll just rest a little longer. I am hurting but hurting doesn't mean I'm dying. Get off it and let's do what we have to do to get out of here. They're gonna come after us in a few hours, maybe sooner."

"Ernie, I don't believe you realize your own condition, but it's too late now. Here's what we'll do. I'm going to help you down to your cabin. You'll stay there gathering what you need and what you think should be destroyed. I'll go down to the hold and prepare the *Eagle* for its demise and for our departure. I'll meet you in my stateroom to get my stuff. And you're right, we've got to get out of here fast."

"I don't need to get anything. I'll just rest here. Someone's got to keep an eye on the yacht. We'll take care of the rest when you're finished. What did Adams say?"

Homer studied Ernie, trying to evaluate his condition. He had an uneasy feeling in his gut. "He heard the noise from the boats. He wants to use our other lifeboat to haul his boxes. We'll be long gone by the time he gets here in the morning. He's had us watched 24/7 since Anchorage. That includes a man on the radar, as well. Let me ask you something. As the boats move away from us they're heading due east, which means the *Eagle* will be blocking the view of the boats from the yacht. Do you think that also applies to the yacht's ability to see the boats on their radar?"

"I think the *Eagle* will shield the boats by distorting the signals," Ernie rasped, his eyes closed. "When the boats get a few miles away, they'll stray a bit. Then they'll be on a direct line of sight from the yacht and could be picked up by their radar, but they present a small target, right on the water. I don't think they'll be spotted."

"Good, that's what I thought."

"Now get out of here and let me rest. We've got to get into our boat soon," he said, coughing.

Homer didn't notice the drop of blood Ernie wiped from his chin. "You look lousy, Ernie. Just sit there. It shouldn't take me more than an hour or so to set up the fireworks, then we're on our way." Homer raced below.

Nick and the engineers had taken care of everything. The boxes had been taken down from the ledge and placed on the deck grates. The thousands of phony hundred dollar bills were piled back in each shipping box—after they were loosened. They even tried to separate the bundles, so they would be scattered. Not all of them were.

He didn't have time to sift through each pile and finish the job. He'd have to soak them well. They'd left him with only one full five-gallon can of gas. It was possible that some bills wouldn't burn and would eventually wash ashore.

After an hour of working on the piles of loose bills, Homer stood there sweating, wondering if he'd get it all done. He found one of the metal nuggets and put it in his pocket. *It's after ten and*

I've still got a shit-load to do. High tide was ebbing, which would make their trip around the rocks more difficult. *I better tell Ernie we'll be delayed and ask him how better to finish this job.* He stopped in the galley for some water. Peering through a starboard side porthole, he could see no activity on the yacht. Both of its lifeboats were on deck. He grabbed a bottle of water for Ernie. "How you doing, buddy?" he asked, entering the bridge.

Ernie sat in the chair motionless.

Homer approached him and placed a hand on his arm. "Ernie, I brought you some water and I've got to pick your brains about something." Homer's breath caught. He shook Ernie's shoulder. His arm dropped off the chair and his head fell to his chest. Homer stepped back. "No, Ernie, no," he whispered. Homer held onto a stanchion and slowly collapsed into a chair. "I'm sorry, Ernie. I'm sorry." He sat for ten or fifteen minutes calming himself and planning, then stood up next to Ernie, placing a hand on his shoulder. "I'll take care of you, old friend." He glanced at the yacht through the starboard doorway. *You'll pay for this, you motherfuckers!*

Homer lifted Ernie out of the chair by his armpits. He backed up, dragging him down the stairway to the hold. He re-arranged the boxes and money to construct a large pile. He found a bucket to haul cleaning fluid up from the engine room, enough to soak everything. It would burn if ignited with a flame. He laid a bundle of rags from the pile about twenty feet along the floor grating. He worked himself into a frenzy, panting, his heart pounding, stopping only briefly to keep from passing out.

Up in his stateroom, he gathered his papers and personal items. He was surprised at how few things he took. He emptied his safe of the money and two pistols then turned to look at the cabin before departing. He checked Ernie's cabin, taking a bag Ernie had packed with his gear, personal papers, and important ship's documents. All of it was hauled out and loaded on the boat, along with a reel of electric wire. The wire had been run up from the hold, and out onto the deck. He was careful not to scrape it or damage it. Their survival suits were in the boat. He had everything. He started the outboard engine; let it run for a few minutes, then set it on idle.

He lowered the acoustic signal device Nick had given him, into the water, moving switches and pushing buttons to arm the signal, and to set it off. He listened for the explosion over the noise of the boat engine. *Nothing! What did I do wrong?* He gathered the acoustic gear, cradling it as he walked back up the gangway. Crossing the ship to the starboard side where he could see the yacht, he sat down on deck with his legs dangling over the side. The yacht looked peaceful. "It's got to work," he said aloud. About to try it again, he paused. *Should I warn them? Should I call to let them get off? Are they all bad? If they get off, they will come after me. With their boat and gear destroyed, what would they do? I'd be dead meat. Just the way Ernie is now. Fuck'em!*

He lowered the device into the water and pushed the switch to acoustically arm the device. He waited a few minutes, watching the yacht, then pressed the button to set it off. Nick had told him at what speed that acoustic signals travel through seawater, but he couldn't remember. A second green light showed on his console, indicating the device was armed. "Yes!" he said. "Do it. Do it." He sat transfixed for a few more seconds—there it was, a muffled blast.

A sheet of water shot up from the aft end of the yacht. A second blast tore it half apart. The two lifeboats fell into the water.

Homer sat, nodding his head, as the back end of the yacht slowly sank. He dropped the acoustic gear into the water and quickly went below deck. In the hold, he poured out the five gallons of gasoline saturating the rags on the pyre and along the grate. He looked at the pile, now a funeral pyre. He remembered what Ernie had once said, *'Homer, I don't have any family. Whether I die at sea or on shore, I want you to bury me at sea. Will you promise me that?'*

"This is as good as I can do, old friend. I don't know what the regulations are here for how far out at sea we should be, but this is the best I can do." With tears in his eyes, choking on the words, Homer continued, "I think you knew, Ernie, sitting up there on the bridge. I think you knew and you wanted it this way. You and our home these many years, our *Alaskan Eagle*, will be buried together. Goodbye and God bless you my friend. I will never forget you." He paused a few moments, breathing deeply, then lit a match at the end of the row of rags.

He watched the flame race to the pyre. He waited until the pyre was burning, then hurried up and out onto the deck and to the gangway.

Standing there on deck, holding a gun and peering down at the lifeboat, was the young lad from the yacht. His clothes were soaking wet. He turned to aim the gun at Homer.

Homer stopped and looked into his face. He felt with some certainty that the boy would not shoot him. "I am glad you were able to get off the yacht. Do you understand what I am saying?"

The boy nodded yes, and in halting English said, "Mr. Adams is in the boat with me and Mr. Marshall is in the boat with me. They are hurt."

"This ship is on fire and will blow up," Homer gestured. "You must get off the ship right now. Where is your boat?"

"The boat is there." He pointed back—indicating out of sight and around to the starboard bow. What do I tell Mr. Adams?" he said, lowering the gun.

"Just tell him you saw a big fire inside the ship, nothing more. You must get off the ship right now." Homer handed him three survival suits from the pile left on deck. "Go fast." Homer headed down the gangway as the boy went running away. He edged the Zodiac out about a hundred feet from the side of the *Eagle*, carefully paying out the electric wire. He stopped near a high rock. He kept the outboard barely running to minimize the noise. The end of the wire on the reel was attached to a battery and a switch. He waited until he heard the noise from the yacht's lifeboat fading away. Hesitantly, he activated the switch, not certain what would happen.

Instantly, the first cake of C-4 exploded within the *Eagle*.

Homer put full power to the outboard, propelling him away from the ship. Six more blasts tore the ship apart. At a safe distance, he stopped to look back. The flames rose high, lighting the way for him to avoid rocks. He headed east.

CHAPTER FORTY-ONE

*A*t the time Homer had been working on his final preparations to leave the Eagle the small flotilla of lifeboats was well clear of the shoal rocks and had changed the tether lines between boats.

The lead boat, carrying Nick and Minnie, was not restrained by lines, giving it freedom to approach others as necessary. Nick felt concerned about a boat going astray. If not for the tethers, they could wander into the darkness while all were asleep. The two smaller Zodiacs were attached at their midpoints. They followed the lead boat. The other two lifeboats followed behind. Polypropylene rope connecting the boats floated on the surface when slack, avoiding fouling problems with propeller blades.

Nick communicated regularly by walkie-talkie with each pair of boats. He told everyone to relax, get comfortable and sleep, if possible. He coordinated his GPS readings with the other two units and asked about the well being of each boatload of people. Fuel consumption information was vital. He calculated that with the back-up cans of gas they should be able to reach the island as planned after first light in the morning. Any time a boat needed to add fuel the entire flotilla would stop and each boat would top off. Nick and Petty Officer Newitt each had satellite phones with spare batteries.

They'd been unable to accurately determine the fuel consumption rate of these ancient boats. If any boat exhausted its fuel supply or if its engine failed, sufficient lines to tow them were available. Oars were carried in each boat as a final back up.

By midnight, the flotilla had been underway for about four hours but had travelled only eight miles from the *Eagle*. Past the shoals, and with reconfigured lines, their speed picked up to about five miles per hour. Nick kept a watchful eye on all the boats and their occupants. Almost all the people, passengers and crew alike, had arranged their positions to look forward. He kept looking backward for three things not associated with the boats. So, it was likely he and possibly only one or two others noticed the bright flash in the sky. He quietly pointed it out to Minnie. "That's our handiwork under the yacht."

"My God, what happened, I didn't hear anything? And why so quickly gone?"

"The charges, including most of the boxed explosives within the yacht, were below the waterline, masking the noise. The noise from our boat engines and the distance from the blast kept us from hearing anything else. I'm sure there was no fire to speak of because the rear end of the yacht would sink pretty fast."

"Did we kill them all?" Minnie asked, shuddering.

"All the cabins are forward, so some of them might have gotten out okay."

Peter Marsden stood in his boat pointing backward—he looked at Nick.

Nick gestured that he didn't know what it was. "Now I'm waiting for the second event," he mumbled to himself." *It shouldn't be long now.*

"Why don't you lie down and rest," Minnie suggested. "You'll have to relieve Jacob in a little while."

"I will, soon. I need to keep checking on things."

About an hour or so later, a series of blasts was faintly heard over the din of the boat engines, and everyone could see a substantial glow. Nick's walkie-talkie buzzed. He responded to all the boats. "Tell everyone that the *Alaskan Eagle* appears to have exploded and has probably been blasted off the rocks to sink. I'm glad we got off when we did. I hope Captain Dixon and First Mate McInnis were able to get off safely. Even though the Captain has one of the walkie-talkies, we're definitely out of range. They should make better time in their boat than we can, so I'll keep trying to contact him. I'm praying for their well-being."

People in all five boats were gazing at Nick in terror but also with admiration. Getting away in the lifeboats had possibly saved their lives. They kept looking at him and waving, wanting to sustain the moment.

He waved back casually.

"Wow," Minnie exclaimed. "They've elevated you to Rock Star or Hollywood status."

"Enough. Cut it out," he said out the corner of his mouth. Once the tumult subsided, he continued his vigil looking for Homer's boat, the third thing he'd been anticipating, though he knew this could take a few hours. "How are you doing?" he asked Jacob. "Ready for me to take over for a while?"

"No, sir, I'm just fine."

"I'll close my eyes for a few minutes," Nick said to him. "Don't hesitate to call me. I don't want you to get over tired."

"Yes, sir."

Nick got comfortable and snuggly with Minnie. It was the first time in a few days he could relax. Exhausted, he fell asleep immediately.

A short while later, he awoke with a start. Some waves were slapping against the boat. He looked around. There were swells but no white caps. A breeze had developed. He could see the moon and some stars. The fog seemed dispersed, but not completely. He looked at Jacob with a questioning gesture.

It was returned with a smile and a thumbs-up sign.

Nice boys Peter has raised. Nick checked his GPS and the chart. They were off course about fifteen degrees. He radioed the other two GPS units. Their readings were the same as his. He got up to talk with his coxswain and identified a star for Jacob to use as a guide. Nick planned to check their position every fifteen minutes. None of the boats had built-in compasses. They all used hand held units. The other boats would keep in line following him. Nick glanced back for Homer, but there was nothing in sight. He keyed the walkie-talkie to Homer's channel. No response. He lay down next to Minnie.

"Mm, Mm," she murmured, but did not wake.

Still in sight of the *Eagle*, Homer stopped his boat again. He couldn't bear turning his back on his ship being destroyed and Ernie's funeral, a life altering moment, never to recover from, never to return.

The successive blasts tore the *Eagle* apart, flinging it off the rocks. It continued to burn, as it gradually floated away and sank. Water depths in the area varied between three and six hundred feet.

I know they'll never consider salvaging it. I hope they never even dive on it. What for? There's nothing worth retrieving and no one knows Smith and Brown were still on board, except some of the crew and the Corps of Engineers people. That might get a little sticky. Coast Guard will have to explain it if it ever comes out. Wait. They were blown up in the blasts, as Ernie was. That's it. Ernie, Ernie, that was the only way I could bury you at sea. He'd say, you did a good job, Skipper! That's what he would say.

The Zodiac bounced off a rock, bringing Homer out of his trance. He studied the area. It was pitch black. He couldn't see the *Eagle* or the yacht or any of the yacht's boats. *Where did that lad come from? Was Adams really with him?* Homer checked a compass to correct his heading. He let the soft-sided boat bounce off the rocks rather than risk shining his flashlight. *The low engine speed and noise make it less likely I'm being followed. I'll open it up when I clear the shoals. It will be a race, but they don't know where I'm going.*

He tried to keep from dozing off, but his fatigue and the drone of the engine were overpowering. He eased his body down to rest the back of his head on the extra survival suit, while keeping his hand on the rudder. He was soon fast asleep.

⊷ ⊶

Nick lay there, wide-awake. The enormity of his responsibility hit him. They were in small boats, out at sea, in the middle of the night. Although there were islands a few miles away, they were still in open-ocean. He needed to protect them all, find the island, and get them off the island to safety. Not what he thought he'd be doing last week when Ernie called. He sat up to look around. *I hope that breeze doesn't develop into anything more.*

His walkie-talkie startled him. Peter Marsden said, "Nick, our engine just quit. We need to stop and add fuel."

"All boats," Nick announced, "idle your engines and add fuel. Peter, let me know when your engine is up and running."

"Will do," Peter responded.

After a few minutes, Nick could feel them drifting off course, and could see his little formation go awry. "All boats, let me know when your fueling is completed." It took about fifteen minutes to get going again. He checked their position and gave Jacob new instructions. The four boats behind formed into position and followed. They needed to repeat the procedure twice more. Then, two boats were out of fuel and needed to be towed by others.

Nick got the hang of adjusting their course. All boats were now low on gas. At first light, he scanned the horizon to spot the island. The three GPS units confirmed their position. The chart showed the island's elevation to be sixty-eight feet. They should have seen it by now.

He and Minnie had been able to grab brief patches of sleep, enough to get them through another day. Morning light brought good visibility, vastly improved from the past few days. They could now see the island ahead. What they saw was a shoreline of mostly cliffs. The island was not as inviting as advertised. Nick looked back at his caravan. People on all the boats were staring at the island and at Nick.

He said they would continue along the coast, looking for a suitable landing. A message from Maria indicated he should find one quickly. Tilly's water had broken, but she was not yet fully dilated. Nick scanned the horizon for any sight of Homer's boat. *I'll wait 'til we get on the island to call them again. I wonder how Ernie is doing? They should be making good time.*

⤛ ⤜

Homer's experience aboard ship had conditioned him to fitful sleep patterns. Even without being wakened by one of the crew, or a shipboard emergency, his mind would keep him aware of his responsibilities and regulate a wake-up signal. He never experienced prolonged nights of sleep. When ashore, usually with Sally, was the only time he could completely relax.

His exhaustion the past few days, exacerbated by the events concerning Ernie and his decision as to how to deal with it—plus the ship grounding and the yacht with its bandits, all experiences so extreme, woke him, shaking and sweating, after only a half hour of sleep.

But that half hour out on the sea in an inflatable craft turned out to be too long. He was way off course. For the next hour, he had to change his heading every ten minutes. The welcome breeze, though slight, was pushing him too far south. *What the fuck is happening here?* He felt almost giddy with his fatigue and the ridiculousness of his situation.

He'd been in storms with forty-foot swells where the waves would crash over the entire ship, forcing him to navigate from the deck above the bridge, the open flying bridge, the highest part of the ship other than the masts. But, he commanded the *Eagle* under him. He'd talk to her. *Stay in there, baby.* And she did. Times like that there was no reason the aging ship wasn't crushed into scrap and sinking to the bottom. But she wasn't crushed, and she didn't sink, and Homer felt so grateful, loving her even more. Now she was gone. She wasn't there to protect him because he'd destroyed her. She'd even found a safe haven up on the rocks, shielding them all, but he'd destroyed her. Maybe she was trying to reunite them, to bring them together at the bottom of the sea.

Homer dozed off again. The engine cutting-out woke him. He refilled the engine's tank with the last of the gas. He hadn't calculated how far he could go on a tank of gas. *I should have, but it doesn't matter now. I'm out here with what I've got.* He wasn't overly concerned. This route from Seattle to Anchorage was his back yard, where he'd roamed safely all these years. He knew it well. The sea around these islands was usually calm.

He checked his position again. He still seemed to be off course. *I could just let the weather take me. I'll land somewhere. No, they'll be worried. I can't do that to them. Sally will be upset. So will Davy and Maddy and Lorraine and others who care for me. All right, Homer, get your act together. Stop this fatalistic shit.* He set his course directly north to counter the wind. If and when his gas ran out, hopefully near or above the island, he planned to row east with partial wind at his back. With the GPS and a chart handy, he checked the oars and stayed awake.

CHAPTER FORTY-TWO

October 25ᵗʰ—9am

Nick finally spotted an area of the island where the cliff was set back from the water. It appeared to be a sandy beach and a gentle protected approach. "This looks promising," he announced to the other boats.

As they neared the cove, he could see water lapping the sand, an indication of the gradual slope of the bottom. He undid the line between his lead boat and the others he was now towing. "I'm going in. Someone should be at the oars in each boat. I'll let you know if it's okay. If so, release all the lines and get control of your individual boat, then come into shore one at a time. Keep a line attached to the bow so we can pull you in as far as possible. The second boat in, will be Maria's, with Tilly."

Nick peered over the bow into the clear water. "It looks good, Jacob. Rev it up to get as far in as possible." He leapt off, landing on firm but moist sand. He helped others in his boat get off, then went over to pull in the boat with Maria and Tilly.

Minnie stayed with Maria to help get Tilly off and comfortable. All five boats were secured to rugged shrubs up on the beach.

"Listen up everyone. We need to unload all the supplies and items onto the beach and layout a campsite. The outdoorsmen we have with us, Peter Marsden and sons Jacob and Jonas, will assist Petty Officer Newitt with the planning. Many factors are involved. I'll continue trying to contact the Canadian Coast Guard by satellite phone to let them know our location. They're out looking for us."

Nick tried Homer again, but still no response. He could not connect with the Coast Guard. The cliff could be blocking the fixed position satellite they needed access to.

"What's the problem?" Minnie asked.

"No contact with a satellite. I'll climb the cliff to try from there."

"I'll come with you. You did a good job, Banner, getting us here. Everyone says you're a hero. I'm happy to be off that ship. It was creepy, with everything going on."

"How's Tilly?"

"Maria said she's ready—anytime now. Tilly told us she's having twins. She said, if one is a girl, she's going to name her Maria, and if a boy, she'll call him Nick. What's the story, Banner?"

"Let's take a walk and I'll tell you, but remember, I've never lied to you and you must believe me."

"Okay," Minnie said, stopping to stare at him.

"Come on, let's keep walking. I want to get to higher ground," Nick said.

"The past two years I did a lot of work up here by myself. Sally's Place is a bar I went into many times. Last winter, yes about nine months ago, the place was not as crowded, winter and all. Though I'd known Sally and Tilly from the previous year as well..."

"You're dragging this on, Banner."

"Relax, I want to tell you everything, tell you the whole story. Well, last winter Tilly got more rambunctious than she'd been the previous year. She had a lot of guys and a lot of dates after work. She also got in the habit of giving me, and some others, a big wet kiss on the lips as we left the club. She had this one guy she used to go out with a lot. One night she was kind of morose and drinking too much. I mentioned it to Sally. She said Tilly's boyfriend dumped her and was going back to his family in the lower forty-eight. Sally said I should be nice to Tilly, that she needed a friend and that she liked me." He paused to study Minnie's reaction.

Minnie drew a brow up, her expression blank.

"Well, this one night she followed me out. She had an apartment nearby. As we got near my hotel, she started feeling faint and wobbly. I told her to come in to lie down. When we get to my room, she went to a bed. When I came out of the bathroom, she was under the covers, fast asleep. I asked if she was okay. She didn't respond. I shook her and all she did was mumble. I went to sleep in the other bed and left before she woke up in the morning. End of story. I never touched her. I never went out with her at all. Case closed."

Minnie smiled. "Okay, Banner, you're off the hook."

While Nick tried to raise Homer on the walkie-talkie, his satellite phone rang. "We're looking for Captain Dixon. This is Commander Carlton with the Canadian Coast Guard Station at Prince Rupert."

"Yes, Commander, it's good to hear from you. We've been trying to call you, but couldn't make contact. This is Nick Banner, Second Mate on the *Alaskan Eagle*. We're off the ship now. Captain Homer Dixon and First Mate Ernie McInnis are in a boat, making their way to the island we're now on. I led five lifeboats with thirty-two people off the ship last night. We made it to the island about an hour ago. Can I give you the coordinates from my GPS so you can record our location?"

"Yes, go ahead, Mr. Banner."

Nick gave him the island coordinates and those of the *Eagle's* location on the shoals to help them track the route of Homer and Ernie's boat.

"You were either very brave or very foolish to make that trip, particularly at night. Those waters can be quite treacherous at times."

"We were neither, Commander. We were desperate. The ship was breaking up on the rocks. It wasn't safe for anyone to stay aboard."

"I've charted your location, Mr. Banner, and you were fortunate to find one of the few beaches in that area. That's the good news. The problem is the island you are on and the tide. The beaches on the island are very low, as you can see. The tide in that area ranges between ten and fifteen feet, meaning the beach will be under water in high tide, which should occur in about six hours. You need to get off the beach and climb to higher ground."

"Yes, we'll do that. I'll get them started in a few minutes. We do have an emergency situation here, though. All of us are physically capable except for one person. She's a young woman about to give birth. How soon can you get a helicopter here to take her to a hospital?"

"Normally, only an hour or two, but you caught us at a bad time. We're a small station with only two helicopters. Unfortunately, one is down for repairs and the other is off station on an operation, many hours away. We'll look into using one of the small commercial helicopters in the area. As soon as we can commandeer one, it'll be on its way to you, weather permitting. Some violent storms are in the forecast for tonight. As for the other thirty people, we'll send out our small but very suitable ship outfitted for rescue missions."

"Commander, what about the U.S. Coast Guard Base at Ketchikan. They have helicopters. Could you notify them of our plight?"

"I've already had someone talking to Ketchikan. They'll be bringing two helicopters, and some people from your government. They expect to be here about noon tomorrow. My suggestion is to let us send our ship. It can't make it by today's low tide, but will be there first thing tomorrow morning. Can your people last that long?"

"Yes, no problem. We have provisions and water and everyone is in a survival suit. Hopefully, the pregnant woman will hold off until tomorrow. We'll be back down on the beach early in the morning. Thank you, Commander, but one other thing. We get satellite contact only when we're up here on the cliff. I'll be going down to organize the move to higher ground. I'll send someone up here with the phone in case you need to call us back. Also, please let Ketchikan know our status."

Nick and Minnie climbed down to the beach, meeting Peter Marsden and Newitt.

"We've got a problem, Mr. Banner," Newitt said. "The tide's coming in. This beach might be under water soon."

"It's come up the beach a few feet since we've been here," Peter added.

"Exactly what I came to tell you. I've just talked with the Canadian Coast Guard at Prince Rupert. A ship will be here first thing tomorrow morning. They've missed the window for today and as long as we're safe it's too risky to try a nighttime rescue. Their helicopters are not available but if necessary, some helicopters from Ketchikan will be at Prince Rupert tomorrow. Peter, would you and your boys climb the cliff, find a good path for everyone to get up there and locate an adequate clearing for all of us to spend the night. Could one of you stay at that location to guide people? Also, whoever stays up there needs to hold on to this satellite phone. It's our link to the outside world, but we can't get a signal except up on the hill."

"We're on it, Nick."

"Newitt, your guys will start hauling the gear up. We should have a few hours to get it done, but first priority will be to help Maria relocate Tilly."

"Will do, Mr. Banner."

"Jacob ran our boat without a break," Nick said to Peter. "He didn't want to be relieved."

"Jonas did the same thing," Peter said. "These kids never seem to go to bed anyway. It's an adventure for them. They were signaling each other on and off all night."

Nick walked up to the group of women around Tilly. "Ladies," he greeted.

"Minnie told us." Maria nodded at him.

"How is Tilly?" he asked.

"Still stable."

"We need twenty-four hours, and she'll be in a hospital. Maria, will your parents be able to climb that cliff?"

"They are both capable. It should not be a problem."

CHAPTER FORTY-THREE

*B*y late morning Homer was still floating about five miles from the island—and about one mile north. He had very little gas left. He shut down the outboard motor to keep a reserve, in case it was needed, and started rowing east. The wind would carry him south. Hopefully, his plan would get him close to the island. He thought he could see cliffs, but the full sun played tricks with his eyesight. In a few hours, he should see it okay.

He rowed hard for an hour and checked his position again. He was only about a half mile closer. *I'll be damned. The wind must be from the northeast. It's keeping me away from the island. At this rate, I'll never make it.* He started the engine, heading northeast. In what seemed like only a few minutes the engine failed, out of gas. He'd gained another half mile. *I'm in trouble now.* He rowed furiously for about two hours, but didn't gain much. *I must be fighting the tide now as well. I'm in deep shit.*

⊰⊱

Nick tried Homer's radio every half hour now. "I can't get him. Either he's out of range, he can't hear it, or the battery's gone," he told Minnie. "The top of this cliff should give us the best view." He scanned the horizon with his binoculars. Visibility was decent and a full sun was coming from a good angle. They would lose daylight in a few hours. "I see something," Nick said. "It looks like a small inflatable, but I can only see one person in it. Maybe the other one is curled up in the bottom of the boat. It's drifting. They're not under power. I've got to go get them. You coming with me?"

"You bet, Banner, let's go."

They siphoned all remaining gas from other boats, pouring most into the boat with the best engine gas consumption. They kept the rest in a reserve gas can.

"That's all there is," Nick said, "but it should be enough." He asked Peter to help him by manning the binoculars on top of the cliff, and let him know by radio if he was heading for Homer. If they lost radio contact, they could be in trouble.

Nick and Minnie took off at a fast pace.

Peter and his sons were guiding them, keeping an eye on the distant boat.

About half way out, the short-range radios lost reception. They tried to follow hand signals and body movements from the Marsdens. Next, three flares were lit on top of the cliff, with the center flare moving back and forth between the two outer flares. "Pretty clever of those Eagle Scouts," Nick told Minnie. "We're going to have problems when we lose daylight. At least we have gas, flashlights, and the Marsdens up on the cliff. Homer and Ernie should see the same lights and signals we do. It's probably frustrating to them that they're not able to get to the island."

"Why shouldn't they be able to get there?" Minnie asked.

"When I saw someone in the boat there was no movement, no activity. Either they're hurt, weak, exhausted, out of gas, or having mechanical problems."

"I can barely see the lights on top of the cliff," Minnie said. "They can't possibly see us in this darkness, but I hope they keep the flares on. Shouldn't we be there by now?"

"I think we should, unless we went too far and overshot their boat. Take our stronger flashlight. Aim it up, rotating it cone-like. That's the best we can do for the cliff to follow us and for Homer and Ernie to see us. Even if the Marsdens can see us now, they can't possibly see the other boat to guide us."

"What do we do if we can't find them? We can't stay out all night. We'd be drifting with no fuel."

"Are our oars here? I didn't even check!"

"Yep, they're here," Minnie said.

"Homer, Captain, Ernie," Nick shouted. "We should have brought some kind of noise maker, but I guess the engine is loud enough. I feel like I'm yelling into a void. That's like shoveling shit against the tide."

"You sure have quaint Navy expressions," Minnie quipped.

Is that a light? I see a light. Homer started waving his own flashlight. He wedged the flashlight so the beam shined up and started rowing. *Damn, I don't think they see me.* He shined his flashlight cone fashion, as they were doing. *They must be looking for me.* He took his walkie-talkie. It still had power. It should, it was turned off. He set the output to all channels. *If that's Nick, he should hear me. Shit, their light is heading away.* He set the shrill, attention-getting signal on the radio, pulsing it on and off.

"That's the radio!" Nick yelled. "Homer, Homer."

"Why the hell are you giving up on me?" Homer yelled into the radio.

"Where are you? We can't see you!"

"Can't you see my flashlight?"

"I see it," Minnie shouted, "Over there. Younger eyes!" She clapped her hands, gleefully.

Once spotting them, Homer started rowing hard to help close the distance. He waved at them.

When they were alongside, Nick asked, "Where's Ernie?"

Homer shook his head.

"What do you mean? What happened, Captain?"

Homer gazed down. "He didn't make it. His bullet wound was more damaging than first thought. He died just before I finished my preparations. We were friends for over twenty years," Homer muttered, his voice breaking. "He had no family. He always told me he wanted to be buried at sea. I'm gonna tell Newitt and the others he died in the blast that decimated the ship." He gradually gained control of himself as he talked—climbing into the larger boat.

They secured a towline to the Zodiac and headed back to the island.

There was a happy crowd that met the boat as it entered the cove, delighted to see Homer. Their elation turned to sadness when hearing about Ernie. Homer made rounds, greeting the crew and all the passengers. Their feelings of security, and well-being, improved. "The Captain is here, we're saved." And for good reason—Homer had filled this role on the *Eagle* longer than any of his crew had been aboard, and he extended the same feeling to passengers who traveled with them.

He was the Captain.

Ernie was gone, and Nick was temporary. There was a large gap between him and anyone else of authority.

He repeated the story of the demise of the *Eagle,* and the death of Ernie, a number of times. Each time he had to re-live, and try to hide, all aspects of his personal grief. It was difficult. It took a toll on him, and he was exhausted.

Nick told him to crash, that he would take care of things.

⊷⊶

Nick inspected the campsite to ensure that all were fed, had something to drink, and that they were comfortable. He told people to keep their survival suits on—that rain was common in the area, and expected. He checked with Maria about Tilly.

Minnie stayed with Maria to help, as did Maria's mother and the other two women.

Maria pulled Nick aside. "She doesn't look good," Maria sobbed. "I think she's dying. Her vital signs are bad. She may have internal bleeding. I can't do anything." Maria looked distraught.

Minnie put her arms around Maria and held her tight. "What do I do if she dies? What about the babies? I would try to induce the births, but I don't have the necessary medications and instruments. I'm lost. I've failed. Her blood pressure is too high. I've got someone checking it every minute." They had a pot of boiling water sterilizing knives and other instruments taken from the ship. "I will not rest until she's in a hospital or under a qualified doctor's care," Maria vowed.

Her mother looked worried.

Newitt reported that all the boats were secure and all useful equipment and supplies had been removed from the boats. He asked Nick what will happen to the six boats.

"That's between the *Eagle's* owners and the insurance company," was Nick's reply.

Nick thanked Peter Marsden for his innovative method to keep them on course when they looked for Homer. "Who's idea was it?

"My boys came up with that one. We tried flashlights and torches first, then they came up with the one that worked, the flares."

An hour later, all seemed quiet in the campsite. After sleeping for a while, noise from the women around Tilly woke him.

Minnie stood with the group surrounding Tilly.

"What is it, what's the matter?" he asked her.

"Maria thinks she may be dying, just giving up," Minnie said sobbing.

"My God, and the babies?"

"Maria might try a cesarean. She's seen it done many times."

"Pick her up," Maria instructed. "Make her stand. Maybe the shock will start something. Tilly, Tilly," Maria shouted in her ear. "You must help me. Do you understand?"

Tilly nodded her head.

"You're ready. We're going to lay you down. You must help me, so you can have beautiful, healthy babies. Start pushing." Maria pinched her arm near the shoulder to keep her alert.

"Ow, ow! It hurts," Tilly cried.

"Good," Maria said, "now push!" The women seemed to be silently pushing.

"Something's happening," Tilly whimpered, "it hurts." She squeezed the hands of the women holding her.

"Bite on this," Maria instructed, placing a stick covered with gauze and tape into her mouth.

"It's coming. I see it," someone said in Spanish. A small head appeared, covered with blood and birth liquids. The little girl practically shot out into waiting hands. Maria cut the cord and handed the baby to a woman who wrapped her. She embraced the screaming child inside her survival suit to keep her warm. The two women from the crew were employed as chambermaids for passengers, and to assist in the galley.

"Keep pushing, Tilly," Maria encouraged, "Keep pushing."

"I can't, damn it!" Tilly cried. "I just can't. "I can't stand the pain!"

"Tilly, you and the baby will die. You must do it."

A moment later, a cry of pain tore from Tilly. A second head appeared, then the shoulders. Tilly seemed to collapse. Maria was able to grab under the arms and pull the baby boy out. With Maria holding the child upside down, they waited anxiously for it to exhibit an effort to live. Maria continued trying all her knowledge and experience skills, the pain and desperation evident on her face. Finally, she gave the baby a strong slap on the back. He took a deep breath and started howling. His face turned from blue to red. Maria and the group watching joined the baby with cries of joy.

Nick watched the entire procedure, his face mimicking the emotions shown by Maria.

Minnie came to him and held him tight, aware of his memories and the pain he must be feeling. She whispered in his ear, and kissed his neck.

⇒+ +⇐

Homer had never seen a birth. The process baffled and terrified him. He breathed a deep sigh of relief when it was over. *Thank God they're all okay.*

He walked through the camp. Away from the burden of the ship and the menace of the yacht, he could again see to his basic responsibility, the well being of his crew and passengers. *What could I have done differently to end up with a better outcome, especially for Ernie?* It would take him many months and many conversations with Sally and Davy, analyzing everything that happened, to ease the pain and guilt he was feeling. Ease, but never do away with.

CHAPTER FORTY-FOUR

October 26th

*T*he *few people awake at first light saw the Canadian Coast Guard ship* as it came around the end of the island. They started rousing the others.

Homer, Nick and Minnie sat with a group of women tending the twin babies, letting them suck on clean wads of gauze soaked in diluted evaporated milk. It was a poor substitute for mother's milk, but Maria said it was better than nothing since Tilly, as yet, seemed unable to produce her own. Others agreed, saying they had seen many children grow up healthy with worse nourishment at birth. The women, all exhausted from the sleepless night, smiled at Tilly.

"Her blood pressure and vital signs are closer to what they should be," Maria announced.

Homer kept staring at the twins. *Sally will be thrilled. I'll call her and Davy as soon as we get to port. It's a good thing I didn't call earlier when it seemed like Tilly might die.* Tilly had named Sally Godmother when she first found out she was pregnant. *I guess that'll make me*

Godfather—a family after all these years. I'll also need to contact the company, but like the rest of the world, they'll have heard about the Eagle's fate by now.

The whap, whap, whap of a helicopter approaching woke up the rest of the crew and passengers. A private company helicopter had been commandeered by the Coast Guard to take Maria, Tilly, and the twins to a hospital in Prince Rupert.

"Thank God," Maria exclaimed, when a doctor came off to greet them.

Nick and Minnie found a spot to spread out inside the Coast Guard ship. They saved room for Homer.

He joined them after paying respects to the Skipper. Homer declined the offer of a cabin and bed, saying he wanted to stay with his crew and passengers.

Homer and Nick were too tired to talk. Shutting out all noise and distractions, they let their fatigue take over, and tried to sleep.

Nick and Minnie shared a sleeping bag. Their fatigue did not prevent them from enjoying each other. Okay, we organize the final report in Seattle and you join me with Hannah in San Diego. Right?"

"I'm not letting you out of my sight, Banner. And you come back with me for a while to my Dad's home on the Eastern Shore of Maryland."

"Absolutely. It ties in with my plan, their plan. Coast Guard wants me back at Headquarters, in D. C."

Relieved of his responsibilities, Homer lay there thinking. There were no tasks to perform and no one to care for. An uncertainty gnawed within him. Someone else was taking care of everything. His whole life, or as far back as he could reasonably remember, he'd carried the weight of responsibilities. He welcomed these responsibilities—he wanted them. They were a part of him. He couldn't imagine life without them.

If he let his mind go blank, it would shift to the core of his memories. The memories that he and all people possess. It's not as if these memories are completely hidden, it's just that they rarely surface except in the individual's own mind. The secrets aren't necessarily wicked or damaging, most being trite and inconsequential, but secrets nonetheless. And the self-doubts, rarely exposed except to closest confidants; and their fantasies—some sexual and others magnanimous.

Yet, just now, Homer was experiencing a feeling of emptiness, a void within him that would take time to fade.

It was almost noon when they glided up the channel toward the Coast Guard pier in Prince Rupert, a city located on Canada's Pacific Coast about six hundred miles north of Seattle.

"Wow," Minnie said. "Look at the crowd. There are even television cameras. One of the crew told me we've been on the news; said they watched the helicopter landing in the hospital parking lot. Tilly and the babies seemed to be okay."

"Good," Homer replied. "I'm sure Sally saw that and will see us. And for anyone else who knows someone who was on the *Eagle*, it will help ease a lot of anxiety."

Nick looked over at him and put a hand on Homer's shoulder. "Captain, you're a good man, and you'll be one—forever."

"But Captain no more," Homer, said. "This is it. This is the end."

"Homer, for some people, the aura of stature and respect never ends. You'll always be the Captain. But, Captain," Nick, said, smiling, "if I were you, I'd get myself washed up a bit. You're going to be the center of attention."

The media and the curious were kept cordoned off at a distance as the ship tied up. Frank Harris and a staff of U.S. Government personnel, with Commander Ellings from the Juneau Coast Guard Station, and an Army Corps of Engineers Colonel, all stayed off to the side, as Commander Carlton greeted Homer and Nick.

After the brief conversation, Homer huddled with his crew, and Nick with the passengers, including Minnie. "Most of the excitement concerning our adventure centers around Maria Sanchez, Matilda Burke and the twins," Homer and Nick told them.

Homer spotted two executives from his Company. He waved at them. "After questioning by the Canadian Coast Guard, we will be flown to Seattle for further interrogations," Homer advised the crew. He pulled Newitt, the Corpsman, and two other Petty Officers aside. "The only thing I ask is that you tell only what you are certain happened, not what could have happened, or what you surmised, or that you heard. But do not speculate, and do not lie."

The four men in front of him, familiar with Homer's grand use of words muttered, "*Aye, aye, Captain,* and *yes, sir.*"

He knew they would not say anything that could harm him or even put him in a bad light. "I want to thank you for all your hard work and support. Who could have imagined, a few weeks ago, that we'd be standing here having this conversation, with the *Eagle* and Ernie McInnis at the bottom of the ocean," Homer stated, barely able to get the words out.

They were quiet and stared at the ground, as the two executives walked up.

Nick's conversation with the passengers carried a similar message, though less gloomy, regarding interrogation by the Coast Guard.

Homer's company seemed cordial in offering various means of transportation to Seattle and compensation for personal items lost.

Now that it was over, most of them considered the events as an adventure. Mr. and Mrs. Sanchez endured the hardship, proud of Maria and her part in saving Tilly and the twins. They were astounded at the television coverage showing Maria.

Nick was effusive with his show of appreciation to Peter, Jacob and Jonas for all their help in the boats and on the island.

"We should thank you!" Peter said, "for letting us participate in an area of our expertise—and to help with our own survival and the survival of others."

The boys, looking at their father, nodded in agreement. "We caught hell from Mom when we called her, but again, the three of us were thrilled at the part we played getting everyone to safety. None of us will ever forget it." The Marsdens decided to take a circuitous bus route through part of the Canadian Rockies, then back to Vancouver for their flight home.

"What are your future plans?" Nick asked Jacob and Jonas.

"We're thinking of applying to the service academies, particularly the Naval Academy."

"I don't know if it would help, but I'd be happy to supply you with one of your recommendations, and, if I end up working for the Coast Guard in Washington, my title should look good on paper."

The circumstances involving the four Corps of Engineers Officers, Homer, Nick and Minnie were somewhat more complex. They were ordered to make no statements and to not even talk about what had happened, other than that they were safe and secure—until after the closed-door meetings in Seattle. As the series of incidents became known to various Government entities, they imposed a secret classification on the events of the previous few weeks, until further investigations could be conducted. The Government's possible culpability, due to delayed action by the Coast Guard, could have been the reason for keeping it under wraps.

"With the counterfeit money burned or lost in the ocean, we will disclose their destruction and the probable demise of the lawbreakers to the public," Frank Harris told them. "The events surrounding the sinking of the yacht will remain a mystery. No one seems to know what actually happened," he said, looking at Homer and Nick. "It's possible that First Mate Ernie McInnis knew, but that's a moot point. I'm pleased that we have recovered seventy-five of the possible seventy-six metal nuggets from the boxes. As yet, we do not know their purpose, other than their possible value."

"Mr. Harris," Homer said, pulling him aside when they were alone during a break. "I found number seventy-six. It's with my gear. It slipped my mind."

"Well, Captain, it'll slip my mind also. Why don't you just keep it as a souvenir, since I have no idea what the government will do with the others." There was no mention of the fifty thousand dollars given to Davy. Homer didn't bring it up.

Homer talked with Sally when he was in Prince Rupert and again from Seattle when she was in Prince Rupert to get Tilly and the twins. "Sally," Homer stressed during each conversation. "You're going to have to bear with me for a while. It will take me time to get through what happened, if I ever get past it. I'll be able to hide my feelings from everyone but you."

"I shudder at the thought of it, and how you managed," Sally said. "But now you'll have a family to distract you. Homer, we're going to have a family."

"I know," he said. "I've always wanted one."

"Tilly has agreed to live with us. She wants to live with us. She said she'd always live with us. I hope so. It's a second life for us, Homer."

"Yes, it is. With what happened to the *Eagle* and Ernie, I felt like I was drifting again without a clear course to steer. You've saved me, Sal. I don't know what I would have done with myself, if not for you."

"We've saved each other, Homer."

"These meetings should last only a few more days. Next, as Davy reminded me, I promised I'd go to Lorraine's for Thanksgiving. I'd like you to come with me, but they'll understand. After that, I'll go from California straight north to Alaska. If I ever leave Ketchikan, it'll be as half of a couple, or as a family."

"I'll hold you to that."

"Maybe we should adopt the twins, Sal. That would make things permanent and official."

"I've thought about the same thing. But we'd have to wait for Tilly to want it. We'll have to make ourselves indispensable."

"We'll want to do that," Homer said. "We can do it. I'm good at that."

"What finally happened between you and the company?"

"It's over. I'm officially retired. Based on their recent attitude, I thought they'd be more contentious in their negotiations, but the whole affair put them on the spot, softened them a little. It worked out well. I think the Coast Guard leaned on them, and that's a lot of weight."

After questioning by Canadian and U.S. authorities in Prince Rupert, some of the *Eagle's* crew and passengers were almost disappointed to leave behind the adventure they'd experienced. The media followed Tilly and the twins back to Ketchikan until their story became less newsworthy.

CHAPTER FORTY-FIVE

*H*omer drove the truck up the winding road to Lorraine's house. "You should move here, Davy. You'd be close to the kids, life is easier, and you're not getting any younger."

"Bullcrap," Davy retorted. "Life couldn't be much easier than where I am. The best weather in Alaska, along with a lot less hustle and bustle. Though, I do like the soft hills in this part of California. They're a little less daunting than the spectacular mountain views we have in Kenai. But I'd miss looking across Cook Inlet at the volcano and the snow capped peaks. And that drive to Anchorage? Can't beat a drive like that anywhere in the world."

"Davy, you come up with reasons for and against any move. Talking with the kids every day isn't the same thing."

"You're right. Maddy's been suggesting it and I do get more aches and pains in the cold, and, as much as I love it, it *is* harder living up there. Homer, we've all been through a hell of a lot of shit the past six weeks. I can't talk about it around Madeline. The memories are too vivid. She starts crying. It's a good thing we're spending Thanksgiving here. I'm not sure when she'll be ready to go home."

"I still can't believe what you did on that car chase out on the cliff. How you were able to stop your car just in time. It saved your ass."

"I know that, and she and Lorraine know it, but it doesn't stop them from giving me hell whenever they think about it. I'll never forget that ride. I didn't know how it was going to end. But when it was over, what a feeling of relief and satisfaction. We're trying to put that period of terror behind us. It was a hell of a thing for Maddy and me at our age.

"What do you hear from Nick?" Davy asked.

"We'll find out when he comes this afternoon with Minnie and his daughter. I'll have to get him aside to talk about it, away from the others."

"What's that van is doing in front of Lorraine's house?" Davy said. He glanced at Homer. "What's the matter, Homer?"

"I don't know. I don't like the feeling I'm getting. It's like when we'd see cloud formations at sea that seemed to be sending us a message that we're coming to get you, and they usually did."

"That last trip on the *Eagle* still has you freaked out," Davy said.

"Maybe so, but it won't hurt to act on my instincts. When I met that boy on the deck of the *Eagle*, he said Adams and Marshall were in the boat with him. I wonder what happened to them? Nick would have let us know if he'd heard anything. What time is it?" Homer asked.

"Twenty 'til two."

"Nick will be here about three. I should call him. Do you have your phone? I left mine in the room."

"No, mine's in the house, too," Davy said. "Maybe that's their van. Maybe they got here early. Someone just opened the door a crack to look out."

"I thought this shit was over," Homer muttered."

"What do you mean? They're all dead," Davy said.

"Open the glove compartment. I put a gun in there."

"What the hell, Homer?"

"I know, I know. Nick told me to keep it for a while. It's one of the Coast Guard's."

"But they're all dead. You told me they're all dead!" Davy exclaimed.

"They're not sure."

"Not sure. Not sure?" Davy cried out.

"That's the last thing Nick said, that they're pretty certain, but not absolutely convinced."

"You've got me panicking. My family is in there."

"Let's go in," Homer said. "Act casual. If it's nothing, we don't want to upset the ladies. I'll take the case of beer. You take the other bags of stuff." Opening the back of the wagon, Homer noticed a box with auto supplies. He picked up a towel rag and a can of grease. With it, he quickly painted the letter U on the back window.

"I'm not going to ask you why you did that," Davy muttered.

"I'll tell you later." As he closed the wagon, he bent the small American window flag so it hung upside down.

"That one I know." Davy nodded. "Your gut feelings are getting to me. Let's get inside to see if everyone is okay."

As they approached the house, the front door opened.

Nick slept late the morning of Thanksgiving Day. He awoke with a start and looked around the room—the same room in the same house in San Diego that his wife and then daughter had lived all these years. *I wake up anxious every day; nothing important to do other than call my Coast Guard contact at noon. They remind me that the possible threat from the yacht people has diminished.* They'd cautioned him to stay vigilant and to report any contact with them, or any unusual happenings. *I still need to carry a gun and so does Minnie; here I am, lying in bed next to her. Hannah is probably asleep in her room; I'm glad she's staying with us, rather than in the dorm near campus.* He'd been reluctant to leave Hannah alone. He still felt uneasy. He'd given her an emergency sound and transmitting device and a can of wasp spray, with instructions to keep them with her, always.

Hannah said how delighted she was to see the person Nick had become, although she'd briefly seen this side of him at times while growing up. 'Thank God for Minnie and that awful adventure you guys went through that forced you to change back to the real you,' she said, when she toasted them both at dinner.

Minnie, with that perfect body. The intensity of our lovemaking has exceeded anything we'd known during our time in Juneau or aboard the ship. Nick pulled the covers off without waking her. His hands gently caressed her skin. He started at the top of her head, moved gently over her face and neck, down each arm, kissing various spots. He continued down her body, along her legs to her toes.

Minnie emerged from her half sleep to full participation. "I've kept count of how many times you've fucked me in your own bed, in your own house, with your daughter in the next room," Minnie whispered. "What if she should walk in? Nick, Nick, oh my. I enjoyed that."

"You love birds up yet? Hannah yelled, "I've got coffee on."

"See?" Minnie said, panting softly.

"Perfect," Nick yelled back to Hannah. "We're getting ready."

"Yeah, right!" Hannah laughed.

"I should have sent you back to the dorm," Nick responded.

"When do we leave for the dinner?"

"In about two hours."

"Okay."

⟛ ⟛

When Homer entered the house, his eyes met those of the young lad from the yacht. His trepidation grew.

"Who the hell are you?" Davy demanded, pushing past the boy. "Maddy, Maddy, Lorraine?" Davy shouted. "Where are they?"

John Adams emerged from the shadows. "They are in the kitchen. Do not be concerned, Captain Masters, they are unharmed."

"Well, I am concerned!" Davy rushed into the kitchen.

"So, we meet again, Captain Dixon."

"Yes, we do, Mr. Adams. I see you survived the open seas," Homer said, uncertain how to respond to the man he tried to kill.

"Homer, get in here!" Davy yelled.

"I'll be right in," Homer shouted back.

"We were able to survive, no thanks to you," Adams snapped. "We have our scars, but they will heal."

They stared at each other.

"What's with the drawn gun?" Homer asked Adams.

"We are not here for one of our philosophical chats, Captain. We are here under delicate, actually desperate, circumstances."

"Damn it, Homer, get in here!" Davy yelled again.

Hearing the sounds of feet pounding on the floor, Homer walked into the kitchen. He saw Maddy, Lorraine, and Lorraine's seventeen-year-old daughter Beth, tied up in kitchen chairs, all with duct tape across their mouths. Davy was on the floor. "You son-of-a-bitch," he snarled at Adams. "What the fuck do you think you're doing?" While Homer helped Davy up, he glared over at another man holding a gun.

"This is my brother, John Marshall," Adams said. "You might remember seeing him when we loaded our boxes in Anchorage."

"You okay, buddy?" Homer asked Davy.

"The bastard whacked me with the butt of his gun," Davy said, trying to calm Maddy, while he held his head. "I'll have a bump, but I don't see any blood."

Homer stared heatedly at Marshall.

"Don't push him, Captain," Adams warned, "he can be a hot head."

The women sat wide-eyed, their bodies stiff with terror.

Marshall waved his gun at Davy and at Homer to back them away.

With an expression of defiance, Homer glared at Adams and Marshall. "I'm going to remove the tape and untie them. They will behave themselves. That's right, isn't it ladies?"

The women nodded.

"If your brother shoots me, you've lost whatever it was you came to achieve, unless your purpose in coming here was to kill me."

"I have sufficient reason to do just that, Captain." Adams paused. He stared at the women. "They made too much noise. If they do not stay quiet, we will strap them down again."

"They'll be quiet now," Homer assured him, as he removed the tape and untied them.

Maddy breathed deeply. She tried to repress her wailing while Davy comforted her.

"They'll be quiet and well-behaved," Homer repeated. He kissed the top of Beth's head.

She held on to him while staring at Adams.

The boy watched her with interest in his eyes.

"These are the two who came to my house," Davy told Homer. He glared at Adams and Marshall.

"Calm down, Captain Davy, the ladies are fine," Adams said. "We secured them for their own safety. Your daughter tried to flee and tried to use the telephone. The dog was making much too much noise and insisted on attacking us. We had to kick him outside. That sent the ladies into hysterics. They thought we were going to harm him. Yes, Captain Masters." He turned to Davy. "Now we have come to your daughter's house to conduct more business." He turned to Homer. "Let's go into the living room, we have much to discuss."

"Yes, Mr. Adams, we do." Homer then calmly addressed the women, "How is dinner progressing?"

Lorraine hesitated, but taking Homer's cue replied, "Everything is under control."

"Good," Homer said, "I hope we have enough for our three new guests."

"I, I think we can manage."

"Good. Let's all sit quietly in the living room," Homer said. "If the dinner needs tending, Lorraine, you or Maddy can go into the kitchen to take care of it." Homer nodded at Adams, receiving a gesture of resignation in return. Marshall grumbled.

"With my brother here, I do not need to show my gun, Adams said. That is his function. My brother says I talk too much. He said to me, 'So these are the two old men who got the best of you'?"

"How did you get away, why are you here, and what do you want?" Homer asked.

"I will be happy to tell you, Captain, as soon as I tell my brother to watch Captain Davy. I am uncertain how to trust him after I read what happened to my two men in Kenai."

"Your man, Brown, told us the two men were instructed to kill Davy and Maddy," Homer said. "Davy was protecting himself in any way he knew how."

"I told the two men to frighten them as only they can do," Adams said. "It is possible they went too far and were unaware of Captain Davy's abilities. As a result, I cannot trust him and I cannot be certain he will not do something foolish before Mr. Banner gets here."

"Okay," Homer responded with exasperation, his voice rising, "What do you want with us, and why do you need Nick, and how the hell did you know we'd all be here today?"

"Too many questions, Captain. It appears my venture planning was not perfect. I did not count on you being such a worthy adversary."

"I told you that in Juneau."

"Yes, you did, but that was just talk. However, we were committed to our plans at that time. I was certain you would listen to me because of your concern about Captain Davy and Mrs. Masters. What turned you around? What caused your resolve to harden?"

"You did," Homer answered. "It was your intent to recover the cargo before we got to Seattle. I wondered what would happen to all of us while you were trying to get the boxes back, and, once you got them, what you would do to keep us quiet. I didn't care about the cargo or your precious contraband. I was concerned about the safety of the people on my ship and my friends. When I realized the threat wasn't going to disappear, that you wouldn't let us all go our separate ways, safe and secure, I knew I couldn't sit back and hope for the best. I knew I had to do something."

The audience sitting in Lorraine's living room followed the talk. Like Homer, John Adams didn't frighten them, but John Marshall did.

Marshall continued to scowl at them and carefully watched Homer and Davy.

"It was your actions," Homer informed Adams. "Your obvious ploy before we got to Ketchikan to see how easy it would be to board our ship, and the instructions to your two men to disable our propulsion."

"We had to do that after you ignored my command to wait for us when we had mechanical problems. I could not let you get away with my cargo. That is when I instructed my two men in Kenai to scare Captain and Mrs. Masters, and for the two on your ship not only disable your ship, but to become a nuisance. How did you overpower my men? Mr. Smith was very capable. Tell me what happened."

Homer thought about his own decisions. *Did I overreact and read the wrong signals? Did I destroy my ship and kill Ernie?* "I couldn't let the actions of your people, and your threatening words, go unanswered. That was the start of my counter-attack."

"So, you killed them. And Captain Davy killed my two men in Kenai. It is too bad you did not contact me, Captain. I would have put a stop to their extreme behavior."

"I had no reason to think you would, Mr. Adams. I'll tell you what happened to the two men. No one here knows this."

Homer studied Marshall's face—a face that expressed nothing. His lips were pursed in anticipation of what Homer would say.

Homer described the confrontation on the *Eagle,* in Smith and Brown's cabin. "After some yelling back and forth, Smith grabbed the pistols and started shooting wildly. He mortally wounded Brown and Ernie. Sometime during that brief period, Ernie fired a shotgun blast into Smith, killing him. Brown died a few hours later. Ernie did not let us know the extent of his wounds. He died before we left the ship," Homer whispered, pausing to take a breath.

The room fell quiet.

Marshall growled, "That is why we could not contact them by radio. You have much more to tell us."

Homer gazed intently at both Adams and Marshall. "Yes, I do. Mr. Brown pleaded with us to save his life. I asked him questions about the female Army Officer, what was going to happen to Davy and Maddy, and what your plans were for the *Eagle*. He told us that Major Flowers was tied up in their closet. When we pulled her out, she was shook-up, but not harmed. She said Smith was going to rape her but that Brown stopped him."

Marshall interjected an obviously jovial statement, in their tongue, to Adams.

Adams' face remained passive but the boy uttered an expression of surprise, which Adams felt a need to explain. "My brother has a primitive way of expressing the needs a man has for a woman. I will not translate the words, in deference to the women present."

Homer ignored the explanation and continued, "John Brown, who still had some goodness in him, said you instructed your people in Kenai to kill Davy and Maddy." Homer glanced at Maddy to see her reaction.

Davy took her hand.

"That is not true. I never gave those instructions. We did not order their execution," Adams said. "We merely wanted to put the fear of God in them before our two men departed Alaska. We needed them just as we needed Mr. Smith and Mr. Brown and the three men you killed on my yacht. It is too bad you think I have no human feelings. I was the product of a very religious family and education; however, as we have discussed, our society and culture have different guidelines than yours. Can you understand that, Captain?"

"I heard what you said, but I couldn't really accept it. After all our private talks, I still didn't know what to believe. Then you seemed to change. Your statements became threatening. That's when I resolved to fight you any way I could. My weakness is that I tried to see the spark of goodness in you, and I think there is that spark, as there is in your youngster here."

All eyes turned to the boy.

He clearly understood the words, his face turning red. He glanced over at Beth.

"You are a charmer, Captain. That is part of your personality. But you are also naïve, living in a naïve society."

"Now you're trying to charm me, Mr. Adams. I can be a nasty son-of-a-bitch when I need to. I think I've shown you that. Don't underestimate me."

"But that is not really you. Tell me, Captain, why did you let this boy here take the survival suits? Did you feel guilty after trying to kill us? The suits saved our lives."

"I'm glad they did. My intent was not to kill you. I merely wanted to destroy your yacht, so you wouldn't kill us."

Adams smiled, and paused. "Captain, I know your language well. It is fortunate for you that my brother does not understand many of your words, but he is very observant. In fact, he just told me that the hand in the front pocket of your trousers is holding a gun."

Homer hesitated, contemplating his reaction. "Your brother is right. I will remove it carefully. Please instruct him to control himself."

Marshall started to move toward Homer to collect the pistol. He backed off at Adams' command.

The boy came to Homer with his hand out. He stepped between Homer and Marshall.

"Why did you do that, Captain?" Adams asked. "What need would you have of a pistol when coming to a family dinner?"

"It's because of you, Mr. Adams. After our unfortunate escapade at sea, I had to modify my normal behavior. You should've checked me when I arrived. And, Mr. Adams," Homer spoke in a louder voice, "you are controlled by your desire to reap ill-gotten gains. That desire has blinded you. You have crossed the line separating good and evil. Don't think that, since your hands are clean, you are clean. You have trapped yourself by coming here. You have no way out. This isn't a situation between two isolated ships at sea, where you can threaten with impunity. You can't just walk out of here unless you plan to kill all of us. What are you doing here?" he shouted, "what the hell do you want?"

The room remained quiet.

Homer glanced around.

Adams was standing still, appearing lost in thought.

His brother looked down, and at Adams, angrily.

The boy glanced back and forth from Homer to Adams.

Marshall turned to Adams and let loose with what sounded like a stream of invective.

Adams, unnerved, shouted back at his brother, then stopped himself and looked at the boy.

The boy looked away.

Adams remained silent for a moment. He looked up when the phone rang. When Lorraine rose to answer it he said softly, "Please sit down." The ringing stopped. It started again after a few seconds. Adams gestured toward Homer. "Captain, if you would, but be careful what you say. I will be listening on the other phone."

"Hello," Homer answered, looking at Adams and at Davy. "Yes, Judy, I remember you. This is Uncle Homer. Yes, I'm okay. I guess everyone heard about our escapade up north. Everything is just fine over here. We didn't realize the dog was crying." Homer glanced over at Adams. He received a nod in response. "Thank you, we'll bring the dog in, and you have a Happy Thanksgiving, thank you."

Beth jumped up. "Can I get him, please?"

Adams motioned for the boy to go with her.

They looked at each other going out the back door. The boy left it open, so everyone could hear and see them. The dog was lying near the door. Beth and the boy crouched down near him. Their hands touched when they both reached to pick him up.

"What is your name?" Beth asked.

"John," he said, but quickly explained that it was his American name. "I cannot tell you my real name."

"Why not?" she asked.

He just shook his head, with a pained expression, indicating he was sorry.

Beth reached up to touch his cheek. "My name is Beth."

He smiled and closed his eyes for a brief moment. "I know."

Beth carried the dog back into the living room. She held him in her lap. Other than being sensitive to touch on his thigh, he seemed fine.

Adams was able to regain his control. "Captain Dixon, you destroyed my cargo, destroyed my yacht, and killed some of my men. I am here to extract some compensation, but do not worry, I will not take risks that could cause me to get caught by the authorities. I have planned my visit here well. I will be able to safely leave here just as I left the yacht. I have no intention of going to prison."

"You don't have to worry about prison, Mr. Adams. Just walk out of here. We will not stop you and we will not call the authorities."

"That is hard for me to believe. I need help to escape. I know where to get help, but that requires American dollars. Your actions, and those of Mr. Banner and possibly his friend Minnie, have deprived me of the 'golden egg' I came to find in your country. I need money. I am a desperate man and desperate men do irrational things. I do not plan to kill anyone, and I am sure it will not come to that, but do not try to back me into a corner. If I need to kill to save myself, I will do so."

Homer absorbed Adams' outburst for a long moment. "Until now, I didn't know I had killed anyone on the yacht. I regret that, and I regret that Brown died. Smith deserved it. Brown told me more, in his effort to purge himself. He told me you planned to come aboard my ship to get your boxes, that you *would kill* were his exact words."

"Again, I said no such thing. Brown exaggerated my words," Adams said.

"Again, Mr. Adams, I had no other information on which to base my reaction to what Brown told me, particularly after Smith destroyed my propulsion, leaving my ship helpless. I needed to protect my crew and my passengers. I'm happy that you survived the yacht explosion, or I will be happy once you depart here, leaving us safe and sound."

"When Mr. Banner arrives, we will be able to conduct and conclude our business. I do not want to harm anyone," Adams said, looking around the room.

"Just what is the important business you need to conduct with Nick Banner?" Homer asked again.

"My operation 'went south', an expression you use, after Mr. Banner joined you on the ship. I did not count on Mr. Banner and his obvious support from Coast Guard. It must have been him who set the underwater charges on my yacht. We need to obtain some satisfaction from him. He owes me. He will pay."

"What sort of satisfaction do you expect to get? Do you plan on harming him, or his family? They don't have a dog, and I am certain Nick does not walk around with a hundred million dollars in his pocket."

"You will see, Captain, you will see."

Homer stared at Adams, trying to decipher his words and expressions. He looked over at Davy for help.

Davy sat tightlipped, shaking his head.

After a brief pause, Homer asked, "How did you survive after the explosion, and escape from the yacht, and why did you carry explosives on board, and again, what do you really want of Nick Banner?"

"I will answer your questions, Captain, but first tell me where you have the fifty thousand dollars we gave to Captain Davy."

"Unlike the phony dollars in your boxes?"

"How did you know that, Captain, if you did not open the boxes?"

"Oh, I did open the boxes, to supply my crew and passengers with the survival suits. We were cautious at first. It turned out there was no chemical gas."

Adams smiled. "So, you deduced that only counterfeit money would be smuggled this way. Genuine dollars can easily be distributed in other parts of the world. It is relatively easy and inexpensive to print more counterfeit money. However, the five-pound lumps of metal, one in each box, have considerable value. They are pure platinum. What happened to them, Captain?"

Homer hesitated a moment before he answered, "I don't know what happened to them. When we opened the boxes, we were in a hurry to get the survival suits. We were surprised to see the money, but didn't open each package in each box. Just before I left the ship, I found a lump of metal on the deck of the hold. It was mixed in with the piles of money. It was strange."

Adams glanced over at his brother. They both looked back at Homer.

"Would you like to have it? It's upstairs in my bag."

"Yes, we would," Adams, said, motioning for the boy to go with Homer.

Marshall went halfway up the stairs to watch the door to the bedroom, as well as the people in the living room.

Homer stared into the boy's eyes as he handed him the bare lump of metal.

The boy gazed back at Homer. He lowered his head.

Adams examined the metal nugget.

"Now that you have an item of great value," Homer urged, "Take it and flee. You remember the fable of the 'golden egg'. It's your greed that could be your downfall, Mr. Adams."

His brother became excited, turning the nugget of platinum over in his hand.

"Where are the others and where is the real money we gave you?"

"The other nuggets and the phony money are in six hundred feet of ocean water. It would be worth organizing a dive party to recover value such as that."

Marshall put his face close to Homer's. "You are lying," he said, raising his hand with the gun.

"We have other ways of getting information!" Adams snapped at his brother. "We cannot get information from him if he is dead. The people here are very dear to you. It's good to have everyone together in one room. I am certain you would not want anything to happen to any of them."

"You motherfucker!" Homer shouted. "I told you once, if you harm any one of them, I will find you wherever you are in the world!"

"You cannot find me if you are dead, Captain."

The living room audience gasped.

Davy stood up, then sat back down to hold a weeping Maddy.

Beth's face held an expression of dread.

"So, a man who says he doesn't kill is again talking about killing," Homer said.

"Enough of this, Captain, we have more important things to discuss before Mr. Banner gets here."

"What the hell do you want with Nick? He has nothing to do with the nuggets or the money, real or fake."

"Do not take me for a fool. As I said, Mr. Banner was your partner in destroying my yacht. It is strange that no news stories mentioned the yacht. He was also working for the U. S. Coast Guard and possibly other government agencies."

How the hell does he know this? "Where did you get such information?"

"Again, Captain, do not take me for a fool. Everything changed once he came aboard. His frequent visits to the Coast Guard in Juneau and again in Ketchikan, his lady friend Minnie, the sudden discovery of my listening devices, and the presence of civilians at the Coast Guard Stations and at Prince Rupert. I wondered why they did they not confiscate my shipment in Ketchikan? After that, I knew I needed to recover the money and the platinum before it got to Seattle. You could have saved yourself much trouble, and saved your ship, had you let me take my cargo."

⛝

Nick was driving Hannah's car. "This is the street, it's down this way." He stopped the car half a block from Lorraine's house.

"This is the wrong house." Minnie looked around.

"I know. The two of you look down a few houses at that truck in the cul-de-sac. What do you notice? Be specific and be detailed."

Noting the intensity in his voice, they both stared at him.

"I see a dirty old truck," Minnie said, "With a big letter U painted on the back window."

"Yes," Hannah agreed, "and the little American window flag is upside down."

"I missed that one," Nick mumbled. "The house numbers are even, jumping two higher every house on this side. What would be the number of the house the truck is parked at?"

They both reported that it was Lorraine's house. "What's going on?" Minnie asked.

"I'll tell you in a minute." Nick backed up a few houses, parked the car, took out his phone and dialed. "Listen carefully," he said

281

into the phone. "I'm near Captain Davy Masters' daughter's house. What address do you have for that house? That's right. I have reason to believe that one or more of the yacht people are inside, along with Davy's family and Captain Homer Dixon. No, I can't take the time to explain how I know. I've got to get in there. I can't wait for back up. It might be too late. Get someone here as fast as you can."

He turned to Minnie and Hannah.

The two women sat there mute, looking stunned.

"Minnie, take your gun out, but don't flash it. Keep it at your side. I'm going in the back way. Don't you come in, but stand outside the back door until I yell for you. Hannah, I'm giving you a gun to hold. You're familiar with them, but don't come into the house at all. I'll come get you."

"Daddy, tell me what's happening," Hannah pleaded.

"That U is the Navy signal flag for danger. An upside down American flag is a sign of distress. Having both together shows that it's not a mistake."

<hr />

Homer walked around the room. He gazed at Davy and the others, and glanced out the window. He saw Nick running up the street about three houses away. Minnie, and a young woman, followed behind. "Your Mr. Smith was the weak link in destroying your plans," Homer spoke to Adams. "It was his actions that upset the apple-cart, requiring responses on my part." He walked away from the window, to the far side of the room, and sat down on an upstairs step. "Because of his harsh methods and your implied threats, I had no other choice."

Both Adams and Marshall noticed Homer's changed demeanor. They became confused and watchful. So, when Marshall walked over and hit Homer with his gun, Adams didn't stop him. When Marshall grabbed one of Homer's arms, hurled him to the floor and pointed his gun, Adams didn't stop him, but pulled out his own gun.

Lying on the floor, Homer reacted by kicking at Marshall. He connected near his groin, pushing him against the wall.

The four onlookers on the couch sat paralyzed with fright, as Adams aimed at Homer. Beth dropped the dog and jumped out of her seat. She lunged at Adams, flailing her arms and yelling, "Don't shoot him!"

Adams looked up, surprised, uncertain what to do. He backed up, hitting a chair.

Homer got up and tried to tackle Marshall.

Marshall fired.

Nick, with gun in hand, charged through the back door.

Marshall now aimed at Nick.

"Drop it!" Nick yelled.

Marshall hesitated.

Disregarding what Nick told her, Minnie came in with her gun held out, as Adams recovered. All four stood with their guns aimed.

The appearance of Nick and Minnie surprised Adams and Marshall. They lowered their arms slightly, but kept their guns out.

Nick and Minnie kept their aim up.

Homer walked into the center, dragging his leg. He stood between Nick and Minnie, and Adams and Marshall. "Okay, Mr. Adams, here's Nick Banner. Can we conclude our business and have you leave us? As I said before, we will neither stop you nor contact the authorities."

"Do not bullshit me," Adams sneered. "I do not trust you. And Mr. Banner is part of your government."

"For the last time, what do you want of us and of Nick?" Homer demanded.

"We came here to recover the money you owe us. We need it to make our escape. Between you, Captain Davy, and Mr. Banner, we want fifty thousand dollars in cash."

"Homer," Davy piped in, "I've got about ten thousand with me, upstairs."

"I've got a good sum in my pocket," Homer offered. "Take all the money and that metal nugget and get out of here."

"I can only offer a few hundred in cash," Nick said.

"We want more than money from you, Mr. Banner."

"Why the hell are we giving them anything?" Minnie grumbled.

"Ah, Miss Minnie," Marshall taunted. "At our last meeting you promised me much more."

"What the fuck are you talking about?" Minnie snapped.

"That word again. Maybe we can include that pretty lady, too," Marshall suggested, staring at Hannah, who'd come in against Nick's wishes.

"You're crazy. Control your brother," Homer said to Adams. "She's Nick's daughter. Take your money and leave while you can."

"We need to complete our mission here, to get revenge. Nick's daughter will not have a father soon."

Nick turned to glance at Hannah when she gasped.

At that moment, Adams barked a command. Both he and Marshall raised their arms to fire at Nick.

But Minnie maintained her vigilance. She fired rapidly, hitting Marshall.

Adams hesitated. He watched his brother fall to the floor. He lowered his arm and faced the boy. He lashed out at him in their native tongue. Adams shot wildly toward the boy, missing him, not aiming, just spraying bullets around the room.

The boy backed up, ducking out of the way. He had an incredulous look on his face.

Nick and Minnie maintained their positions, observing the scene.

Adams continued to berate the boy. He raised his gun hand toward him again.

"Don't!" Beth yelled.

The boy, now controlled by fear and anger, responded with a few wild shots of his own. One of them accidentally hit Adams in the chest. The boy lowered his arm.

Homer's gun dropped from the boy's hand. His face now showed a mixture of terror and remorse, as he knelt near Adams. He reached a shaky hand out to touch the body.

It was all over in a moment. Marshall and Adams were dead. Nick had been hit in the hand.

Homer stood up, pressing his side. "Don't shoot him!" he yelled, holding up his hand at the others. "Come here, son," he called to the boy. "Go out the door. Run away, quickly. People will be coming soon. Hide, and find yourself, in this big country. Take this," Homer gave him the wad of bills from his pocket. "Go now. If you stay here you'll go to prison."

The boy, still in a state of shock, took the money. He pressed Homer's hand in both of his.

"What are you doing, Homer?" both Davy and Nick yelled.

"I know what I'm doing. The boy is blameless. Let him go. Hurry, son!" He motioned forcefully to him.

The boy paused to look at Adams and Marshall on the floor and at Beth.

Beth nodded at him as he went out the door, her face still contorted by the terror she had witnessed. She, too, had seen his youthful innocence. She stood up, heading toward the door.

"Beth!" Lorraine yelled,

Beth halted and turned to look at Lorraine. "Mom, I have to help him." She ran through the doorway.

Lorraine gasped and rushed over to the door. Davy and Maddy came up behind her. They saw Beth running down the street, still holding the dog. The boy turned to wait. He took the dog. Mother and grandparents watched in shock as Beth walked out of sight. After a few minutes, they went back to sit on the couch. They were dazed.

Nick and Minnie covered Adams and Marshall.

Homer let out a moan, as he collapsed into a chair. Blood was oozing from his side.

"Uncle Homer!" Lorraine yelled, crouching beside him. "You're hurt."

"That John Adams, couldn't figure him out," Homer groaned. "Nick, if I don't make it, you'll have to contact Sally."

"You'll make it, Homer."

"I hope so," Homer gasped, "but I don't know."

"Oh, Uncle Homer," Lorraine cried.

"Well, I always did want to be a hero," Homer whispered.

"Oh, my God, Uncle Homer, you *are* a hero!" Lorraine said, her wet cheek touching his.

Outside, two police cars passed a girl and boy with a dog.

EPILOGUE

Ketchikan had changed. In Homer's early years on the *Eagle* the town had seemed to be a sleepy hamlet that expanded in population every summer with fishermen, tourists and cruise ships. At that time, the downtown area merchants were locally owned and operated. When Homer retired, new hotels and shopping outlets had crowded out many of the established stores, turning the town into a lopsided community, in that many of the newer businesses closed their doors for seven or eight months of the year, re-opening each summer.

Ketchikan gradually adjusted. Many stores and shops that had once been within walking distance of the cruise ship docks moved to other areas of town, accommodating the all-year residents and year-round fishermen.

Sally's Place remained a local hangout and was not adversely affected by the end of summer exodus. Though Sally welcomed the increased summer business, she survived nicely the rest of the year with a following of regulars and bluegrass lovers.

One afternoon in early September, a young woman entered alone. Sally had trained her staff to appraise all who came in. A group of boisterous men could be disastrous. Local hookers and habitual drunks knew her place was off-limits.

The young woman stood looking over the sparsely crowded room. She decided to sit at the bar.

The bartender stared at her with a dubious expression.

"I'll have a ginger ale."

"Good thing." He smiled. "I was about to card you. The fine print in the regulations says you can't even have that in here, but we never get checked. Everyone knows that Sally's Place is straight. Even if we did get checked, unlikely at this time of day, a young woman of your age, whatever age that is, could be taken for fifteen or even thirty."

"Thanks a lot. In that case, I'll have a beer. I'm joking," she said, seeing him hesitate. "A ginger ale will be fine. Do you spend this much time with all the customers or are you curious to find out where I am in the fifteen to thirty range."

"Well, it's a little slow, as it is most days at this time, and seeing a young woman come in by herself piques my curiosity. Almost everyone wants to chat, particularly if they're alone. I talk with them all, men or women. More so with women, they're easier to draw out. The men, mostly the older ones, don't always open up to someone my age. The best part of working behind a bar is that I hear all kinds of things and some of them are gems. When that happens, and it's rare, I use this recorder to save my thoughts. One of my teachers stressed that. She said that, when we're inspired or impressed by something, or witness something unusual, we should save it because someday we'll want to bring that memory back."

"This is weird," she said.

"What's weird?"

"My father always told me similar things. Okay, here's part of my story, but it's not very interesting. I'm not from Ketchikan, or Alaska."

"Well, I knew that."

"Okay, smarty pants, you can't make snide remarks after everything I say."

"Sorry, I'll just listen. And my name is Nick by the way. So, can I ask questions?"

"Questions are good, Nick. I'll start as soon as you get my ginger ale."

"Oh, right."

"My father was in Alaska a few years before I was born, no, that's not where to start. I'm in college. I'll soon begin my junior year."

"What school?"

"That's not relevant. That's just curiosity," she quipped.

"You're right, and you're also very strict."

"Yes, I am. My course of study is English Literature. I would like to write. My Dad was delighted with that. He wasn't born in the United States and has always had a difficult time expressing himself in English. I mentioned to him that I needed to have my own experiences to be able to write. He wasn't too happy hearing that. He said by observing people and incidents during my daily activities, I could witness a wealth of life. I said I needed something more exotic. He frowned at that. As I said, he'd been to Alaska once. After thinking it over, he said that at my age Alaska was about as exotic as he could let me experience, but that I couldn't go alone. He said the people here were friendly, talkative and all have stories to tell; that it could be due to the weather, isolation, loneliness or everything combined. He said I should go to Ketchikan. He had enjoyed his visit here. He even mentioned Sally's Place. He must have overlooked the fact that it's a bar."

The bartender started to say something, but hesitated.

"Please, speak your piece," she said. "You look like you're bursting."

"I was going to say that Sally's Bluegrass Place is not just a bar, it's a happening that also serves drinks. How come your Dad let you come at your age, and where's your traveling partner?"

"My friend and I wanted to do different things today. She went to see the totem poles. I wanted to come to Sally's Place again.

We're leaving tomorrow and I couldn't go without trying one more time. So, besides your stories, and I'm sure they're great, where are the other people I can talk with who can tell me their tales?"

"Okay," he said, grinning at her. "Here's what I've been waiting to tell you. You came to the right place at the right time. My Grandpa should be here any minute. He says that we've all had experiences going back to our childhood, things we've done, seen and thought. He's got more stories than anyone I know. He and my Grandma Sally are loaded with them. Imagine someone like my Grandma running a bar for about forty years. I've asked her if she ever kept notes or a diary. She said, 'no, anything left is what's in my head.' Here he is now. Hey, Grandpa."

"Good afternoon, young people. Who's your friend, Nicky?"

"She wants to be a writer, Grandpa, and needs a good story."

"How do you do, Grandpa? I'm Bette Hancock."

"How are you, Bette, I'm Homer Dixon."

Bette gasped. "That, that's my brother's name, Homer Dixon Hancock."

Homer, still holding her hand, kept staring at her. "Is your father's name, John Hancock, by any chance?"

"Yes, how do you know? Did you know him?"

"Wow, what a coincidence," Nick exclaimed.

"Do you have a photo of him, my dear?" Homer asked.

"Why, yes," Bette said, surprised at his request, looking for the photo in her wallet.

Homer sat down and studied the photograph. He was visibly moved.

Bette and Nick glanced at each other. "You okay, Grandpa?"

"It isn't a coincidence, Nicky. I can't tell you how many times, through the years, I've wondered what happened to him," Homer said, his eyes full of moisture. "Bette, how did you happen to come in here?"

"My Dad said if I go to Ketchikan I should be sure to visit Sally's Place. I've been here a few times this week, but couldn't find anyone to talk with, until I met Nicky."

"I've got a story to tell you, Bette. You might have heard parts of it from your father. I've wanted to tell Nicky and my granddaughter, Maria, also, but I can't tell you unless your father says it's okay. I hope it won't change your opinion of him. I met him four or five times, about twenty years ago. Our meetings had an impact on my life, and I always hoped they changed his life as well."

"My God," Bette exclaimed, taking Homer's hand. "I'm sure he wanted me to meet you. That's why he directed me here. Can I call and ask him?"

"Yes, please do." Homer nodded. "Nicky, is Maria here?"

"She just walked in with Mom and Grandma. This is the damnedest thing, isn't it Grandpa?"

"It sure is," Homer said, giving his grandson a hug.

Bette returned with a big smile. "He said it's fine with him. In fact, he'd like to hear it sometime also. From what he's told us, it seems it was a difficult time for him."

"I'd like to hear the events from him as well." Homer smiled. "I hope we can arrange it. I've always wondered what happened to him. His survival and life must be fascinating."

"Hi, Grandpa," Maria greeted, walking up to the bar. "Is it true? Are we going to hear *the story*? Are we old enough, now?"

"Maria, sweetheart, meet Bette, and sit down. You're just as feisty as your Grandma."

Homer started at the beginning; the loading of the *Eagle* in Anchorage, and his meeting with Davy in Kenai. He needed to give them some background and give himself a little time, time to put into words the events he never forgot—memories that were always simmering within him. Through the years, he'd discussed certain incidents with Sally and Davy, but never the whole experience. Most of his conversations had been when he visited Davy.

They used to kid each other, "*Damn it, Davy, or damn it, Homer, here we are enjoying our beers and the fine view of Cook Inlet, and you have to ruin it by bringing up those weeks of terror and death!*"

Homer recalled and narrated that six-week period of his life and, at times, submerged himself in a dream-like state, occasionally closing his eyes as the memories floated up to his conscious mind. He looked at the three young listeners in front of him, and glanced at Sally and Tilly sitting nearby.

"Grandpa, when it all started, why didn't you or Davy just call the police and be done with it?" Maria asked.

"It was the threats made by those people. Remember the dead dog and the warning that they knew where Davy's daughter and granddaughter lived? When the Coast Guard got into the act, they told us of people who'd been killed. Also, when we heard they might have more guys in the lower forty-eight working with them. That knuckled us under."

"Weren't you scared that first night when they were chasing you in the car?"

"I was more scared than at any other time during the six weeks. I didn't know what to expect. Everything seemed so new and uncertain. But it didn't compare to the time Davy and Maddy had when they were heading for the cliff with that car banging into them. On one of our trips to see Davy in Kenai, after it was all over, we drove down that cliff road. He showed me how he tricked those two guys into crashing on the rocks. He was really proud of it. And I was proud of him, too. We never told Maddy we went there. It would have brought up terrible memories for her. The next time we all visit that area of Alaska, we'll drive out to see the cliff road. It's just as it was when Davy lived there, still unpaved and no homes or other construction. But they did replace the barrier at the edge."

"I'd like to see that," Nick said. "It must have been pretty hairy that night the boxes were opened on the ship."

"It was an anxious night for your namesake 'Nick', and for those in the hold of the ship. I was on the bridge, but we were tense the whole time."

"How were you able to do what you did with Ernie," Maria asked, "and how were you able to blow up the ships and kill people?"

"It was the hardest thing I've ever had to do, blowing up the *Eagle* and taking care of Ernie. It wasn't easy," Homer answered, staying quiet for a while. "I still get misty thinking about Ernie, but I had to do it."

Sally came up to hug him from behind.

"Ernie was a good friend. You only have a few good friends in your life, people you can rely-on and trust completely. Just like the love you have for your family. As the years go by, you realize that the most precious thing in your life is having someone, many someones, you can love."

"Grandpa, why are you looking at us with that glow on your face?"

"I just told you." Homer smiled. After a pause, he continued, "The killing was very difficult, but it's like being a cop or a soldier. Sometimes the decisions are made for you based on the circumstances of the moment."

"My Dad told me and my brother about sliding out of control down the glacier and about the man who helped him. Was that you?" Bette paused, frowning. "But he has never told us the details of his involvement in the overall events."

"Yes, it was me." Homer nodded. "It was the first time I met your father. Are you certain he wanted me to tell you all the details?"

"Yes," Bette's face contorted, as if she were trying not to cry. "He said he could never tell us about it, but he wanted us to know. He said it was a part of his life he wasn't proud of, even though he was tricked into being there, whatever that meant."

"Your father was told to follow me when I went up on the glacier. The bear freaked him out and made him lose his phone and gun."

"He told us about the bear," Bette said.

Homer thought for a moment, and continued, "He was told to aim a gun at me on three different occasions. Each time, I knew he didn't want to do it. He was just a kid. I could see it in his face, in his eyes, that he wouldn't shoot me. The time I saw him when I was ready to leave the *Eagle*, I wanted to take him to safety in my boat, but couldn't because of Adams and Marshall."

Bette started weeping.

Nick, sitting between Maria and Bette, put his arm around her.

"Are you sure you want me to continue, my dear?"

"Yes, please continue. He said he wanted to tell me but couldn't bring himself to do it. He said when I come home, he'll fill in the gaps."

"I'd like to hear that also," Homer said, again. "I'd like to know how or why he got mixed up with John Adams, and who Adams was to him. It's interesting that I never felt Adams himself was a killer, yet he was able to have others do it for him, except for that last incident in Carlsbad. Maybe your Dad could shed some light on that for me."

"Grandpa, how were you able to deal with someone like Adams?"

"I had to build up to it. As you guys get older and have experiences with people in different situations, you'll get to the point where you can sit back, look at other people and think—what do they want? How can I get what I want in my dealings with them? Use emotion as a tool. Be calculated and controlled, so you don't show weakness. That's what Adams was doing in dealing with me until I was able to turn the tables, or at least even things out."

"How did you prepare yourself for the battle with Smith and Brown?"

"Very insightful question, Nicky. It was very unlike anything I'd ever done but it was one of those things you know you must do, at the time. We didn't hesitate, but never thought it would come to that—the killing."

"You were out at night, all alone in that small boat in the middle of the ocean. How did you handle that?"

"You've got to remember, I spent my whole career at sea. I felt concerned, but comfortable out there, and then Nick and Minnie found me."

"You haven't told us how you recovered from getting shot."

"I'll tell you that," Sally said. "I had to come down for a week to take care of him. So, a few weeks after I took you twin babies from Prince Rupert to Ketchikan, I went to San Diego to get this big baby. The wound bled a lot but fortunately, it wasn't serious."

"I hope you could meet my Dad, or at least talk," Bette said. "Do you know anything about the stranger who gave him money and told him to find himself in this country? That's the only other thing he has told us about staying in the United States and getting started."

Homer smiled.

Bette jumped up. "It was you, it was you!" She lunged at Homer to embrace him. "He said you changed his life. He mentions that often, but no matter how much my brother and I asked, he would always put us off."

"Bette," Nick said, "You said your Dad named your brother after Grandpa. Did he name you after someone?"

"He told us that before he was free on that last day in Carlsbad, there was this young girl who, he felt, believed in him. He never explained. Her name started with a B, so he picked Bette for me."

"He came close. That B might have been Davy's granddaughter, Beth," Homer said. "They met at Lorraine's house. They seemed to understand each other, have an instant bond. Beth traveled with him. They left Carlsbad by bus, ending up in the Midwest. She helped him get settled for about a month, until he got a job and then returned home to go to college. I hope I'm not telling you secrets that your mother doesn't know."

"My Dad said he's told my Mom everything." Bette looked at Nick and Maria. "What happened to your mom Tilly, and to Maria and Luis?"

"Mom is sitting right over there, next to our Grandma Sally," Maria answered. "She's the one who's smiling and crying at the same time. Many years ago, she told us about the details of our birth on the island, and about the time when she went to Luis and Maria's wedding in Acapulco. Grandpa, do you ever hear from any of the crew or passengers?"

"Not much. We did get an invitation to the wedding in Acapulco. We stayed here to take care of you guys when your Mom went, and we got mail from Peter Marsden, when Jacob and Jonas graduated from the Naval Academy. Everyone's got his or her own lives to live. But you've seen some of my old crew come in here, now and then, when their ships stop at Ketchikan."

"All right, Grandpa, what did you do with the fifty thousand dollars and the nugget of platinum?"

"My share of the money paid for part of your education. Davy did the same for his family. Do you recall how you've always asked me what that shiny metal is in the thick glass case over the bar? Now you know. But you can't tell anyone. It's too valuable for people to know about. That will be yours someday."

"Wow, what a story!" Nick said. "I wish you'd told us sooner."

"It wasn't complete, or almost complete, until now, until Bette found us," Homer said. "I'll contact Bette's Dad and ask to meet with him to exchange stories."

"Oh, I'm sure he'll want that!" Bette said.

They continued to talk for a few hours through dinner. Homer's whole family; Sally, Tilly, Maria and Nicky, and now Bette. Having Bette there, helped fill a void in past events and in Homer's life.

He watched all of them, talking and laughing. Homer had to turn away. He didn't want them to see him tear-up, a more frequent emotion as he got older.

"Grandpa, what about Nick and Minnie?" Maria asked, "Did they get married?"

"After the incidents at Lorraine's house in Carlsbad, they went back east—Nick for a job at Coast Guard Headquarters in Washington, and Minnie to her home in Maryland. When Nick came through here a few years ago, he was working for the Department of Homeland Security, Coast Guard's boss. We talked over the events still classified by the government, involving the *Eagle* and the yacht, things that only Minnie and the two of us knew. He told me a very interesting tale of what happened between him and Minnie. "But that," Homer said, smiling at the group, "is another story."

THE END

ABOUT THE AUTHOR

Hal Dorin is a Professional Mechanical and Ocean Engineer.

His writing draws from a career in Underwater Construction and his period on a Navy Rescue and Salvage Vessel, including training as a Navy Diver.

He lives in Pikesville, Maryland.

Initial Editing and Format By:
Bonnie Lea Elliott

Book & Cover Design By:
Wicked Muse Productions

www.ingramcontent.com/pod-product-compliance
Lightning Source LLC
Chambersburg PA
CBHW071252170626
46809CB00001B/192